PROGRESS · RUSSIAN CLASSICS SERIES

A. S. Pushkin
Portrait by V. Tropinin. 1827

ALEXANDER PUSHKIN

Selected Works
in Two Volumes

Volume Two
PROSE WORKS

PROGRESS PUBLISHERS
MOSCOW

Translated from the Russian

Александр Пушкин
ИЗБРАННЫЕ ПРОИЗВЕДЕНИЯ В ДВУХ ТОМАХ
Том 2. Проза

На английском языке

П $\dfrac{70301-885}{014\,(01)-79}$ без объявл.   4702010000

CONTENTS

THE TALES OF THE LATE
IVAN PETROVICH
BELKIN

MISTRESS PROSTAKOVA

Aye, Sir, he was fond of listening to
tales from a child.

SKOTININ

Mitrofan takes after me.

"The Dunce" *

FROM THE EDITOR

Having undertaken to publish the tales of
I. P. Belkin, now presented to the reader, we should
like to preface them with a brief account of the life
of the deceased author, thereby satisfying in part
the legitimate curiosity of lovers of our native
literature. For this purpose we appealed to Marya
Alexeyevna Trafilina, the next of kin and the
heiress of Ivan Petrovich Belkin. Unfortunately,
however, she was unable to furnish us with any
information about him, never having had the
slightest acquaintance with the deceased. She advised us to apply on this subject to a certain worthy
gentleman, who was a friend of Ivan Petrovich. We
followed her advice, and our letter received the
satisfactory reply given below. We print it without
any alterations whatever, as a precious monument
to a refined understanding and a touching friendship, and at the same time a perfectly adequate biographical statement:

Respected Sir,
   I had the honour to receive your kind letter of the
15th of this month on the 23rd day of the same, in

---

* A comedy written in 1782 by Denis Fonvizin (1745-
1792), a major Russian playwright and publicist of the day.

which you made known to me your desire to receive detailed information concerning the birth and death, the service, the home life, occupations and character of the late Ivan Petrovich Belkin, my erstwhile sincere friend and neighbour in the country. I undertake the fulfilment of your desire with the utmost satisfaction to myself, and am sending you, my dear Sir, all that I can remember of his conversation and also some observations of my own.

Ivan Petrovich Belkin was born of honourable gentlefolk in the year 1798, in the village of Goryukhino. His late father, Second-Major Pyotr Ivanovich Belkin, married the spinster Pelageya Gavrilovna, of the Trafilin family. He was not wealthy, but thrifty, and thoroughly capable of managing his practical affairs. His son received his early education from the parish clerk. To this worthy man he seems to have owed his love of reading and his taste for writing in his native tongue. In 1815 he joined a Jager infantry regiment (I cannot recall its number), in which he remained right up to 1823. His parents dying within a short time of one another, he was compelled to send in his papers and go to live in his native village of Goryukhino, on his hereditary estate.

Entering upon the management of his estate, Ivan Petrovich, owing to his inexperience and soft-heartedness, very soon let his property fall into neglect and relaxed the strict discipline maintained by his late parent. Discharging the conscientious and efficient village-elder with whom the peasants (as is their wont) were dissatisfied, he left the management of the village to his former housekeeper, who had earned his confidence by her skill in telling stories. This gullible old woman had never been able to distinguish a twenty-five-ruble note from a fifty-ruble note; the peasants, to many of whose children she was godmother, stood in no fear of her. The peasants chose a new elder, who indulged them inordinately, conniving with them to cheat their master, so that Ivan Petrovich was obliged to give up the system of corvée, substituting for it extremely low quit-rents; even so his peasants, taking advantage of their master's weakness, wheedled out of him certain quite superfluous favours in respect to the first year, and in the next year paid over two-thirds of their rents in nuts, bilberries and the like; and even here there were arrears.

As a friend of Ivan Petrovich's late father, I considered it my duty to offer my advice to the son also, and volunteered several times to restore the former order, which he had been unable to *maintain by himself. For this purpose I went to visit him one day, demanded the account-books, summoned the rascal of an elder, and began looking through them in the presence of Ivan Petrovich. The youthful proprietor at first followed my investigations with the utmost attention and diligence, but when the accounts showed that during the past two years the number of peasants had increased, while that of the poultry and cattle had noticeably decreased, Ivan Petrovich was content with these preliminary calculations, and would listen to no more, and at the very moment when I had reduced the rascally elder, by my investigations and stern questions, to extreme confusion, and silenced him completely, what was my vexation to hear Ivan Petrovich snoring loudly in his chair! From that moment I ceased to interfere in the arrangements of his estate, leaving his affairs (as he did himself) to the will of the Almighty.*

The friendliness of our relations was by no means affected by all this, for, while deploring his weakness and the disastrous slackness common to our young gentlefolk, I was sincerely attached to Ivan Petrovich. It would indeed have been impossible not to love so kindly and honourable a youth. And Ivan Petrovich, for his part, paid me the respect due to my years, and was very fond of me. We met almost daily, up to the very end, for he valued my simple conversation, though, as regards habits, manner of thinking, and dispositions, we had very little in common.

Ivan Petrovich was extremely moderate in his tastes, avoiding all forms of indulgence; I never saw him the worse for drink (a perfect miracle this, in our parts); he had a great weakness for the female sex, but was himself as bashful as a maid.*

In addition to the tales to which you refer in your letter, Ivan Petrovich left behind a number of manuscripts, some of which are in my possession, and some of which have been used by the house-keeper for various domestic purposes. Thus, last winter, all the windows in her wing of the house were pasted up with the first part of a novel which he never finished. If I am not mistaken the above-mentioned tales were his first literary attempts. Most of them, according to Ivan Petrovich, are true, and were related to

---

* Here follows an anecdote which we omit as superfluous. At the same time we can assure the reader it contained nothing injurious to the memory of Ivan Petrovich.

him by various persons.* Almost all the names are, however, fictitious, while the hamlets and villages are taken from our parts, my own village being referred to among others. This was not owing to any evil intentions whatsoever, but simply to lack of imagination.

In the autumn of 1828 Ivan Petrovich caught a severe cold which developed into a high fever, and died, despite the indefatigable efforts of the local apothecary, a man of great skill, especially in the treatment of long-standing diseases, such as corns and the like. Ivan Petrovich died in my arms in his thirtieth year, and was buried in the churchyard at Goryukhino, beside his parents.

Ivan Petrovich was of middle height, had grey eyes, fair hair and a straight nose; he was light-complexioned and lean of countenance.

This is all, dear Sir, that I have been able to recollect of the life, occupations, disposition, and appearance of my late neighbour and friend. If, however, you should see fit to make any use of my letter, I would ask you to be so kind as not to mention my name; for though I greatly esteem and love men of letters I have no desire to appear in that guise myself; indeed, considering my years, it would be unbecoming.

With sincere respect, I remain . . . .

November 16th, 1830,
Village of Nenaradovo.

Considering it a duty to respect the will of our author's friend, we proffer him our profound gratitude for the information furnished by him, and trust that our readers will appreciate the sincerity and frankness of his contribution.

A. P.

---

* As a matter of fact, every tale in the manuscript of I. P. Belkin bears the inscription, in the author's hand: "Told me by So-and-so (rank or title, and initials). We may cite the following for the curious: *The Postmaster* was related to him by Titular Counsellor A.G.N., *The Shot* by Colonel I.L.P., *The Undertaker* by B. V., a shop-assistant, *Blizzard* and *Lady Into Lassie* by a young lady K.I.T.

was attached to me; at any rate I was the only one
he desisted from his usual malicious persiflage,
various topics with simplicity and extraordinary
the remembrance of that unfortunate evening,
ain on his honour was not washed out by his own
ver left me, and prevented me from treating him as
ashamed to meet his eyes. Silvio was too clever and
nced not to observe this and guess at its cause. It
distress him, at any rate I once or twice observed in
esire to open his heart to me. But I avoided such
ies and Silvio left me to myself. From this time I only
the company of my comrades, and our former frank
e to an end.

mpered inhabitants of great cities can have no con-
f many sensations which are familiar to the inhabitants
s or country towns, such as, for example, the waiting
-day to come round again. On Tuesdays and Fridays
al headquarters were always crowded with officers,
pecting money, some letters, some newspapers. Letters
a rule unsealed then and there, and items of news
ed, so that the office presented a scene of great animation.
who received his letters through the regiment, was usually
too. One day he was handed a letter, the seal of which
ke with an air of the utmost impatience. His eyes gleamed
glanced swiftly over its contents. The officers, each occu-
ith his own letters, noticed nothing. "Gentlemen," cried
, "circumstances require my instant departure. I must
to-night. I trust you will not refuse to dine with me for
st time. I shall expect you," he continued, addressing me,
must come!" With these words he hastened out of head-
ters, and the rest of us, agreeing to meet at Silvio's house,
each his own way.

arrived at Silvio's house at the appointed hour and found
ost the entire regiment gathered there. His things were
ady packed; nothing remained but the bare, bullet-riddled
ls. We sat down to table; our host was in the best of spirits,
his gaiety was soon communicated to his guests. Corks
pped incessantly, the wine frothed and hissed in the glasses,
we indefatigably wished the departing one a good journey
d the best of luck. It was late in the evening when we rose
om the table. While we were getting our caps, Silvio took

THE SHOT

> We fought a duel.
>
> *Baratynsky**
>
> I vowed I would shoot him by right
> of duel (I still owed him a shot).
>
> *"Evening at the Bivouac"***

I

We were stationed at the small town of X. Everyone knows
what the life of an army officer is like. In the morning, drill and
the riding-school; dinner at the Regimental Commander's, or
in some Jewish tavern; punch and cards in the evening. There
was not a single house open to us in X., not a single marriage-
able girl. We forgathered in one another's quarters, where there
was nothing for us to look at but one another's uniforms.

There was only one person in our circle who was not a military
man. He was about thirty-five, and we considered him quite old.
His experience gave him great advantages over us; and in addition to this, his habitual gloom, harsh disposition and malicious
tongue exercised a powerful influence on our youthful minds.
His fate was shrouded in mystery; he seemed to be a Russian,
and yet he bore a foreign name. At one time he had served in
the Hussars, and with every prospect of a successful career.
Nobody knew what it was that had made him resign his commission and settle in a wretched little town, where he lived at the
same time meanly and lavishly, going about on foot, in a

---

* Pushkin's friend the poet Yevgeny Baratynsky (1800-1844).

** Lines from a story by Alexander Bestuzhev-Marlinsky (1797-1837),
a participant in the Decembrists' uprising, 1825. Pushkin could not give
his name for reasons of censorship, but by quoting from Bestuzhev-
Marlinsky's story he showed that his sympathies lay with the Decembrists.

worn black frock-coat, but keeping open house for all the officers of our regiment. True, his dinner consisted of two or three dishes, cooked by an ex-soldier, but champagne flowed unchecked at his table. Nobody knew what his fortune or his income was, and nobody dared to question him about them. He had a good supply of books, mostly military texts and novels, which he was always ready to lend, and never asked for again. And he himself never returned to its owner a book he had borrowed. His principal occupation was shooting from a pistol. The walls of his room were riddled with bullet-holes, and looked like the sections of a honeycomb. His rich collection of pistols was the only luxury of the wretched clay hut in which he lived. The skill which he had achieved was of the highest order, and if he had suggested shooting a pear from somebody's cap, there was not a man in our regiment who would have hesitated to place his head at his disposal. Our conversation frequently turned on the subject of duelling, but Silvio (as I will call him) never took any part in it. When asked if he had ever fought a duel he would reply curtly that he had, without entering into any details, and it was obvious that such questions displeased him. We decided that he had some unfortunate victim of his terrible skill on his conscience. It certainly never entered our heads to suspect that there was anything like cowardice in him. There are some people whose very appearance forbids such suspicions. And then an event occurred which took us all by surprise.

One day some ten of our officers were dining at Silvio's quarters. We drank about as much as usual, which is to say a great deal. After dinner we begged our host to keep the bank for us. He held out for a long time, for he seldom played cards. But at last he ordered cards to be brought in, scattered fifty or so ten-ruble pieces on the table, and began dealing out the cards. We all surrounded him, and the game was on. It was Silvio's habit to maintain absolute silence while playing, neither arguing, nor offering explanations. If the punter happened to make a mistake Silvio either paid up immediately or jotted down the surplus. We were well aware of this and allowed him to dictate his own rules. But among us was an officer lately transferred to our regiment. While playing, this man absent-mindedly raised the stakes a point; Silvio picked up a piece of chalk and, according to his wont, righted the score. The officer,

thinking Silvio had ma... Silvio went on with the... tience, picked up the br... had been wrongly entere... the figures down again. ... gambling, and the laughte... mortally insulted, and se... table flung it at Silvio, wh... impact. We were greatly p... gleaming, Silvio rose. "Sir,"... thank God that this happene...

We had no doubt of the ou... comrade as a dead man. The... was ready to answer for the... gentleman in charge of the b... minutes longer, but we all felt t... mind to the cards, and one by... making for our respective quarte... soon to be expected.

At the riding-school the next da... if the poor lieutenant was still alive... appearance among us; we put the... replied that he had had no word fron... us. We went to Silvio's house, and ... after another right in the middle of an... He received us in his usual manner, ... previous day's incident. Three days p... was still alive. Could it be that Silvio... we asked one another in astonishmen... He contented himself with a very sligh... up with the lieutenant.

This might have lowered him consider... young men. Lack of courage is the last th... young people, who usually regard bravery ... covering a multitude of sins. Gradually, ... thing was forgotten, and Silvio regaine... fluence.

I alone was unable to feel the same about... nature with a romantic imagination, I had fo... devoted than all the rest to the man whose... enigma, and whom I regarded as the hero of...

tale. And he... with whom... and discuss... charm. But... when the s... volition, ne... usual. I wa... too experi... seemed to... him the d... opportuni... met him i... talks cam... The p... ception o... of villag... for mai... regimen... some e... were a... exchan... Silvio, ... there, ... he bro... as he... pied ... Silvio... leave... the l... "you... qua... wen... I... alm... alr... wa... an... po... as... a... f...

leave of each one separately; taking my hand in his, he stopped
me just as I was leaving. "I want to speak to you," he said in
low tones. I stayed behind.

The guests had gone, and we remained alone, facing each
other and lighting our pipes in silence. Silvio was preoccupied,
not a trace of his spasmodic gaiety was left. His sombre pallor
and gleaming eyes, and the thick smoke issuing from his mouth,
made him look like a veritable demon. A few minutes passed,
and then Silvio broke the silence.

"Perhaps we shall never meet again," he said. "Before parting
I should like to have a talk with you. You may have remarked
that I do not care much what others think of me, but I like you,
and it would pain me to leave you under a false impression."

He paused and began to refill his pipe. I looked down without
uttering a word.

"You thought it strange," he continued, "that I did not
demand satisfaction from that drunken fop R. You will agree
that I, being entitled to choose the weapons, held his life in
my hands, while my own was scarcely threatened. I might allow
you to ascribe my moderation to sheer magnanimity, but I have
no desire to deceive you. If I could have punished R. without
endangering my own life in the least, I would never have for-
given him."

I gazed at him in astonishment. His admission quite took me
aback. Silvio continued:

"Yes—I have no right to risk my life. Six years ago I was
struck in the face, and my enemy is still alive."

My curiosity was strongly roused. "And you didn't fight
him?" I asked. "I suppose you were parted by circumstances?"

"I did fight him," replied Silvio, "and I have here a souvenir
of our duel."

He rose and extracted from a cardboard box a braided red
cap with a gilt tassel (the kind that the French call a *bonnet de
police*). He put it on, and I saw that there was a bullet-hole in
it an inch above the forehead.

"You are aware," continued Silvio, "that I once served in
the Nth Hussar regiment. And you know my disposition. I am
accustomed to be first in everything; but in my youth it was a
passion with me. Rowdiness was the fashion in our day, and I
was the greatest fire-eater in the army. We were proud of getting drunk, and I once drank the famous Burtsov, immortalised

by the poet Denis Davydov,* under the table. Duels took place almost every minute in our regiment, and there was hardly one in which I was not either a second or an active participator. My comrades idolised me, while the regimental commanders, who were constantly changing, regarded me as an inevitable evil.

"I was calmly (or perhaps not so calmly!) enjoying my fame, when a wealthy youth, the scion of a distinguished line whom I will not name, joined the regiment. Never had I seen one so brilliant and so favoured by fortune! Figure to yourself youth, brains, looks, boisterous spirits, reckless courage, a resounding name, money which he expended lavishly, and which never seemed to come to an end, and try to imagine the impression he was bound to make on us. My title of champion was shaken. Attracted by my reputation, he tried at first to cultivate my friendship, but I received his advances coldly, and he desisted without the slightest regret. I conceived a bitter hatred for him. His popularity in the regiment and among women drove me to utter desperation. I tried to pick a quarrel with him—he capped my epigrams with epigrams of his own, which always seemed to me wittier and fresher than mine, and which were certainly infinitely more amusing. He merely jested, my shafts were poisoned. At last one evening at a ball given by a Polish landowner, seeing him the cynosure of all the ladies, especially of the lady of the house, with whom I was having an affair, I uttered some words of vulgar raillery in his ear. He flushed up and struck me in the face. Our hands flew to our sword-hilts. Ladies swooned, we were forcibly parted, and we set off to fight a duel that very night.

"It was the hour of dawn. I stood at the appointed place with my three seconds. I awaited my opponent with indescribable impatience. It was spring and the sun rose early, so it was already hot. I caught sight of him from afar. He was on foot, carrying his tunic on his sword, and accompanied by a single second. We went to meet him. He approached with his cap, full of cherries, in his hand. The seconds paced out twelve steps between us. I

---

* Denis Davydov (1784-1839), a poet and military writer, was Pushkin's good friend. In 1812, Davydov commanded an army partisan detachment which, together with the peasant partisans, fought against the invading French troops. Burtsov, also a participant in the Patriotic War of 1812, is often mentioned in Davydov's poems.

was to shoot first, but I was so shaken with rage that I could not
rely on the steadiness of my hand, and yielded the first shot to
him. But this my opponent would not agree to. It was decided
to draw lots—the lot fell to him, the perpetual favourite of
fortune. He took aim and shot through my cap. Then it was my
turn. At last his life was in my hands. I gazed keenly at him,
trying to discern the slightest trace of anxiety. He faced my
pistol, selecting ripe cherries out of his cap and spitting out the
stones, which almost reached to where I was standing. His cool-
ness infuriated me. What's the good of depriving him of his life,
I thought, when he doesn't even value it? A fiendish thought
passed through my mind. I lowered the hand holding the
pistol.

"'I see you are too busy to think of death,' I said, 'it is your
pleasure to breakfast. I do not wish to disturb you.' 'You don't
disturb me in the least,' he retorted, 'be so good as to fire. Just
as you please, however. You owe me a shot, and I shall always
be at your service.' I turned to the seconds and told them I did
not intend to shoot at the moment, and the duel ended
at that.

"I resigned from the army and retired to this little place.
Ever since, not a single day has passed without my meditating
revenge. My hour has now struck...."

Silvio drew from his pocket the letter he had received in the
morning, and gave it to me to read. Somebody (his lawyer,
apparently) wrote to him from Moscow that *a certain person* was
soon to enter into holy matrimony with a beautiful young
lady.

"You have guessed," said Silvio, "who this *certain person* is.
I am going to Moscow. We will see if he meets death on the eve
of his wedding as indifferently as he once awaited it over a capful
of cherries!"

With this, Silvio rose, dashed his cap on the floor and began
pacing up and down the room like a caged tiger. I stood quite
still, and heard him out, agitated by strange and conflicting
emotions.

The servant came in to say that the horses were in readiness.
Silvio pressed my hand warmly; we embraced. He got into the
carriage, in which lay two trunks, one containing his pistols,
the other his personal effects. We once more bade each other
farewell, and the horses galloped off.

II

Several years passed, and domestic circumstances compelled me to take up my abode in a poverty-stricken village in the X. district. While occupied with the management of my estate, I never ceased to sigh for my former noisy, carefree life. The thing I found it hardest of all to accustom myself to, was the utter solitude of the evenings in autumn and winter. Till the dinner-hour I contrived, somehow or other, to fill up my time, talking to the village-elder, driving about the estate to see how the work was going, or visiting newly-started enterprises. But as soon as dusk began to fall I did not know what to do with myself. I already knew by heart the contents of the few books which I had discovered in various closets, and in the store-room. The housekeeper Kirilovna had related her store of tales again and again; the songs of the women reduced me to a state of melancholy. I might have taken to drinking bitters, if they had not made my head ache. Moreover I have to freely admit that I was afraid of becoming a drunkard out of sheer ennui, that is to say, the worst of all drunkards, of whom I have seen innumerable examples in our district. My only neighbours were two or three of these unfortunates, whose conversation consisted mainly in hiccoughs and sighs. Solitude was more tolerable than such company.

Four versts away was the rich estate of the Countess B. But no one lived there except the steward, the Countess having visited her estate only once, during the first year of her marriage, and then stayed not much over a month. But during the second spring of my seclusion it was rumoured that the Countess and her husband intended to visit their estate in the summer. And in the beginning of June they actually arrived.

The arrival of a wealthy neighbour marks an era in the lives of country-dwellers. The landowners and their domestics talk about it for two months before the occurrence and three years after. In my own case I admit that the tidings of the arrival of a young and beautiful neighbour had a powerful effect on me. I burned with impatience to see her, and set off for the village of C. after dinner on the first Sunday after her arrival, to introduce myself to their Excellencies as their nearest neighbour and most humble servant.

The footman led me to the Count's study and went away to

announce me. The spacious study was furnished with the utmost luxury; against the walls were well-filled book-shelves, each with a bronze bust on the top. Above the marble fireplace was a great mirror; the floor was carpeted with green cloth, over which rugs were scattered. Having grown unaccustomed to luxury in my humble nook, and long ceased to witness the wealth of others, I was seized with timidity, and awaited the Count with nervous anxiety, as a suitor from the provinces awaits the coming of the Minister. The door opened, admitting an exceedingly handsome man of about thirty-two. The Count approached me with a cordial and friendly air. Endeavouring to recover my composure, I was about to introduce myself, but he forestalled me. We sat down. His conversation, which was courteous and easy, soon vanquished the shyness born of my long solitude; I was just beginning to feel at my ease, when the Countess entered, and I was seized with still greater embarrassment than before. She was indeed a lovely creature. The Count introduced me. I wished to appear at my ease, but the more I tried to assume a nonchalant air, the more embarrassed I felt. In order to give me time to recover my presence of mind and get used to being among strangers, they began talking to each other, treating me without ceremony, as a good neighbour. In the meanwhile I walked up and down, looking at the books and pictures. I knew very little about pictures, but there was one which attracted my attention. It depicted a Swiss landscape, but it was not the picture itself that attracted me so much as the fact that it bore the marks of two bullet-holes, one exactly over the other. "That was a good shot," I said, turning to the Count. "Yes," he replied, "a remarkable shot. Are *you* a good shot?" he went on. "First-rate," I answered, glad that the talk had at last turned on a subject so close to my heart. "I wouldn't miss a card at thirty paces—from pistols I was used to, of course." "Really?" said the Countess, with an air of great attention. "Could *you* hit a card at thirty paces, my love?" "We'll have a try one day," said the Count. "I wasn't a bad shot in my time. But I haven't had a pistol in my hand these four years." "Oh," I remarked, "in that case I will wager Your Excellency would not be able to hit a card at twenty paces—pistol-shooting requires daily practice. I know that from experience. I used to be considered one of the best shots in our regiment. But once I passed a whole month without touching a pistol—mine were undergoing repair. And

what do you think, Your Excellency? The first time I tried to
shoot after that, I missed a bottle at twenty-five paces, four
times running. Our captain, who was a wag and a joker, was
there and he said to me: 'Anyone can see you can't bear to hit
a bottle, friend.' Oh no, Your Excellency must not neglect that
exercise, or you'll get out of practice in no time. The best shot
I ever knew used to try his hand every day, shooting at least
three times before dinner. It was just as much a habit with him
as a glass of vodka before a meal." The Count and Countess
were glad that I had found my tongue. "Tell me something
more about his shooting," the Count asked. "I'll tell you what,
Your Excellency—sometimes he would see a fly settle on the
wall—I see you are laughing, Countess, but what I say is true,
I swear. Well, so he would see a fly and shout out: 'Kuzka, my
pistol!' and Kuzka would bring him his loaded pistol. And
bang, the fly would be squashed against the wall." "Marvellous!"
exclaimed the Count. "What was his name?" "Silvio, Your
Excellency." "Silvio!" cried the Count, jumping up. "Did you
know Silvio?" "Indeed I did, Your Excellency. He and I were
great friends. He was received in our regiment like one of ourselves. But I haven't heard a word of him for five years now.
And so Your Excellency knew him, too?" "I did. I knew him
very well. Did he never tell you ... but that is hardly likely ...
did he never tell you of a certain remarkable episode in his
life?" "Does Your Excellency mean the time a young fop struck
him in the face?" "And did he never tell you the name of that
young fop?" "No, Your Excellency, he didn't," I said. Then,
the truth suddenly dawning on me—"Oh, Your Excellency,"
I exclaimed, "forgive me! I had no idea ... was it you?" "It
was," replied the Count, looking extremely distressed. "And the
picture with the bullet-holes is a souvenir of our last meeting...." "Oh, my dear," said the Countess. "Do not talk about
it, I implore you. You know it always frightens me...." "Ah,
but I will, I will relate it all," said the Count. "He knows how
I insulted his friend. Let him hear how Silvio avenged himself
on me." The Count pulled up an armchair for me, and I listened
with the most lively curiosity to the following narrative:

"Five years ago I got married. The first month, the honey-
moon, I spent here, in this village. I owe the happiest moments
of my life to this house and one of my saddest memories.

"One evening we were out riding together. My wife's horse

became restive. She was alarmed, and handing the reins to me went back to the house on foot. I rode ahead. I saw a travelling carriage in the yard, and was told that there was a man waiting for me in my study who had refused to give his name, simply saying that he had business with me. I went into this room and saw in the dusk a man, covered with dust and unshaven, standing before the fire-place, just here. I went up to him, trying to remember who he was. 'Don't you know me, Count?' he said in a trembling voice. 'Silvio!' I cried, and I have to admit that I could feel my hair standing on end. 'Quite so,' he said. 'It is my turn to fire! I have come to discharge my pistol. Are you ready?' A pistol was sticking out of his breast-pocket. I measured out twelve paces, and stood over there in the corner, begging him to be quick, and fire before my wife got back. He delayed, asking for lights. Candles were brought. I locked the door and gave orders for no one to be admitted, and once more asked him to fire. He drew out the pistol and took aim. I counted the seconds.... I thought of her.... A minute of terrible suspense passed. Silvio let his hand fall. 'I regret,' said he, 'that my pistol is not loaded with cherry-stones, bullets are so heavy. I can't help feeling as if this were not a duel but murder. I'm not used to aiming at an unarmed man. Let us begin all over again—draw lots for the first shot.' My head reeled ... as far as I remember, I did not agree.... At last we loaded another pistol, twisted up two lots, which he put into the cap I had once shot through. Again I drew the lucky number. 'You have the devil's own luck, Count,' he said, with a smile I shall never forget. I cannot understand what came over me, and how I could have allowed him to make me do it.... But I fired, and hit that picture." (The Count pointed to the picture with the bullet-holes. His cheeks flamed; the Countess was whiter than her shawl; I was unable to suppress an exclamation.)

"I fired," continued the Count, "and thank God I missed. Then Silvio ... he was a terrible sight at that moment ... began to take aim at me. Suddenly the door opened, and Masha rushed in, shrieking and throwing herself on my shoulder. The sight of her gave me back my presence of mind. 'My dear,' I said to her, 'don't you see we are joking? What a state you are in! Go and have a drink of water, and then come back to us. I want to introduce my old friend and comrade to you.' Masha still did not believe me. 'Tell me, is it true what my husband

says?' she asked, turning to the formidable Silvio. 'Is it true
that you are both only joking?' 'He is always joking, Countess,'
replied Silvio. 'Once he struck me in the face just for a joke, he
shot through my cap for a joke, and just now he missed his
aim for a joke. And now *I* feel inclined to have a joke....'
With these words he again made as if to aim at me—in front
of her! Masha threw herself at his feet. 'Get up, Masha, for
shame!' I cried in a frenzy. 'And you, Sir, will you stop mocking
at an unfortunate woman? Do you intend to fire, or do you not?'
'I do not,' replied Silvio. 'I have received satisfaction. I have seen
you anxious, alarmed. I made you shoot at me, and I have had
enough. You will remember me. I leave you to your conscience.'
Here he made as if to go, but standing in the doorway he glanced
at the picture I had hit, fired at it almost without taking aim,
and vanished. My wife was in a swoon. My servants, who did
not dare to detain him, merely looked aghast at him. He stepped
into the porch, called to his coachman, and was gone before I
had time to realise what had happened."

The Count said no more. And thus it was that I discovered the
end of the tale, the beginning of which once made such an
impression on me. I never again met its hero. It is said that
Silvio led a detachment during the Alexander Ipsilanti* rising,
and was killed in the battle of Skulyani.

---

* Alexander Ipsilanti—a General in the Russian Army. In 1820, he
headed a hetaireia, a secret revolutionary society fighting for the liberation
of Greece from Turkish invaders. His company was routed by the Turkish
army on June 29, 1821, near Skulyani on the river Prut.

BLIZZARD

The steeds fly o'er the rugged ground,
Trampling the snow beneath their hoofs....
When lo! Amidst the solitude
Appeared the lonely house of God.

. . . .
And sudden blizzard covers all,
The snow descends in whirling flakes;
And a fable crow with whistling wing
Sweeps low above the bounding sleigh.
Its cry prophetic bodes no good!
The flying horses strain their sight,
Peering into the distant gloom,
Their manes erect in fear.

*Zhukovsky**

Towards the end of the year 1811, that never-to-be-forgotten period of our history, there lived in his estate of Nenaradovo the worthy Gavrila Gavrilovich R. He was known throughout the district for his hospitality and kindliness; neighbours visited him incessantly, to eat, drink and play Boston for five-kopek stakes with his wife, while some came to look at their daughter Marya Gavrilovna, a maiden who was pale, slender and seventeen. She was considered a good match, and there were many who hoped to win her for themselves or their sons.

Marya Gavrilovna had been brought up on French novels, and consequently was in love. The object of her choice was an ensign with a pale countenance, on leave of absence in his hereditary village. It goes without saying that the young man burned with an equal passion, and that the parents of his beloved, observing their mutual inclination, forbade their daughter to think of him, and received him as coldly as if he were a retired assize-magistrate.

Our lovers kept up a correspondence, and met every day in

---

* From *Svetlana*, a ballad by the Russian poet and translator Vassily Zhukovsky (1783-1852).

the solitude of a pine copse, or at an ancient chapel. There they vowed eternal love, bewailed their sad lot, and made all sorts of plans. As a result of such correspondence and conversation they came (naturally enough) to the following conclusion: since we cannot exist without each other, and cruel parents stand in the way of our happiness, why not dispense with their consent? It will easily be imagined that the young man was the first to arrive at this happy thought, and that it greatly pleased the romantic fancy of Marya Gavrilovna.

Winter came, putting an end to their meetings: but this only made their correspondence more animated. Vladimir Nikolaye-vich implored his beloved in every letter to become his, to marry him in secret, live in concealment for a short time, after which they would throw themselves at the feet of her parents, whose hearts could not fail to be touched by the heroic fidelity and suffering of the lovers, and who would surely exclaim: Come to our arms, children!

Marya Gavrilovna was long in making up her mind: innumer-able plans for flight were rejected. At last she agreed: on the day appointed she was to absent herself from the suppertable, and take refuge in her bedroom, pleading a headache. Her maid was let into the secret. Both girls were to go into the garden through the back-entrance, to find a waiting sleigh, get into it and drive the five versts from Nenaradovo to the village of Zhadrino, straight to the church, where Vladimir would be waiting for them.

On the eve of the decisive day Marya Gavrilovna did not sleep all night; she went through her wardrobe, making a bundle of her linen and dresses, indited a lengthy epistle to a certain sentimental young lady-friend of hers, and another to her parents. She bade them farewell in the most moving terms, ascribing her action to the overwhelming power of passion, and ending her letter with the declaration that she would consider the moment when she would be permitted to throw herself at the feet of her beloved parents as the happiest of her life. Sealing both letters with a Tula seal—two flaming hearts above an appropriate inscription—she flung herself on her bed just before daybreak and fell into a light doze, but was aroused every few minutes by terrible dreams. Once she dreamed that at the very moment when she was getting into the sleigh to drive to the church, her father stopped her, dragging her over the snow with agonising speed and flinging her into a dark, bottom-less dungeon ... she plunging rapidly downwards, her heart almost stopping; another time she dreamed she saw Vladimir lying pale and bleeding on the grass. Dying, he begged her in piercing accents to hasten their marriage.... Visions, hideous and chaotic, passed before her mind one after another. At last she rose, even paler than usual, with a genuine headache. Her father and mother noted her perturbation; their tender solicitude and incessant questions: "What is the matter with you, Masha? Are you ill, Masha?" smote her heart. She endeavoured to allay their fears and appear cheerful, but did not succeed in this. Evening came. The thought that this was the last day she would spend in the bosom of her family, made her heart ache. She could hardly breathe; in secret she bade farewell to all the persons and objects so familiar to her. Supper was served; her heart beat violently. In a trembling voice she announced that she did not want any supper, and said good night to her father and mother. They kissed her and gave her their blessing, in the usual way; she almost wept. Once in her bedroom, she flung herself into an arm-chair and burst into tears. Her maid begged her to calm down and recover her cheerfulness. All was in readiness. Half an hour later Masha was to bid farewell for-ever to her parents' home, her own room, her tranquil girl-hood.... Outside a blizzard was raging; the wind was howling, the shutters shaking and rattling; everything seemed to her like a threat or a mournful omen. Soon the whole house was wrapt in sleep. Masha covered her shoulders with a shawl, put on a warm cloak, picked up her trinket-box, and left the house by the back-door, her maid following her with two bundles. They went into the garden. The blizzard had not abated; the wind blew in their faces, as if endeavouring to stop the youthful sin-ner. It was all they could do to get to the end of the garden. In the road a sleigh was awaiting them. The horses, chilled through, could hardly stand still; Vladimir's coachman was pacing up and down in front of the shafts, in his efforts to control the mettlesome steeds. He helped the young lady and her maid to seat themselves and settle their bundles and trinket-box in the sleigh, gathered the reins into his hands, and the horses sprang forward with a will. Leaving our heroine to the mercy of fate and the skill of the coachman Tereshka, we will turn to our youthful lover.

Vladimir had been driving from place to place all day. In the morning he visited the priest at Zhadrino and persuaded him, not without difficulty, to comply with his request; then he went in search of witnesses from among the neighbouring landowners. The first one he visited, Dravin, a forty-year-old retired cornet, gave his consent readily, declaring that the adventure reminded him of former times and Hussar pranks. He persuaded Vladimir to stay and dine with him, assuring him that there would be no difficulty in finding the other two witnesses. Indeed, immediately after dinner, land-surveyor Schmidt, moustached and spurred, made his appearance, accompanied by the son of the district police officer, a lad of some sixteen summers, who had recently entered a regiment of the Uhlans. They not only agreed to Vladimir's proposal, but they declared their readiness to sacrifice their lives for him. Vladimir embraced them warmly, and went home to make his preparations.

Dusk had long fallen. He dispatched his *troika* with his trusty Tereshka, fully instructed, to Nenaradovo, and ordering his small one-horse sleigh to be harnessed, he drove himself to Zhadrino, where, in two hours' time, Marya Gavrilovna was to arrive. The road was familiar to him, and the drive should not have taken more than twenty minutes.

But hardly had Vladimir left the village behind and found himself in open country, when the wind rose and the blizzard became so dense that he could see nothing. The road was snowed up in a minute; the surroundings vanished in a snowy haze, dim and yellowish, in the midst of which whirled white snow-flakes; the sky merged with the ground; Vladimir found himself in the middle of a field, and tried in vain to get back to the road; the horse stepped out into the unknown, now blundering into a snow-drift, now tumbling into a hollow; the sleigh was continually overturning. All Vladimir's efforts were concentrated on trying not to lose his way. But after what seemed to him half an hour, he had not reached the copse at Zhadrino. Another ten minutes or so passed, and the copse was still not to be seen. Vladimir drove over open country, criss-crossed by deep gullies. The blizzard had not subsided, and the sky was still overclouded. The horse began to show signs of fatigue, and Vladimir perspired freely, despite the fact that he was continually plunging up to his waist in snow.

At last he discovered that he had been travelling in the wrong

No one in the house knew that flight had been intended. The letters written the evening before had been burned; Masha's maid said not a word to anyone, fearing the wrath of her master. The priest, the retired cornet, the bewhiskered land-surveyor and the youthful uhlan were discreet for reasons of their own. Tereshka the coachman never let fall an unnecessary word, even when tipsy. And so the secret shared by more than half a dozen conspirators was kept. But Marya Gavrilovna herself gave away her secret in her uninterrupted delirium. Her words were, however, so inarticulate that her mother, who never left her bedside, was only able to make out from them that her daughter was hopelessly enamoured of Vladimir Nikolaye-vich, and that this love was probably the cause of her illness. She consulted her husband and a few of the neighbours, and at last it was unanimously agreed that Marya Gavrilovna's fate was probably predestined, that there is no escape from fate, that poverty is no crime, that one has to live not with money-bags but with a human being, and so on. Platitudes are exceedingly helpful when we cannot find much justification for our actions.

In the meantime the girl gradually recovered. Vladimir had not been seen in the house of Gavrila Gavrilovich for a long time. He had been frightened off by the reception usually accorded him. Now he was sent for, and informed of his unexpected happiness—consent to his marriage. But what was the amazement of the owners of Nenaradovo when in reply to their invitation they received a half-crazy letter from the young man. He assured them that he would never again cross their threshold, and asked them to forget an unhappy wight, for whom the last remaining hope was death. A few days later they learned that he had gone back to the army. This was in the year 1812.

It was long before anyone ventured to tell the convalescent Masha of this. She herself never mentioned Vladimir. A few months later, discovering his name amongst those decorated for bravery, and dangerously wounded after the battle of Borodino*, she swooned, and it was feared that the fever would set in again. But the swoon, thank God, had no evil consequences.

---

* The battle of Borodino was fought on August 26, 1812, between the Russian and the French armies at the village of Borodino, 110 kilometres from Moscow.

She was soon visited by a fresh sorrow—her father gave up
the ghost, leaving her heiress to his whole estate. But her heritage
did not console her; she sincerely shared the grief of poor
Praskovya Petrovna, vowing never to part from her; they both
left Nenaradovo, with its melancholy associations, and went to
live on their estate in the village of X.

Here also there were plenty of suitors hovering around the
charming and wealthy heiress, but she never gave any of them
the slightest encouragement. Her mother sometimes tried to
persuade her to choose a life-mate, but Marya Gavrilovna only
shook her head and became pensive. Vladimir was no longer
among the living; he had died in Moscow, on the eve of the
French entry into the city. Masha held his memory sacred; at
any rate she preserved everything that might remind her of
him—the books he had once read, his drawings, the music and
verses he had copied out for her. The neighbours, learning of
this, were astounded at her constancy, and awaited with curiosity
the hero who was fated to triumph finally over the mournful
fidelity of this chaste Artemis.

In the meantime the war came to a victorious end and our
regiments returned from foreign parts. The people ran out of
their houses to meet them. The bands played songs captured
from the enemy—*Vive Henri Quatre*, Tyrolese waltzes, and arias
from *La Joconde*. Officers who had joined the campaign as
mere lads, returned matured by the air of the battlefield, and
hung with crosses. Soldiers chatted gaily to one another,
besprinkling their speech with French and German words.
Unforgettable days! Days of glory and enthusiasm! How
violently the Russian heart beat at the words *native land*! How
sweet were the tears of reunion! How unanimously we combined feelings of national pride with love for the tsar! And what
a moment it was for him!

The women, the women of Russia, were inimitable in those
days. Their habitual frigidity deserted them. The enthusiasm
was veritably intoxicating, when, meeting the conquerors,

> *The women cried: Hurrah!*
> *And threw their bonnets in the air!**

---

* From *Wit Works Woe*, a comedy by Alexander Griboyedov.

Self-portrait. Ink. 1829

Pyotr Vyazemsky (1792-1878). Son of a courtier of Catherine
the Second, a poet and critic, a famous wit and author of pungently
satirical verse, one of Pushkin's closest friends

Self-portrait. Ink. Pushkin portrayed himself astride a horse, wearing a shaggy Cossack cape and with a lance in his hand. The picture is based on an episode which occurred on June 14, 1829, when while travelling in the Caucasus, Pushkin found himself involved in a skirmish

Yekaterina Ushakova (1809-1872), the eldest daughter in a cultivated family of Moscow nobility. In the 1820s Pushkin was a frequent and welcome guest at the Ushakovs' and was good friends with Yekaterina. Water-colours. 1830s

Anna Olenina (1808-1888), daughter of Alexei Olenin, President
of the Academy of Arts. Pushkin was deeply in love with her,
asked for her hand in marriage, but was refused.
A drawing. 1833

What officer of those days but admits that he was indebted to some Russian woman for his best, most precious reward?

During this dazzling period Marya Gavrilovna lived with her mother in the gubernia of X., and did not see how the two capital cities celebrated the return of the troops. But the general enthusiasm may be said to have been still greater in the uyezds and villages. The appearance of an officer in such places was always triumphant, and the lover in a frock-coat had a hard time of it.

We have already stated that, despite her coldness, Marya Gavrilovna was surrounded by suitors as before. But all were forced to retreat when a wounded colonel of the Hussars, Burmin by name, made his appearance in her stronghold with a St. George's cross in his button-hole and a countenance of *interesting pallor*, as the local young ladies put it. He was about twenty-six years old. He was on leave of absence on his estate, which was quite close to the property of Marya Gavrilovna. Marya Gavrilovna showed him great preference. In his presence her usual melancholy yielded to a certain liveliness. There was no hint of coquetry in her behaviour towards him; but the poet, observing her, might have said:

Se amor non è che dunque? . . .

Burmin was certainly a most prepossessing young man. His was precisely the kind of mind which women like—decorous, attentive, without the slightest pretensions, and tinged with easy mockery. In the presence of Marya Gavrilovna he bore himself with simplicity and freedom; but whatever she said or did, his thoughts and his glances invariably followed her. He seemed to be very quiet and discreet, but rumour had it that at one time he had been a fast liver, and this did him no harm in the eyes of Marya Gavrilovna who (like most young women) gladly forgave pranks betraying audacity and ardour.

But it was the reserve of the youthful hussar which, more than anything else—more than his gentle manners, his pleasing conversation, his interesting pallor, his bandaged arm—fired her with curiosity and stirred her fancy. She could not help realising that she had made a great impression on him; and no doubt he, with his brains and experience, had already observed that she was far from indifferent to him—how was it then that she had not yet seen him at her feet, and heard his declaration of love?

What was it that restrained him? The diffidence inseparable from genuine love? Pride? Or was it the cunning of an experienced lady's man? He was an enigma for her. After much thought she decided that diffidence was the sole cause of his reserve, and took it upon herself to encourage him by still more marked attentions and, when occasion arose, even by a display of tenderness. She thought out an issue that should be altogether unexpected, and impatiently awaited the moment of romantic declaration. A mystery of any sort is always exasperating to the heart of woman. Her military manoeuvres were crowned with success, at least to the extent that Burmin sank into such reveries, and his black eyes dwelt so ardently on Marya Gavrilovna's face, that the decisive moment seemed to be imminent. The neighbours were already talking of the wedding as of a settled affair, and the good Praskovya Petrovna rejoiced that her daughter had at last found a suitor worthy of her.

One day the old lady was sitting in her drawing-room spreading out the cards for *grande patience*, when Burmin entered and asked for Marya Gavrilovna. "She's in the garden," answered the old lady. "Go to her, and I'll stay here and wait for you both." Burmin went out and the old lady crossed herself, thinking: "Perhaps everything will be settled today."

Burmin found Marya Gavrilovna at the pond, beneath a willow-tree, a book in her hand and in a white dress, just like the heroine of a novel. After the usual inquiries, Marya Gavrilovna purposely refrained from keeping up the conversation, thus intensifying their mutual embarrassment, which could only be removed by a sudden and determined declaration. And this is what happened. Burmin, conscious of the awkwardness of his situation, informed her that he had long been seeking an opportunity to lay bare his heart before her, and requested a moment of her attention. Marya Gavrilovna shut her book and lowered her eyelids as a sign of consent.

"I love you," said Burmin. "I love you passionately." (Marya Gavrilovna blushed and let her head droop still lower.) "I acted indiscreetly in yielding to the delightful habit, the habit of seeing and hearing you daily...." (Marya Gavrilovna was reminded of St. Preux's first letter.) "It is too late for me to resist my destiny; the memory of you, your sweet, incomparable image, will henceforth be the torment and joy of my whole life; but there still remains for me to fulfil a painful obligation, and disclose

to you a terrible secret, which will place an insuperable barrier between us...." Marya Gavrilovna interrupted him eagerly: "It always existed ... I could never have become your wife...."
"I know," he replied softly. "I know that you once loved another, but death, and three years of grief.... Dear, kind Marya Gavrilovna, do not seek to deprive me of my only consolation! The thought that you might have consented to make my happiness if ... be silent, I pray you, be silent! You torture me. I know, I feel, that you would have been mine, but—I am an unfortunate man—I am married!"

Marya Gavrilovna glanced at him in astonishment.

"I am married," continued Burmin. "I have been married these four years and know not who my wife is, or where she is, or if I am destined ever to meet her."

"What!" exclaimed Marya Gavrilovna. "How very strange! Go on; I will tell you later ... but go on, I implore you!"

"Early in the year 1812," said Burmin, "I was hastening to Vilna, where our regiment was stationed. Arriving at a posting station late one evening, I ordered fresh horses to be harnessed immediately, when a terrible blizzard sprang up all of a sudden and the keeper of the station and the drivers counselled me to wait for it to pass. I heeded their advice, but a strange feeling of anxiety overcame me; it was as if I was being urged on. The blizzard did not become any less violent; I lost patience and again gave orders for horses to be harnessed, and set out in the teeth of the storm. The driver took it into his head to go by the river, which should have shortened the journey some three versts. The banks were snowed up; the driver went past the place where we should have gone on on to the road, and we found ourselves in an unfamiliar neighbourhood. The storm showed no signs of subsiding; I saw a light and told the driver to go towards it. We arrived at a village; there was a light in the wooden church. The door was open and there were several sleighs drawn up inside the fence; people were moving about inside the porch. 'This way! This way!' shouted several voices. I told the driver to go up to the church. 'What on earth delayed you?' said someone to me. 'The bride is in a faint; the priest doesn't know what to do; we were just going to go home. Come in quick!' I leaped from the sleigh without a word and entered the church, which was faintly illuminated by a few candles. A young girl was seated on a bench in a dark corner; another was rubbing her temples. 'Thanks be to God,' said the latter. 'You've only just come in time. You have almost killed my young lady.' An old priest approached me with the question: 'Shall we begin?' 'Begin, Father, begin,' I answered abstractedly. The girl was helped to her feet. She seemed to me quite pretty . . . inexplicable, unpardonable levity. . . . I stood beside her at the altar; the priest was in a hurry; three men and a serving-maid supported the bride, and gave thought to no one else. We were made man and wife. 'Kiss!' they told us. My wife turned her pale countenance towards me. I was just going to kiss her. She shrieked: 'Oh, it is not he! It is not he!' and fell down unconscious. The witnesses directed a scrutinising gaze upon me. I turned, left the church all unhindered, dashed into my sleigh, and shouted: 'On!'"

"Dear God!" cried Marya Gavrilovna. "And you do not know what became of your unfortunate wife?"

"No," replied Burmin. "I do not know the name of the village where I was married; I do not remember what posting station I came from. At the time I ascribed so little importance to my reprehensible prank that I fell asleep as we left the church behind, and did not wake up till the next morning, at the third posting station. The servant who was then with me died during the campaign, so I have no hope of seeking out the person I mocked so cruelly and who is now herself so cruelly revenged."

"Good God!" said Marya Gavrilovna, seizing him by the sleeve. "So it was you! And you didn't recognise me!"

Burmin turned pale . . . and threw himself at her feet.

THE UNDERTAKER

> Do not we coffins everywhere behold,
> Those grey hairs of our ageing universe?
>
> *Derzhavin**

The last of the domestic effects of undertaker Adrian Prokhorov had been loaded on to the hearse, and the pair of lean
horses trudged for the fourth time from Basmannaya Street to
Nikitskaya Street, where the undertaker had moved with his
entire household. Locking up the shop, he nailed an announcement over the entrance, to the effect that the house was to be
let or sold, and set off on foot for his new abode. As he approached the yellow walls of the house which had so long been
the object of his desires, and which he had at last bought for a
substantial sum, the old undertaker discovered to his surprise
that he felt no joy. Stepping over the unfamiliar threshold into
the new dwelling, where all was as yet chaos, he sighed for the
rickety hovel in which, during the course of eighteen years, the
strictest order had prevailed; chiding his two daughters and
the serving-maid for their slowness, he began to help them.
Order was rapidly restored; the iconostasis, the china-closet,
the table, the couch and the bed were all installed in their
several corners in the back-room; the property of the master
of the house—coffins of all colours and dimensions, and
wardrobes full of mourning headgear, cloaks and torches—was
stacked in the kitchen and parlour. Over the gate was hung a
sign depicting a stout Cupid, bearing a torch upside down in

---

* From *Waterfall*, an ode by Gavriil Derzhavin (1743-1816), a distinguished Russian poet.

his hand, above the inscription: "Coffins plain and coloured sold and upholstered, also let out on hire, and old coffins repaired." His daughters retired to their own chamber, and Adrian, after inspecting his new dwelling, seated himself at the window and ordered the samovar to be heated.

The well-informed reader is aware that both Shakespeare and Sir Walter Scott represented their grave-diggers as light-hearted and waggish, in order, by force of contrast, to make a greater impression on our minds. Our respect for the truth, however, prevents us from following their example, and we are obliged to admit that our undertaker's disposition was in complete accord with his dismal trade. Adrian Prokhorov was a grave and gloomy individual. On the rare occasions when he broke silence it was to reprove his daughters when he came upon them looking idly out of the window at the passers-by, or to demand an exorbitant price for the works of his hands from those who were so unfortunate (or, as the case might be, so fortunate) as to stand in need of them. And so Adrian sat at the window over his seventh cup of tea, absorbed as usual in melancholy reflections. He remembered the torrents of rain which had greeted the funeral procession of the retired brigadier the week before, just as it was passing through the toll-gate. As a consequence many cloaks had shrunk, and many hat-brims were warped. He foresaw considerable expenditure, for the ancient stock of funeral raiment in his possession was in a pitiable state. He had hoped to compensate for his losses by the funeral of old Tryukhina, the merchant's widow, who had been lingering on the verge of the grave for a whole year. But Tryukhina was dying at Razgulyai, and Prokhorov feared that the heirs, despite the promise made to him, would not trouble to send so far for him, and would come to terms with the nearest contractor.

These meditations were suddenly interrupted by three Masonic knocks at the front door. "Who's there?" cried the undertaker. The door opened, and a man, immediately recognisable as a German craftsman, entered the room and approached the undertaker with a cheerful air. "Forgive me, dear neighbour," he said, speaking broken Russian in the manner which we are still unable to hear without laughter. "Forgive me if I interrupt you, but I wish to make your acquaintance as soon as possible. I am a shoemaker, my name is Gottlieb Schultz, and

I live just across the street in the little house you can see from
your window. I am celebrating my silver wedding tomorrow,
and I want to invite you and your daughters to come and dine
with me in a friendly way." The invitation was graciously
accepted. The undertaker asked the shoemaker to sit down and
drink a cup of tea with him, and soon, thanks to the frank disposition of Gottlieb Schultz, they were chatting in the most
friendly manner. "How goes it in your trade?" inquired Adrian.
"Heigh-ho," replied Schultz. "We have our ups and downs. I
can't complain. Of course my wares are not like yours—the
living can do without boots, but a dead man cannot live without
a coffin." "Perfectly true," agreed Adrian. "At the same time,
if a living man has no money to buy boots with, he can go barefoot, saving your presence; but a dead beggar will get his coffin
for nothing." The conversation proceeded in this manner a
little longer, till the shoemaker rose and took leave of the undertaker, at the same time repeating his invitation.

The next day, precisely at noon, the undertaker and his
daughters stepped out of the gateway of the newly-purchased
house, and set off to visit their neighbour. I will not attempt to
describe the Russian *kaftan* of Adrian Prokhorov, nor the
European attire of Akulina and Darya, thereby deviating in this
respect from the approved custom of modern novelists. It may,
however, not be superfluous to remark that both damsels wore
yellow hats and red slippers, which they only put on for special
occasions.

The shoemaker's small room was crowded with guests, most
of whom were German craftsmen with their wives and apprentices. The only Russian official present was Police Constable
Yurko, a Chukhon, who, in spite of his modest rank, enjoyed
the special favour of the host. For twenty-five years he had truly
and faithfully pursued his calling, like Pogorelsky's famous
postman. The fire of 1812, destroying the ancient capital,
annihilated also his yellow sentry-box. But as soon as the enemy
was driven away, a new sentry-box, painted grey and adorned
with white Doric columns, appeared in its place, and Yurko
resumed his pacing up and down in front of it, armed *cap-à-pie*.
He was acquainted with most of the Germans inhabiting the
streets around Nikitsky Gate, some of whom even found themselves obliged to spend their Sunday nights in his sentry-box.
Adrian hastened to make his acquaintance, regarding him as a

person of whom he would certainly stand in need sooner or later, and when the guests sat down to table, these two sat next to each other. Herr and Frau Schultz and their daughter, the seventeen-year-old Lottchen, while dining with their guests, waited at table and helped the cook to dish up. Beer flowed freely. Yurko ate for four. Adrian was not behindhand. His daughters minded their manners. The conversation, which was carried on in German, grew ever louder. Suddenly the host called for attention, and, uncorking a bottle besmeared with tar, cried out loudly, in Russian: "To the health of my good Luise!" The light champagne frothed. The host kissed the fresh-complexioned face of his middle-aged help-mate, and the guests noisily drank the health of the good Luise. "To the health of my dear guests!" announced the host, uncorking another bottle, and the guests returned their thanks, draining their glasses again. The toasts now began to follow thick and fast—they drank to the health of each person singly, toasted the city of Moscow, and a round dozen small German towns, then came toasts to all trades as such, and to each in turn, and to the health of all the craftsmen and apprentices in them. Adrian drank conscientiously, at last becoming so elated that he actually proposed a whimsical toast. Then one of the guests, a stout baker, raised his glass with the exclamation: "To the health of those for whom we work—*unserer Kundleute!*" This toast, like all the preceding ones, was drunk with cheerful unanimity. The guests began bowing to one another—the tailor bowed to the shoemaker, the shoemaker to the tailor, the baker to them both, the entire company to the baker, and so on. In the midst of these mutual salutations, Yurko turned to the undertaker, crying: "Come on, neighbour, drink the health of your dead men!" Everyone laughed but the undertaker, who took umbrage and frowned. No one noticed this, and the guests went on drinking; by the time they rose from the table the bells were ringing for vespers.

The guests dispersed at a late hour, most of them tipsy. The stout baker, and the bookbinder, whose face seemed to be "bound in crimson morocco", led the constable to his shelter with a hand under each of his arms, observing, in this instance, the Russian proverb—a debt is crowned in the payment. The undertaker arrived home angry and befuddled. "After all," he reflected aloud, "why is my trade less honourable than the others? An undertaker is not brother to the hangman, is he? What do those foreigners find to laugh at? Is an undertaker a fool in motley for them? And I was going to invite them all to my house-warming. Oh, no, I won't do that! I will invite those for whom I work—my Christian corpses." "Oh, Sir!" exclaimed the serving-maid, who was taking off his boots. "Think what you are saying! Cross yourself! Invite the dead to a house-warming! It's horrible!" "Before God, I will do it!" continued Adrian. "And tomorrow, too! Do me the honour, my bene-factors, to feast with me tomorrow night. You shall share my little all." With these words the undertaker got into bed and was soon snoring.

It was still dark outside when Adrian was roused. Tryukhina, the merchant's widow, had died during the night, and a mes-senger from her factotum had galloped up on horseback to bring the tidings to Adrian. The undertaker rewarded him with ten kopeks for vodka, dressed hastily, hailed a *droshky* and drove to Razgulyai. Policemen were already posted at the entrance to the house of the deceased, and merchants were strutting up and down like crows sensing carrion. The corpse was laid out on a table, her countenance waxy, but the features not yet deformed by decay. Relatives, neighbours and domestics crowded round her. All the windows were open; there were candles burning; the priests were reading the prayers for the dead.

Adrian went up to the dead woman's nephew, a youthful merchant in a fashionable frock-coat, and informed him that the coffin, candles, pall, and other funeral paraphernalia would be supplied immediately in good condition. The heir thanked him absentmindedly, remarking that he would not haggle over the price, but would trust entirely in the undertaker's good faith. The undertaker, as was his wont, vowed that he would not charge a kopek too much, after which he exchanged a significant glance with the factotum, and drove back to make his prepara-tions. All day he drove backwards and forwards between Raz-gulyai and Nikitsky Gate. By evening everything was in order, and he went home on foot, dismissing the driver. It was a moonlit night. The undertaker arrived safely at Nikitsky Gate. As he was passing the Church of the Ascension our friend Yurko challenged him, and recognising the undertaker wished him good night. The hour was late. The undertaker was approaching his house when all of a sudden it seemed to him that somebody came up to the gate, opened it, and disappeared through it. "What can it mean?" wondered Adrian. "Who else could be needing me? Is it a thief breaking in? Can it be that young men visit my little fools by night?" He even thought of calling his friend Yurko to his aid. Just then another person approached the gate and was about to enter, but catching sight of the undertaker hurrying towards the house, he stood still and raised his cocked hat. Adrian fancied he knew the face, though in his haste he had not been able to examine it closely. "You were coming to see me," he panted. "Step in, please." "Don't stand on ceremony, friend," said the unknown in hollow tones. "You go in first—show your guests the way." Adrian was in much too great a hurry to stand on ceremony. The gate was unlatched, and he went up the steps to the house, the other following him. It seemed to Adrian that there were people moving about in his rooms. "What the deuce does it all mean?" he thought, hastening to let himself in, and ... his knees gave way. The room was full of corpses. Through the window the moon lit up their yellow and blue visages, their fallen mouths, dim, half-shut eyes and peaked noses.... Adrian recognised with horror people whom he had assisted to bury, and in the one who entered with him he beheld the brigadier buried during the pouring rain. They all, ladies and gentlemen alike, clustered round the undertaker, with bows and words of greeting, with the exception of one poor fellow buried free of charge not long before, who did not come near, but stood humbly in a corner of the room as if ashamed of his ragged attire. All but he were decently attired, the women in ribboned caps, the defunct officials in uniforms, but unshaven, the merchants in their best robes. "You see, Prokhorov," said the brigadier, speaking on behalf of the whole company, "we have all risen to accept your invitation. Only those who are quite helpless, who have completely decayed, have stayed behind, and those who are nothing but fleshless bones, but one of these latter could not resist coming, so anxious was he to visit you...." Just then a small skeleton elbowed its way through the crowd and approached Adrian. Its fleshless visage leered affectionately at Adrian. Straps of bright green and red cloth and threadbare linen clung here and there to it, as to a pole, and its shin-bones rattled in high riding-boots, like a pestle in a mortar. "Don't you recognise me, Prokhorov?" said the skeleton. "Don't you

remember retired sergeant of the Guards Pyotr Petrovich Kurilkin, the man you sold your first coffin to (a deal one, but you
said it was oak), in 1799?" With these words the skeleton
extended his arms in a bony embrace, but Adrian, mustering up
all his strength, cried out and pushed him away. Pyotr Petrovich
swayed and fell to the ground, a mere heap of disjointed bones.
A hum of indignation arose from the corpses. All were anxious
to defend the honour of their comrade, advancing upon Adrian
with curses and threats and the unfortunate host, deafened by
their cries, and almost crushed by their onslaught, lost his presence of mind and in his turn fell unconscious upon the bones of
the deceased sergeant of the Guards.

The sun's rays were already lighting up the bed on which
the undertaker lay. At last he opened his eyes and saw before
him the servant-maid blowing on the embers in the samovar.
Adrian remembered with horror the events of the night.
Tryukhina, the brigadier, and Sergeant Kurilkin vaguely
haunted his imagination. He waited in silence for the maid to
open the conversation and tell him what the consequences of
the nocturnal adventure had been.

"How late you slept, Adrian Prokhorovich, Sir," said Aksi-
nya, handing him his morning robe. "Our neighbour the tailor
came to see you, and the police constable ran in to say that it
was the police inspector's name-day today, but you were asleep,
and we didn't like to wake you."

"And did anyone come from the late widow Tryukhina?"

"Tryukhina? Why? Is she dead?"

"What a fool you are! Didn't you help me make the preparations for her funeral yesterday?"

"Have you gone mad, Sir, or are the fumes of yesterday's
drinking still hanging about you? There wasn't any funeral
yesterday! You feasted at the German's all day and came back
drunk, and fell on to your bed and you've been asleep up till
now, and the bell has stopped tolling for service."

"Have I?" exclaimed the undertaker, in relief.

"Of course you have," replied the maid.

"In that case, hurry up with the tea, and call my daughters."

THE POSTMASTER

He was a Civic Counsellor,
And the despot of a posting station.

*Prince Vyazemsky**

Show me the man who has never cursed the master of a posting station, or who has never wrangled with one; the man, who,
in a moment of fury, has not demanded the fatal volume in
which to enter useless complaints of arbitrary behaviour, rude-
ness and unpunctuality; who does not consider postmasters as
monsters in human form, as bad as certain defunct officials, or
at any rate no better than the Murom robbers. We will endeav-
our to be just, however, and to put ourselves in their place,
and then, perhaps, we shall judge them with much greater
indulgence. What is a postmaster? He is a veritable martyr
among petty officials, protected from blows and cuffs by nothing
but this official rank of his, and even this does not always save
him (I appeal to the conscience of my readers). And how
difficult is the position of this despot, as Prince Vyazemsky
playfully calls him? Is not his work veritable hard labour? No
rest either by day or by night! The traveller pours out all the
vexations accumulated during the tedious journey upon the
postmaster. The weather is atrocious, the roads abominable, the
driver stubborn, the horses lazy—and for all this the postmaster
must take the blame. The traveller who enters his poor dwelling
regards him as a foe; and the postmaster is fortunate if he suc-
ceeds in soon getting rid of the uninvited guest. And if there

---

* From *The Station*, a poem by Pyotr Vyazemsky (1792-1878).

should happen to be no horses available! Heavens, what oaths, what threats are showered on his head! He is forced to run from house to house in rain and mud; he goes out into the porch while the storm rages and the frosts of January prevail, just to get a moment's respite from the shouts and pushes of the irate traveller. A general arrives, and the trembling postmaster gives him his last two *troikas*, one of which was being reserved for the mail-coach. The general departs, without so much as a word of thanks. Five minutes later comes the sound of bells and a state-messenger flings on the table an order for fresh horses. Weigh all these circumstances, and instead of indignation, your hearts will be filled with sincere sympathy. A few more words on this subject: I have travelled all over Russia in the course of twenty years. I know almost all the posting routes; I am acquainted with several generations of drivers; there is scarcely a single postmaster whom I do not know, and with whom I have not had dealings; I hope at no distant time to publish the interesting stock of observations I have accumulated while travelling; but for the present I will merely state that the race of postmasters has been grossly misrepresented to the public. These much abused postmasters are as a rule peaceable folk, of an accommodating disposition, sociably inclined, with no exaggerated sense of what is due to them, and by no means grasping. Much that is curious and instructive may be gleaned from their conversation, which many esteemed travellers make a great mistake in neglecting. For my own part, I admit I prefer it to the speeches of your second-rate official, travelling on government business.

It will easily be guessed that I have friends among the estimable class of postmasters. Indeed there is one of them whose memory is very precious to me. Circumstances brought us together at a certain period of my life and it is his story that I now intend to relate to my indulgent readers.

In May of 1816 I chanced to travel in the province of X., by a route which no longer exists. I held the rank of a petty official, and travelled post, my means only sufficing for two horses. This caused postmasters to treat me with scant ceremony, and I frequently had to take by force that which I considered to be mine by right. Being young and impetuous I was indignant at the baseness and pusillanimity of some postmaster who gave away to some high official the horses which had been prepared for my use. It took me just as long to get used to being passed over during one of the courses at the Governor's table by some perspicacious lout of a waiter. Now both these situations seem to me quite in the order of things. After all, what would become of us if for the rule, so universally accepted, *let rank yield to rank*, another were to be substituted, for instance—*let mind yield to mind*? What disputes would arise! And whom would the domestics have to serve first? But I will return to my narrative.

It was a hot day. Three versts from the posting station of X. a light drizzle began, and a minute later I was soaked to the skin by a downpour. On arriving at the station my first care was to change my clothes as quickly as possible, my second to ask for tea. "Hey, Dunya!" cried the postmaster. "Get the samovar ready, and go and fetch some cream." In response to these words a girl of some fourteen summers emerged from behind a partition-wall and scampered to the porch. I was struck by her beauty. "Is that your daughter?" I asked the postmaster. "Yes," he replied with an air of complacency. "And she's so clever, so quick, just like her dear mother before her." He began then and there copying out my order and I fell to examining the pictures which adorned his humble but neat and clean dwelling. They illustrated the story of the Prodigal Son. In the first picture a venerable old man in night-cap and dressing-gown was bidding farewell to a restless youth who was hastily receiving his blessing and a bag of money. Another displayed in vivid detail the dissolute conduct of the young man, who was depicted seated at a table surrounded by false friends and shameless women. Then came a picture of the ruined youth in a ragged cloak and cocked hat, herding swine and sharing their meal; his face expressed profound melancholy and contrition. The last of the series showed his return to his father; the good old man, still in his night-cap and dressing-gown, ran out to meet him; the prodigal son knelt at his feet; in the background could be seen the cook slaughtering the fatted calf, and the older brother asking the servants the reason for these rejoicings. I read the appropriate German couplets beneath each picture. All this is still fresh in my memory, together with the pots of balsam and the bed with the bright-patterned curtain and other objects by which I was then surrounded. I can still see before me the master of the house himself, a man of about fifty, hale and cheerful, his long green frock-coat adorned with three medals dangling from faded ribbons.

Hardly had I paid off my old driver, when Dunya came back with the samovar. The little coquette was not slow to observe the impression she had made on me, and lowered her great blue eyes demurely. I entered into conversation with her and she answered without the slightest signs of embarrassment, like a girl who had seen something of the world. I offered her father a glass of punch. To Dunya, I handed a cup of tea, and we all three chatted together as if we had known one another for ages.

The horses were in readiness, but I was loath to part from the postmaster and his daughter. At last I took leave of them, the father wished me a good journey, and the daughter saw me to my carriage. I stopped in the porch and asked her to allow me to kiss her. Dunya consented.... I can pass in review innumerable kisses,

Since I began this pastime to enjoy,

but not one of them has left such a delightful and lasting memory.

Several years passed, and circumstances again conspired to take me along the same route, to the same places. I remembered the postmaster's daughter, and rejoiced at the thought that I should see her once more. And then I reflected that the old postmaster might have been dismissed, and that Dunya was probably married by now. The thought of the death of the one or the other also flashed through my mind, and I approached the posting station of X. with melancholy forebodings.

My horses drew up before the postmaster's little house. Going into the room I immediately recognised the pictures illustrating the story of the Prodigal Son. The table and bed were in their old places, but there were no longer flowers on the window-sill, and everything in the room spoke of decay and neglect. The postmaster was asleep covered with a sheepskin coat. My arrival woke him, and he sat up.... It was Samson Vyrin himself, but how he had aged! While he was copying out my order I noticed his grey hair, the deep lines in his unshaven cheeks and his bowed shoulders, and could not contain my astonishment that three or four years should have transformed a robust man into a frail ancient. "Don't you know me?" I asked. "You and I are old friends." "Quite possible," he replied morosely. "It's a busy route, a great many travellers come here." "And how is your Dunya?" I continued. The old man frowned. "God knows," he said. "Is she married, then?" I asked. The old man pretended not to have heard my question, and went on reading over my order in a whisper. I discontinued my questions and asked to have the kettle put on. I was beginning to feel the prickings of curiosity, and hoped that punch would loosen my old friend's tongue.

I was not mistaken—the old man did not reject the proffered glass. I observed that rum dispersed his gloominess. By the second glass he became talkative, remembering, or at least pretending to remember, who I was, and I learned from his lips a tale which at the time interested and moved me strangely.

"So you knew my Dunya?" he began. "Ah, who did not know her! Ah, Dunya! Dunya! What a girl she was! Everyone who came here used to praise her, no one had a word to say against her. The ladies used to give her presents—some a kerchief, some a pair of ear-rings. When gentlemen came to the posting station they would stop on purpose, as if for dinner or supper, but really for the sake of looking at her a little longer. However angry a gentleman might be, he would calm down at the sight of her, and speak graciously to me. You will hardly believe it, but couriers and state-messengers would talk to her by the half-hour. My home depended on her—she found time to clean house, to cook, to do everything. And I, old fool, could not take my eyes off her, could not contain my joy in her. Did not I love my Dunya, did not I cherish my child? Did not she have an easy life? But you can't stave off disaster by prayers—there is no escape from destiny." Here he began to give me a detailed account of his misfortune.

Three years before, one wintry evening when the postmaster was ruling himself a new ledger, and his daughter was sitting behind the partition making a dress, a *troika* drew up and a traveller in a Circassian cap and military great-coat, and a thick muffler, entered the room and demanded horses. The horses were all out. On hearing this, the traveller raised his voice and his whip, but Dunya, who was familiar with such scenes, came running out from behind the partition, and addressed the traveller graciously, asking him if he would like something to eat. The appearance of Dunya produced its usual effect. The traveller's rage left him; he consented to wait for horses and ordered supper. After taking off his wet shaggy fur

The village of Boldino, the estate of Pushkin's father in Nizhni-Novgorod Gubernia. In the autumn of 1830s, Pushkin went there to assume ownership of the neighbouring village of Kistenevka which his father had turned over to him on the occasion of his marriage. During the three months which he spent in Boldino, Pushkin wrote five "Small Tragedies", "The Tales of Belkin", the long poem "A House in Kolomna", 30 short poems and many articles

The countryside around Boldino. The Luchinnik wood, Pushkin's favourite haunt

The manuscript of Pushkin's story "The Undertaker", 1830s, with his drawings.
The drawing shows the cobbler Gottlieb Schultz and the undertaker Adrian
Prokhorov having tea together

A drawing in Pushkin's manuscript of "The Undertaker". 1830s. "The Funeral"

St. Petersburg. The Arsenal. A lithograph. 1830s.

Natalia Golitsina (*née* Chernyshova) (1741-1837), the
mother of Moscow's Governor-General Dmitry Golitsin.
She was a lady in waiting of five Russian empresses.
A striking figure in Petersburg high society, she was
nicknamed *Princesse Moustache*. Pushkin endowed his
Old Countess in "The Queen of Spades" with some of
Golitsina's traits of character and biographical details.
A miniature. 1810s

cap, unwinding his muffler, and throwing off his great-coat, he was seen to be a slender young hussar with a small black moustache. He made himself quite at home in the postmaster's house, and was soon chatting gaily with the postmaster and his daughter. Supper was served. Meanwhile the horses had returned and the postmaster ordered them to be harnessed to the traveller's sleigh, without even being fed. But when he got back to his room he found the young man lying almost unconscious on the bench. He felt faint, his head ached, he was not fit to travel.... There was no help for it! The postmaster gave up his bed to him, and it was decided, should the patient not be better by the morrow, to send to C. for the apothecary.

Next day the hussar was worse. His servant rode to the neighbouring town for the apothecary. Dunya laid a handkerchief soaked in vinegar round his head, and sat beside his bed with her sewing. In the postmaster's presence the patient moaned and could scarcely utter a word, though he drank two cups of coffee and moaned out an order for dinner. Dunya never left his side. He constantly begged for a drink, and Dunya as constantly brought him a mug of the lemonade she had prepared with her own hands. The patient moistened his lips, and every time he returned the mug he pressed Dunya's hand in his feeble grasp, by way of showing his gratitude. The apothecary arrived at dinner-time. He felt the patient's pulse, spoke to him in German, and declared, in Russian, that all he needed was rest, and that he would be able to resume his journey in a couple of days. The hussar handed him twenty-five rubles in payment for his visit, and invited him to dinner. The apothecary accepted the invitation and the two of them ate heartily, drank the contents of a bottle of wine, and were vastly pleased with each other.

Another day passed and the hussar recovered completely. He was extremely gay, joking incessantly, now with Dunya, now with the postmaster, whistling tunes, chatting with travellers, entering their relays in the ledger, and making the kindly postmaster so fond of him that by the morning of the third day he could hardly bear to part with his pleasant lodger. It was a Sunday, and Dunya got ready to go to church. The hussar's sleigh was brought round. He bade the postmaster farewell, rewarding him generously for his board and lodging. He said good-bye to Dunya, too, offering to drive her as far as the church, which was at the other end of the village. Dunya seemed perplexed.... "What are you afraid of?" her father said. "His Honour isn't a wolf—he won't bite you; let him drive you to the church." Dunya got into the sleigh and sat down next to the hussar, the servant leaped on to the box-seat, the driver whistled, and the horses galloped off.

The unfortunate postmaster could never understand how it was that he had allowed his Dunya to go with the hussar, how he could have been so blind, what could have possessed him! Hardly half an hour passed when he began to feel a gnawing at his heart, and was overcome by anxiety to such an extent that he could no longer contain himself, and went to the church to look for her. As he approached it he saw the people already coming out, but Dunya was neither in the churchyard, nor in the porch. He hastened into the church; the priest had left the altar, the sexton was extinguishing the candles, two old women were still saying their prayers in a corner; but there was no Dunya to be seen. The unhappy father forced himself to ask the sexton if she had been at the service. The sexton replied that she had not. The postmaster returned home more dead than alive. He had only one hope left—Dunya with the levity of youth might have gone on to the next posting station, where her godmother lived. He awaited the return of the horses which he had sent with the carriage in an agony of impatience. But the day passed, and the driver did not come back. At last, towards night, he rode up alone, tipsy, and the bearer of appalling tidings: "Dunya had gone on from the next posting station with the hussar."

The old man never got over his misfortune, and that evening took to his bed—the very bed on which the youthful impostor had lain the day before. The postmaster, reviewing all the circumstances, now guessed that the young man's illness had been feigned. The poor old man was seized with a raging fever and was taken to C., another postmaster being temporarily appointed in his place. He was attended by the very same doctor who had visited the hussar and who now assured the postmaster that the young man had been perfectly well, and that he had guessed his evil intentions at the time, but had said nothing, for fear of the hussar's whip. Whether the German spoke the truth, or merely wished to show off his perspicacity,

he did not afford his unhappy patient the least consolation. The
postmaster had hardly recovered from his illness when he asked
the authorities at C. for two months' leave, and, without a word
of his intentions to anyone, set off on foot to look for his
daughter. From the ledger he discovered that Captain Minsky
had travelled from Smolensk to Petersburg. The coachman who
drove him said that Dunya had wept all the way, although
apparently going of her own free will. "God willing," thought
the postmaster, "I shall bring my strayed lamb home." Inspired
by this thought he arrived in Petersburg, putting up at the bar-
racks of the Izmailov Regiment, in the house of a retired non-
commissioned officer, and old comrade-in-arms of his from the
days of his military service. And from there he began his
search. He quickly discovered that Captain Minsky was in
Petersburg, living at the Demutov tavern. The postmaster determined to see him.

Early in the morning he arrived at the hussar's front door and
requested the servant to inform his honour that an old soldier
wished to see him. The servant, polishing a riding-boot on a
boot-tree, told him that his gentleman was asleep, and did not
receive anyone before eleven o'clock. The postmaster went
away and returned at the appointed hour. Minsky himself
came out to him in his dressing-gown and a crimson fez.
"What can I do for you, brother?" he asked. The old man's
heart seethed with emotion, tears welled up in his eyes, and he
could only mutter, in trembling accents: "Your Honour! For
God's sake, Your Honour...." Minsky cast a rapid glance at
him, flushed crimson, took him by the hand, led him to his study,
and locked the door from the inside. "Your Honour," went on
the old man. "What is lost is gone forever, but give me back my
poor Dunya! You have had your joy of her—do not ruin her
for naught." "What has been done cannot be undone," said
the young man, who was evidently quite overcome. "I have
wronged you and am willing to ask your forgiveness. But you
must not think me capable of deserting Dunya. She will be
happy, I give you my word of honour. What do you want
with her? She loves me, she has become unused to her former
condition. Neither you nor she could ever forget what has
happened." Then, thrusting something into the postmaster's
cuff, he unlocked the door and the old man, hardly knowing
how, found himself in the street.

He stood motionless for a long time, and at last noticed that there was a bundle of paper beneath his cuff. He drew it out, and unfolded a number of crumpled five- and ten-ruble notes. Tears welled up afresh in his eyes, tears of indignation. He crumpled the notes into a ball, flung them on the ground, trampled them beneath his heel, and went away.... After walking a few yards he stood still, bethought himself and ... retraced his steps. But the notes were no longer there. A well-dressed young man, on seeing him, ran up to a *droshky*, and got in hastily, shouting: "Drive on!" The postmaster made no attempt to pursue him. He decided to go back to his posting station, but first wanted to see his poor Dunya, if only once. And so, two days later, he went to Minsky's quarters again. But the military servant told him sternly that his gentleman received no one, shouldered him out of the hall, and slammed the door in his face. The postmaster stood outside for some time—and then he went away.

That same evening he was walking along Liteinaya Street, having attended a service at the Church of All Martyrs. An elegant carriage dashed past him, and the postmaster recognised Minsky. The carriage stopped in front of a three-storey house, drawing up at the door, and the hussar leaped into the porch. A happy thought passed through the postmaster's mind. Turning back till he got to the carriage, he asked the coachman: "Whose horse is this, brother? Not Minsky's?" "Yes, it is," said the coachman. "Why do you ask?" "I'll tell you why—your master told me to take a note to his Dunya, and I've forgotten where she lives, this Dunya." "Why, she lives here, on the next floor. But you're late with your note, brother. He's with her himself, now." "No matter," said the postmaster, with a strange fluttering at his heart. "Thanks for putting me right, but I must keep my promise." And with these words he mounted the steps.

The door was locked. He rang the bell and passed a few seconds in an agony of suspense. The key rattled in the lock and the door was opened. "Does Avdotya Samsonovna live here?" he asked. "Yes," replied the young maid-servant. "What do you want with her?" Without replying the postmaster entered the hall. "You can't go in!" the servant called after him. "Avdotya Samsonovna has company." But the postmaster, taking no notice, walked on. The two first rooms he passed through were

in darkness, but there was a light in the third. He made for the
open door and came to a stop. Minsky was seated deep in
thought in the splendidly furnished room. Dunya, attired in
the height of fashion, was perched on the arm of his chair, as
if riding side-saddle in the English manner. She was gazing
tenderly at Minsky, twisting his black curls round her fingers,
which gleamed with jewels. Poor postmaster! Never had his
daughter seemed lovelier to him; he watched her with involuntary admiration. "Who's there?" she cried, without raising her
head. He stood silent. Not receiving an answer, Dunya looked
up ... and fell on the carpet with a shriek. Minsky, alarmed,
rushed to pick her up, but catching sight of the old postmaster
at the door, left Dunya and approached him, shaking with
rage. "What do you want?" he said through clenched teeth.
"Why do you follow me about like a thief? Are you after my
life? Get out!" And seizing the old man by the collar of his
coat with his strong hand, he shoved him out on to the stairs.

The old man went back to his lodging. His friend advised him
to lodge a complaint, but the postmaster, after thinking it over,
dismissed the idea with a wave of his hand, and decided to leave
things as they were. Two days later he left Petersburg and went
back to his posting station, where he resumed his former work.
"And it is now almost three years," he said in conclusion, "since
I have been living without Dunya, with never a word of her.
Whether she is alive or dead God alone knows. Anything is
possible. She is not the first and will not be the last to be
seduced by a passing fop, to be first kept by him, and then
abandoned. There are plenty of young fools like her in Petersburg, today dressed up·in satin and velvet, and tomorrow, look
you, sweeping the crossings with the riff-raff. Sometimes when
I think Dunya may be languishing there, I can't help the sinful
wish that she were in her grave...."

Such was the tale of my friend the old postmaster, a tale
constantly interrupted by tears, which he wiped away pic-
turesquely with the hem of his coat, like the zealous Terentyich
in the exquisite ballad of Dmitriev. These tears were partially
called forth by the punch, of which he imbibed five glasses in
the course of his narrative, but they nevertheless moved me
powerfully. After I took my leave of him it was long before I
could get the thought of the old postmaster out of my head, or
stop thinking of the unfortunate Dunya.

Not so long ago, passing through the hamlet of X., I remembered my old friend. I learned that the posting station which he had ruled over no longer existed. No one could give me a satisfactory answer to the question: "Is the old postmaster still alive?" I felt a desire to visit the familiar parts, and hiring horses drove to the village of N.

It was autumn. The sky was covered with grey clouds, a cold wind was blowing from the empty cornfields, bearing red and yellow leaves from the trees in its passage. I arrived at the village just before sunset, and stopped in front of the post-master's house. A stout woman came out into the porch (where poor Dunya had once kissed me), and replied to my inquiries that the old postmaster had been dead a year, that his house now belonged to a brewer and that she herself was the brewer's wife. I began to regret my useless journey and the seven rubles expended in vain. "What did he die of?" I asked the brewer's wife. "He drank himself to death, Sir," quoth she. "And where is he buried?" "Just beyond the village, beside his late wife." "Couldn't someone take me to his grave?" "Why, certainly. Hi, Vanka! Let that cat alone! Take the gentleman to the cemetery and show him the postmaster's grave."

A ragged urchin, red-haired and squint, ran up and led me to the end of the village.

"Did you know the postmaster?" I asked him on the way.

"Oh, yes, I knew him! He taught me to make whistles. When he came out of the tavern (God rest his soul!) we used to run after him and say: 'Uncle! Uncle! Give us some nuts!' And he would give us all nuts. He was always playing with us."

"And do travellers ever ask after him?"

"There aren't many travellers any more. Unless it's some assize-judge and he never thinks about dead people. But there was a lady this summer, she asked about the old postmaster and went to see his grave."

"What sort of lady?" I asked inquisitively.

"A lovely lady," said the boy. "She was in a coach-and-six, with three children and a nurse, and a black pug. And when they told her the old postmaster was dead, she cried, and said to the children: 'You stay here quietly, while I go to the cemetery.' I offered to take her there. But the lady said: 'I know the way myself.' And she gave me a silver five-kopek piece—such a kind lady!"

We arrived at the cemetery, a bleak spot with no railings, dotted with wooden crosses, and quite unprotected from the sun's rays. Never in my life have I seen such a melancholy cemetery.

"This is the grave of the old postmaster," said the little boy, leaping on to a mound of sand in which a black cross bearing a brass icon had been stuck.

"And did the lady come here?" I asked.

"She did," replied Vanya. "I watched her from the distance. She lay here, a long time she lay. And then she went to the village, the lady, and called for the priest, and gave him some money and went away and me she gave a silver five-kopek piece —a very nice lady!"

I, too, gave the small boy a five-kopek piece, and did not regret either my journey or the seven rubles it had cost me.

LADY INTO LASSIE

In any attire, sweetheart, you are charming.

*Bogdanovich**

The estate of Ivan Petrovich Berestov was situated in one of our remotest provinces. Ivan Petrovich served in the Guard in his youth, obtained his discharge in the year 1797 and went to live on his property, never again to leave it. He married a poor gentlewoman who died in child-birth during his absence, when he was some distance away on a hunting-expedition. He soon found consolation for his loss in the management of his property. He had his house built according to plans drawn up by himself, set up a cloth-factory on the estate, increased his income, and regarded himself as the wisest man in the whole district, which opinion his neighbours, who got into the habit of paying him long visits with their families and their hunting-dogs, did nothing to shake. On weekdays he went about in a velveteen jacket, on holidays he donned a frock-coat of home-spun cloth; he kept all the accounts himself, and read nothing but the Proceedings of the Senate. On the whole he was well-liked, though considered proud. His nearest neighbour, Grigori Ivanovich Muromsky, was the only person who did not get on with him. And he was a Russian gentleman of the old school. Having frittered away the greater part of his property in Moscow, and become a widower, he went to live in the sole village remaining to him, and there continued to waste his sub-stance, but this time in a different manner. He laid out a garden

---

* From the poem *Dear Heart* by Ippolit Bogdanovich (1743-1803).

in the English style, on which he expended almost all the money
he had. His stableboys were attired as English jockeys. His
daughter had an English governess. He farmed his land according to the English system.

But alien ways do not suit Russian corn, and despite considerable diminution of expenditure, the income of Grigori Ivanovich
did not increase; even in the country he found ways of accu-
mulating fresh debts; and with it all he was accounted an able
man, being the first landowner to think of mortgaging his estate
with the Court of Chancery—a manoeuvre in those days considered extremely complicated and audacious. Among those
who censured him, his sternest critic was Berestov, whose chief
characteristic was a dislike of innovations. He was unable to
speak calmly of his neighbour's Anglomania, and never tired
of finding fault with him. When showing visitors over his estate
he would reply to their praises of his management with sly
irony: "Well, well! We don't do things here the way neighbour
Grigori Ivanovich does. It's not for us to ruin ourselves in the
English style. We are thankful if we get enough to eat the Russian way!" Thanks to the zeal of the neighbours, these and
other quips, which you may be sure lost nothing in the telling,
were brought to the ears of Grigori Ivanovich. The Anglomaniac was no more able to bear criticism than are our jour-
nalists. Infuriated, he dubbed the rural Zoilus a bear and a
provincial.

Such were the relations between these two proprietors when
Berestov's son came to visit him. Educated at the university
of X., he intended to go into the army, but his father would not
give his consent to this. The young man felt himself to be completely unfitted for government service. Neither would give in,
and in the meantime the youthful Alexei lived the life of a
gentleman at large, cultivating a moustache so as to be ready
for any exigency.

Alexei was indeed a fine young fellow. It certainly would be
a pity if his graceful figure were destined never to be enclosed
in a military uniform, and if, instead of cutting a figure as a
dashing horseman, he would have to spend his youth stooping
over official documents. When the neighbours saw him at the
hunt, always galloping in the forefront, regardless of obstacles
in his way, they agreed unanimously that he would never make
a good government official. Glances full of interest, which not

seldom grew to admiration, were cast at him by the young ladies in the neighbourhood; but Alexei took very little notice of them, so that they felt bound to ascribe his coldness to a love affair. By way of corroboration of this view a paper was passed from hand to hand, bearing a copy of an address from one of his letters: *Akulina Petrovna Kurochkina, Moscow, opposite the Monastery of St. Alexis, at the house of the copper-smith Savelyev, you are kindly requested to hand this letter to A.N.R.*

Those of my readers who have never lived in the country can have no idea how delightful these provincial young ladies are. Brought up in the fresh air, in the shade of their apple-orchards, they derive all their knowledge of life and society from books. Solitude, liberty and reading early develop in them emotions and passions unknown to our pampered beauties. For these country maidens the jingle of bells is an adventure, a visit to the nearest town a momentous event in their lives, and visitors leave lasting, sometimes lifelong memories behind them. Anybody is entitled, of course, to laugh at certain oddities which may characterise these young ladies; but the jests of a superficial observer cannot destroy their essential qualities, of which the principal one is distinction of character, that *individualité* without which, according to Jean-Paul Richter, no human being can be great. It may be that in the great capitals women receive a superior education; but the ways of society soon exercise their levelling influence on character, and make the minds of women as alike as their headgear. This is said neither in judgement nor censure, but nevertheless *nota nostra manet,** as an old writer has it.

It is easy to conceive the impression bound to be made on our young ladies by Alexei. He was the first gloomy, disillusionised being they had met, the first to speak to them of spent pleasures and blighted youth; and to crown all he wore a black ring set with a death's head. All this was quite new to the province. All the girls were frantic about him.

But none of them devoted so much thought to him as the daughter of the Anglomaniac, Lisa (or Betsy, as her father usually called her). The fathers did not visit each other's houses, so that she had not yet seen Alexei, whereas all the young women of the neighbourhood talked of nothing but him. Lisa was

---

* The observation rests.

seventeen years old. Her attractive, olive-skinned countenance was lit up by a pair of black eyes. Being an only child, she was, of course, spoilt and petted. Her liveliness and incessant pranks were the delight of her father and the despair of her governess, Miss Jackson, a starched spinster of forty, who enamelled her cheeks and dyed her eyebrows, read *Pamela* right through every six months, for all of which she received two thousand rubles a year, and nearly died of boredom in this *barbarous land of Russia*.

Lisa was attended by her maid Nastya, who was a little older, but just as flighty as her young mistress. Lisa was very fond of her, let her into all her secrets, and enlisted her aid in the preparation of her pranks. In short, Nastya was a much more important personage in the village of Priluchino than many a *confidente* in a French tragedy.

"May I go out visiting today?" asked Nastya while dressing her mistress one morning.

"Certainly! When are you going?"

"To Tugilovo, to the Berestovs'. It's the name-day of their cook's wife, and she came yesterday to invite us to dinner."

"Oh, indeed!" said Lisa. "The masters are at odds, but the servants entertain one another!"

"Our masters' quarrels are no business of ours," retorted Nastya. "Besides, I'm *your* servant, not your Papa's. You and young Berestov have not quarrelled yet, you know, so let the old folk fight it out among themselves!"

"Try and get a sight of Alexei Berestov, Nastya, and tell me exactly what he's like and what sort of person he is."

Nastya promised, and Lisa waited impatiently all day for her maid's return. Nastya came back in the evening. "Well, Lisaveta Grigoryevna," she said, as soon as she got into the room. "I've seen young Berestov; I had a good look at him. We were together all day."

"What? Tell me, tell me everything right from the beginning!"

"Certainly. We all got there, I, Anisya Yegorovna, Nenila, Dunya...."

"Never mind all that! Well, and then?"

"Let me tell you everything from the very beginning. So we got there just at dinner-time. The room was full of people. The servants of the Kolbins and the Zakharyevs were there, the steward's wife and daughters, the Khlupin servants...."

"Tell me about Berestov!"

"Wait a minute. So we sat down to table, the steward's wife next to the hostess, I next to her ... the daughters pouted, but what do I care about them?"

"Oh, Nastya, how tiresome you are with your everlasting details."

"And how impatient you are! Well, so we got up from table ... the dinner lasted three hours, very good it was—there were blue, red, and stripy *blanc-manger* tarts.... So we got up, and went to play catch in the garden, and the young master came there."

"Well? Is it true he's so good-looking?"

"He's ever so good-looking, really handsome. Slim, tall, red-cheeked...."

"Really! And I was sure he would be pale. Well? How did he strike you—mournful, pensive?"

"Not a bit of it! I never saw such a mad fellow in my life. He took it into his head to play catch with us."

"*He* play catch with you! You don't mean it!"

"But he did! And what's more—whenever he caught anyone he gave her a kiss."

"Oh, Nastya, you're telling stories!"

"I'm not then! I could hardly get away from him. He stayed with us the whole day."

"But everyone says he's in love, and never looks at anyone."

"That's as it may be, he certainly looked at me and at Tanya, the steward's daughter. And he didn't overlook the Kolbins' Pasha—come to think of it, he didn't overlook any of us, the scamp!"

"Astonishing! Well, and what do they say about him in the house?"

"They say he's a very nice gentleman, ever so kind and cheery. The only thing wrong with him is that he's too fond of running after the girls. But I don't see much harm in that myself—he'll get over it."

"How I should like to see him!" sighed Lisa.

"Well, that's easy enough. Tugilovo isn't far from us—only three versts. Take a walk over there, or go on horseback, you're sure to meet him. He goes out every morning early, with his gun."

"Oh, that would never do! He might think I was running after him. Besides, our fathers are on bad terms, so I can't get to know him anyhow.... Oh, Nastya! I'll tell you what! I'll dress myself as a peasant girl!"

"Do that! Put on a homespun blouse, and a *sarafan*, and walk boldly over to Tugilovo. I vouch for it Berestov won't overlook you!"

"And I can talk just like the village people. Oh, Nastya, dear Nastya! What a splendid idea!" And Lisa went to bed with the firm intention of carrying her entertaining scheme out.

The next day she went to work on its execution, sending to the market for thick homespun, blue print and brass buttons. With Nastya's aid she cut out a blouse and a *sarafan*, and set all the servant-girls to work on it, so that by evening everything was ready. Lisa tried on her new attire and, looking at herself in the mirror, could not but own that she had never seen herself so pretty. To rehearse her part, she bowed low and walked about, tossing her head from side to side like one of those clay cats whose heads move in a socket, spoke in the local dialect, covering her mouth with her sleeve when she laughed, and earned the full approval of Nastya. The only difficulty arose when she tried walking about the yard barefoot, for the sand and gravel hurt her tender feet. Here, too, Nastya came to her aid. She took the measure of Lisa's foot, and ran into the fields to find the shepherd Trofim, from whom she ordered a pair of bast shoes. Lisa was awake the next day before day-break, while the rest of the household was still sleeping. Nastya stood waiting at the gate for the shepherd to pass. The horn sounded and the village herds wound their way past the landowner's house. As he went by, Trofim handed Nastya a pair of small, brightly coloured slippers, for which he received fifty kopeks from her in payment. Lisa slid noiselessly into her peasant attire, gave Nastya whispered instructions with regard to Miss Jackson, left the house by the back-porch and ran through the kitchen-garden into the open fields.

Dawn was brightening the eastern sky, and the clouds seemed to be drawn up in golden ranks, awaiting the sun, like courtiers awaiting the appearance of their tsar; the transparent sky, the morning freshness, the dew, the breeze and the singing of birds filled Lisa's heart with childish gaiety; in her fear of encountering someone she knew she seemed to fly rather than walk.

When she arrived at the copse which marked the limits of her
father's property, she slowed down. It was here that she was to
wait for Alexei. Her heart beat violently—why, she could not
have said; but it is the trepidation accompanying our youthful
ventures which constitutes their principal charm. Lisa entered
the twilight of the copse. Muffled sounds greeted the girl's ears
from its depths, and her gaiety was instantly subdued. Little
by little she gave herself up to blissful meditations. She
thought ... but who can say exactly what a girl of seventeen
thinks about in a copse, between five and six o'clock of a spring
morning? She walked on, absorbed in her thoughts, along a
pathway shaded on either hand by tall trees, when suddenly a
fine pointer ran barking towards her. Lisa cried out in alarm.
Almost at the same moment a voice was heard, exclaiming:
"*Tout beau, Sbogar, ici!*" and a young huntsman appeared from
behind some bushes. "Don't be afraid, pretty one!" he said to
Lisa. "My dog doesn't bite." Lisa, who had quite recovered
from her fright, was quick to take advantage of the situation.
"But I *am* afraid, Sir," she said, feigning a mixture of fear and
shyness. "Look how fierce he is! He'll jump on me again."
Alexei (the reader will have guessed the stranger's identity),
gazed steadily the while at the peasant lass. "I'll go with you if
you're afraid," he said. "Will you allow me to walk beside
you?" "Who's to prevent you?" returned Lisa. "Anyone is
free to use the road." "Where do you come from?" "From
Priluchino. I'm the daughter of Vasili, the blacksmith. I've
come to gather mushrooms." (Lisa dangled a bark basket from
a string.) "And who are you, Sir? From Tugilovo?" "Quite
right," replied Alexei. "I'm the young master's valet." Alexei
wished to meet her on an equal footing. But Lisa looked at him
and laughed. "No, you're not," she said. "You can't take *me* in!
I can see you're the master himself." "What makes you think
so?" "Everything about you." "But tell me what!" "As if one
couldn't tell the master from the man! You're dressed differently,
you talk differently, and you don't call your dog the way we
do." Lisa's charms grew upon Alexei. Accustomed to treat the
pretty village girls with scant ceremony, he tried to put his arm
round her; but Lisa sprang back and suddenly assumed an
expression so cold and forbidding that Alexei, though amused,
refrained from further advances. "If you want to be friends
with me in future," she said primly, "you mustn't forget your-

self." "Who taught you to talk like that?" asked Alexei, laughing heartily. "Was it my friend Nastenka, your young lady's
serving-woman? Now we see how education is spread!" Lisa
felt that she had been speaking out of character, and hastened
to get back into her assumed role. "Well," she said, "do you
suppose I never go to the big house? I see and hear all sorts
of things there, you know! But I shan't get many mushrooms,
standing here and chattering with you. You go your way, Sir,
and I'll go mine. Good morning, Sir." Lisa made as if to go.
Alexei seized her hand and held her back. "What's your name,
pretty one?" "Akulina," replied Lisa, trying to extricate her
fingers from Alexei's hand. "Let go of me, Sir—it's time for me
to go home." "Well, friend Akulina, I shall certainly go and
see your father, Vasili the blacksmith." "What?" cried Lisa.
"For God's sake don't do that! If they were to find out at home
that I had been talking to a gentleman all alone in the copse I
should get it. My father, Vasili the blacksmith, would beat me
black and blue." "But I must see you again." "I shall be coming
here for mushrooms." "But when?" "I don't know—tomorrow
perhaps!" "Akulina dear, I would kiss you, if I dared. Make it
tomorrow, at the same time—do!" "Very well." "And you
won't disappoint me?" "No, I won't." "Swear you won't!"
"I swear by the Holy Cross that I'll come."

The young people parted. Lisa went out of the wood, crossed
the field, crept into the garden, and rushed headlong to the
farmstead, where Nastya was waiting for her. Here she changed
back into her own clothes, answering the eager questions of her
confidente with an abstracted air, and hastened to make her
appearance in the drawing-room. The table was laid, breakfast
was ready, and Miss Jackson, powdered and wasp-waisted even
at this early hour, was cutting bread into thin slices. Lisa's
father praised her for being out so early. "There is nothing
healthier," he observed, "than getting up at daybreak." He then
cited several instances of longevity culled from English periodi-
cals, remarking that all those who had lived to over a hundred
had abstained from vodka, and got up at daybreak summer
and winter. Lisa hardly heard what he said. She was mentally
reviewing all the circumstances of the morning's rendezvous, the
entire conversation between Akulina and the young hunter, and
was beginning to feel qualms of conscience. She assured herself
in vain that their conversation had not overstepped the limits

of decency, that her prank could not possibly have any untoward consequences—conscience spoke louder than reason. The chief cause of her uneasiness was the promise she had given for the morrow, and she was within an ace of breaking her solemn vow. But Alexei, after waiting for her in vain, might go to the village to look for the true Akulina, the blacksmith's daughter, a plump pock-marked lass, and in this way guess at the trick Lisa had played on him. The thought of this appalled her, and she made up her mind to go again to the copse the following morning, disguised as Akulina.

Alexei's ecstasy was unalloyed, all day he thought of nothing but his new acquaintance, and when night came his dreams were haunted by visions of the dusky beauty. He was up and dressed almost before the dawn. Without waiting to charge his musket he went out with his faithful Sbogar, and hastened to the place of the promised rendezvous. About half an hour passed in what was unbearable suspense for him; at last he caught sight of a blue *sarafan* flitting among the bushes, and rushed to meet his dear Akulina. She received his ecstatic gratitude with a smile, but Alexei was quick to note the traces of dejection and anxiety on her countenance. He inquired the reason for them. Lisa confessed to him that she now regarded her conduct as indiscreet, and regretted it, that she had been unwilling to break her word this time, but that this would be their last meeting, and that she begged him to break off an acquaintance which could hold nothing good for them. Of course, she expressed all this in country dialect, but thoughts and feelings so unusual in a simple girl astonished Alexei. He exerted all his eloquence to make Akulina retract her decision; he assured her of the innocence of his intentions, vowed never to give her grounds for regret, to obey her will in all things, imploring her not to deprive him of the joy of meeting her alone, if only every other day, or two days a week. He employed the language of true passion, and, at the moment, really felt that he was in love. Lisa heard him out in silence. "Give me your word," she said, when he had finished, "that you will never look for me in the village, or make any inquiries about me. Give me your word never to seek a meeting with me, beyond those which I myself appoint." Alexei was about to promise "by the Holy Cross," but Lisa stopped him with a smile. "I don't ask for vows," she said. "Your word is enough for me."

They then conversed in the friendliest fashion, walking about the wood side by side till the moment when Lisa said: "It is time for me to go." They parted and Alexei, left to himself, could not understand how it was that a simple village lass had been able to get such unmistakable power over him in a mere two meetings. His relations with Akulina held the charm of novelty for him, and though the edicts of the strange peasant girl appeared to him onerous, the thought of breaking his word never so much as entered his head. Truth to tell, Alexei, despite the sinister ring, the mysterious correspondence, and his air of disillusion, was just a good-hearted, impulsive youth, with an unspoilt heart, capable of enjoying the most innocent pleasures.

Had I no one but myself to please I should now embark upon a detailed description of the young people's trysts, of their ever-increasing mutual liking and confidence, their occupations, their talks; but I am aware that the majority of my readers would not share my enjoyment of this. Such details invariably appear insipid, and I will therefore omit them, merely remarking that before two months had passed, my Alexei was head over ears in love, and Lisa, though less articulate, was almost equally so. They both rejoiced in the present, and gave little thought to the future.

The thought of indissoluble bonds crossed their minds frequently, but they never spoke about this to each other. The reason is not far to seek—attached as Alexei was to his dear Akulina, he fully realised the distance between himself and a poor peasant girl; and Lisa, knowing the hostility which existed between their fathers, did not dare to hope for a reconciliation between them. Moreover, her vanity was secretly tickled by an obscure romantic hope of at last seeing the heir to Tugilovo at the feet of the daughter of the Priluchino blacksmith. And then an important event bade fair to alter their standing in each other's eyes.

One fine cold morning (one of those mornings which are so frequent in our Russian autumn), Ivan Petrovich Berestov went out riding, taking with him, just in case anything should turn up, five or six greyhounds, his groom, and a few serf boys with rattles. At the very same moment, Grigori Ivanovich Muromsky, tempted out by the fine weather, ordered his mare to be saddled, and trotted over his anglicised estate. As he rode up to the wood, he caught sight of his neighbour, proudly erect in the saddle, wearing a jacket lined with fox-fur, and awaiting the appearance of the hare which his lads were chasing with shouts and rattles out of the bushes. If Grigori Ivanovich could have foreseen this encounter he would undoubtedly have turned in another direction, but he came upon Berestov quite unexpectedly, and found himself within a pistol shot of him. There was no help for it. Muromsky, every inch the urbane European, rode up to his enemy and greeted him courteously. Berestov responded as cordially as a chained bear bidden by his leader to bow to the gentry. Just then the hare leaped out of the wood and made for the open field. Berestov and his groom hallooed at the top of their voices; they unleashed the dogs, and galloped after the hare at full speed. Muromsky's horse, which had never been used for hunting, took fright and bolted. Muromsky, who gave himself out for a fine horseman, let it have its head, secretly pleased at the accident which had rid him of an unpleasant encounter. But his horse, galloping to the brink of a gully which it had not seen till then, suddenly shied, and Muromsky was unable to keep his seat. Falling rather heavily on the frost-hardened earth, he lay there, cursing his dock-tailed mare, which, as if coming to her senses, halted as soon as she felt herself to be riderless. Ivan Petrovich galloped up and asked Grigori Ivanovich if he had hurt himself. In the meantime the groom had brought back the culprit, and stood holding her by the bridle. He assisted Muromsky to mount, and Berestov invited the latter to his house. Muromsky felt obliged to accept the invitation, and thus Berestov returned in triumph, having caught a hare and led his enemy home, wounded and almost a prisoner of war.

The neighbours conversed in a perfectly friendly manner over their breakfast. Muromsky asked Berestov to let him have a carriage, admitting that the shaking-up he had received had unfitted him to ride his mare back. Berestov accompanied him to the entrance and Muromsky did not leave until he had received Berestov's word of honour to bring Alexei to take pot-luck with him the very next day. Thus it happened that the old, deep-rooted enmity showed promise of coming to an end, through the timidity of a dock-tailed mare.

Lisa came running out to meet Grigori Ivanovich. "What's the matter, Papa?" she cried in astonishment. "Why are you limping? Where's your horse? Whose carriage is that?" "You'll never guess, *my dear*," replied Grigori Ivanovich, who was fond of using English forms of address. He gave her an account of the whole incident. Lisa could not believe her ears. Grigori Ivanovich, giving her no time to recover from her astonishment, told her that the two Berestovs were coming to have dinner with them the next day. "What!" she exclaimed, turning pale. "The Berestovs—father and son? Dining with us tomorrow! You can do as you like, Papa, but *I* shall certainly not appear." "Are you mad?" exclaimed her father. "What makes you so shy all of a sudden? Or is it that you feel a hereditary hatred for him, like the heroine of a novel? I won't have any more of this fooling...." "No, Papa, not for anything in the world will I appear in front of the Berestovs!" Grigori Ivanovich, who knew full well that there was nothing to be gained by opposing her, shrugged his shoulders, gave up the argument, and betook himself to rest after his memorable ride.

Lisaveta Grigoryevna went to her room and called Nastya to her. The two held a lengthy conference on the subject of the morrow's visit. What would Alexei think when he recognised in the well-bred young lady his own Akulina? What would be his opinion of her conduct, her principles, her prudence? At the same time Lisa was extremely anxious to see the impression made on him by so unexpected a meeting.... Suddenly she had a bright idea. She instantly communicated it to Nastya. Both were delighted with it and determined to put it into practice at all costs.

The next day at breakfast Grigori Ivanovich asked his daughter if she still intended to hide from the Berestovs. "Since you wish it I will receive them, Papa," replied Lisa, "but only on condition that, whatever the guise in which I appear before them, and whatever I do, you will not scold me and will not show the slightest sign of astonishment or dissatisfaction." "Up to your tricks again!" said Grigori Ivanovich, laughing. "Very well, I agree. Have your own way, my black-eyed madcap!" With these words he imprinted a kiss on her brow, and Lisa ran off to make her preparations.

Punctually at two a home-built carriage drawn by six horses entered the drive, rolling past the circle of bright green turf. Berestov senior, supported by two of Muromsky's liveried footmen, mounted the steps of the porch. His son came in his wake on horseback, and accompanied him to the dining-room, where the table was laid in readiness. Muromsky received his guests with the utmost cordiality, inviting them to inspect his garden and menageries before dinner, and leading them along well-swept gravel paths. Old Berestov secretly deplored the time and labour wasted on such useless whims, but kept silent from courtesy. His son shared neither the disapproval of the thrifty landowner, nor the enthusiasm of the complacent Anglomaniac. He was waiting impatiently for the appearance of the host's daughter, of whom he had heard much, and although his feelings were, as we know, engaged, a beautiful young woman was always sure of stirring his imagination.

The three of them returned to the drawing-room and sat down. The old men recalled former times and exchanged stories of military life, and Alexei busied himself with thinking of the part he should play in the presence of Lisa. He decided that an air of cold *hauteur* would be the most appropriate, and prepared himself accordingly. The door opened; he turned his head with an indifference and elaborate scorn, calculated to make the heart of the most hardened coquette throb. Unfortunately it was not Lisa, but Miss Jackson, powdered, corsetted, her eyes lowered, who entered the room dropping a curtsey, so that Alexei's grand military manoeuvre was quite lost. Hardly had he time to recover his senses, when the door again opened, and this time Lisa came into the room. All rose: the father was just going to introduce the guests, when he stopped short and hastily bit his lip. . . . Lisa, his dusky Lisa, was powdered to the ears, tricked out to rival Miss Jackson; false curls, much fairer than her own hair, were frizzed like the wig of Louis Quatorze; sleeves *à l'imbécile* stuck out like Madame Pompadour's farthingale; she was laced in till her figure was like the letter X, and all her mother's diamonds which had not yet been pawned blazed at her fingers, her throat, and her ears. Alexei could not possibly have recognised his Akulina in this brilliant, but ludicrous female. His father rose to kiss her hand, and Alexei unwillingly followed his example. As his lips brushed her slender fingers it seemed to him he noticed a slight tremor pass over them. At the same moment he caught sight of a little foot, obviously advanced with the purpose of showing off the extravagantly coquettish shoe. This reconciled him somewhat to the rest of her attire. As for the powder and paint, it must be admitted that in the simplicity of his heart he did not at first notice them, and even later he did not suspect them. Grigori Ivanovich remembered his promise and endeavoured to evince not the slightest astonishment. But his daughter's whim amused him mightily, and he could hardly keep a straight face. But it was no laughing matter for the prudish Englishwoman. She guessed at once that the paint and powder had been filched from her dressing table, and a crimson flush of vexation showed beneath the artificial pallor of her cheeks. She cast furious glances at the youthful miscreant who, postponing explanations to some future date, pretended not to notice them.

They took their seats at the table. Alexei continued in his role of an absent-minded, pensive individual; Lisa simpered, speaking through her teeth in a sing-song voice, and only in French. Her father kept looking at her, ignorant of her purpose, but finding it all extremely amusing. The Englishwoman was reduced to speechless fury. The only person who felt at ease was Ivan Petrovich, who ate for two, drank his usual fill, laughed at his own jokes, and conversed with ever-increasing friendliness.

At last the time came to leave the table. The guests took their departure, and Grigori Ivanovich was free to indulge in laughter and questions. "What put it into your head to fool them?" he asked Lisa. "And by the way, powder suits you! I don't understand the secrets of a lady's toilet, but if I were you I'd start using powder. Not too much, of course, just a little." Lisa was charmed with the success of her idea. She flung her arms round her father's neck, promised to think over his advice, and ran off to propitiate the infuriated Miss Jackson, who could hardly be brought to open her door and listen to Lisa's excuses. Lisa told her she had been ashamed to show herself before strangers with her dark skin; she had not ventured to ask ... she was sure dear, good Miss Jackson would forgive her ... and so on, and so on. Miss Jackson, when convinced that Lisa had not meant to make fun of her, calmed down, kissed Lisa, bestowing upon her as a token of reconciliation a jar of English whitening, which Lisa received with every sign of sincere gratitude.

The reader will easily surmise that Lisa did not fail to appear at the trysting-place on the following day. "You went to see our gentlefolk yesterday," she said the moment she met Alexei. "What do you think of our young lady?" Alexei replied that he had not noticed her. "A pity!" ejaculated Lisa. "Why?" asked Alexei. "Because I wanted to ask you if it's true what they say...." "What do they say?" "... if it's true what they say ... that I'm like her." "What nonsense! She's a fright compared to you!" "Oh, Sir, you shouldn't say that; our young lady is so fair, so elegant! How can I be compared with her!" Alexei vowed that she was better than all the fair young ladies in the world, and in order to allay her doubts entirely, proceeded to describe her mistress in such comic detail that Lisa laughed heartily. "And yet," she sighed, "my young lady may be ridiculous, but I am a mere unlettered dunce compared to her." "Eh," cried Alexei, "is that what worries you? If you like I'll start giving you lessons this very minute." "And why not?" exclaimed Lisa. "Why shouldn't I try?" "Do, my dear; let us start here and now." They sat down. Alexei produced a pencil and a note-book from his pocket and Akulina learned the alphabet in a remarkably short time. Alexei could not contain his astonishment at her quickness. The next morning she wanted to try writing; at first the pencil would not obey her, but in a few minutes she was writing the letters quite well. "It's a marvel," said Alexei. "Why, we're getting on faster than they're supposed to under the Lancaster system!" Indeed, by the third lesson Akulina was able to spell out *Natalya, Daughter of the Boyar*,* interrupting her reading with remarks which amazed Alexei, and blotting a sheet with aphorisms copied from the same novel.

A week passed, and they were exchanging letters. Their post-office was a hollow in an ancient oak-tree. Nastya secretly fulfilled the function of postman. Alexei brought to the oak-tree letters written in a bold hand, and found there missives on cheap blue paper, scrawled over by his beloved. Akulina's style improved with every letter, and her mind formed and developed noticeably.

In the meantime the relations which had so lately sprung up between Ivan Petrovich Berestov and Grigori Ivanovich Muromsky were steadily improving, and soon turned into friendship, thanks to the following circumstances: Muromsky often reflected that at the death of Ivan Petrovich all his property would go to Alexei Ivanovich, when the latter would become one

---

* Historical novel by N. M. Karamzin (1766-1826).

of the wealthiest proprietors in the district, and that there was
no reason whatever why he should not marry Lisa. Old Berestov,
for his part, while noting in his neighbour certain eccentricities
(or, to borrow his own expression, a craze for everything English),
did not, however, deny that he had many excellent qualities,
among which unusual ingenuity was to be counted. Grigori
Ivanovich was closely related to Count Pronsky, a distinguished
and powerful man. The count might be of great use to Alexei,
and Muromsky (thought Ivan Petrovich) would doubtless be
glad of a chance to marry off his daughter advantageously. For
some time the two old men kept their thoughts to themselves,
but there came a day when they at last opened their hearts to
each other and embraced, promising to look into the matter
thoroughly. Each set about it in his own way. Muromsky foresaw a difficulty—namely, the bringing together of his Betsy and
Alexei, whom she had not seen since the memorable dinner. It
appeared that they were not greatly drawn to each other. At any
rate, Alexei did not come to Priluchino again, and Lisa retired
to her chamber whenever Ivan Petrovich honoured them with a
visit. But Grigori Ivanovich said to himself, "If Alexei comes
every day Betsy is bound to fall in love with him. It is in the
nature of things. Time will settle everything."

Ivan Petrovich felt less uncertainty as to the success of his
plans. That very evening he called his son into his study, lit his
pipe, and said, after a short pause: "How is it, Alyosha, that
you have quite stopped talking about a military career? Don't
you sigh for a hussar's uniform any more?" "No, Sir," replied
Alexei respectfully. "I see it is not to your liking that I should
enter the Hussars—it is my duty to submit to your wishes."
"Good," said Ivan Petrovich. "You are a dutiful son, I see.
That is a great consolation to me. And I, too, have no desire
to force you. I shall not compel you to enter the government
service—at present. And in the meanwhile I intend you to get
married."

"Whom do you wish me to marry, Sir?" inquired the
astonished Alexei.

"Lisaveta Grigoryevna Muromskaya," replied Ivan Petrovich. "Not a bad choice, I think."

"But, Sir, I am not thinking of marriage as yet."

"You are not thinking, and therefore I have thought for you,
and made up my mind."

"But, Sir, I don't like Lisa Muromskaya."

"You'll like her afterwards. Love follows on habit."

"I do not feel myself capable of making her happy."

"Never mind her happiness. What? Is this your respect for your parent's wishes? For shame!"

"Like it or not, Sir, I do not wish to marry, and I will not do so."

"Either you get married, or I will curse you and, as God is my judge, I will sell the property and fritter away the price I get for it, without leaving you a kopek. I give you three days for reflection, and till then keep out of my sight!"

Alexei knew that if his father got an idea in his head there was no getting it out, not even, as Taras Skotinin* put it, "with a nail". But Alexei took after his sire, and it was just as difficult to get him to change his mind. He went to his room and pondered over the limits of parental authority, the personality of Lisaveta Grigoryevna, his father's solemn threat of making him a beggar, until finally his thoughts came to rest on Akulina. For the first time he became clearly aware that he was passionately in love with her. The romantic idea of marrying a peasant girl and living by his own labours passed through his mind, and the more he thought about this determined act, the more reasonable did it seem. The trysts in the copse had ceased for some time on account of rainy weather. He sent Akulina a letter in which the writing was a model of clarity and the style frenzied, informing her of the imminent threat to their happiness and at the same time offering her his hand. He took the letter at once to the post-office in the hollow oak, and went to bed well satisfied with himself.

The next day, firm in his resolution, Alexei went early in the morning to see Muromsky, and speak frankly to him. He hoped to arouse his magnanimity and get him on his side. "Is Grigori Ivanovich at home?" he asked, reining in his horse in front of the porch of the Priluchino mansion. "No, Sir," replied the servant. "Grigori Ivanovich went away early this morning." "How vexatious!" he thought. "Well, is Lisaveta Grigoryevna at home?" "Yes, Sir." Alexei jumped off his horse, handing the reins to the servant, and went in unannounced.

---

* Taras Skotinin—a character in Fonvizin's comedy *The Dunce*.

"Everything will be settled," he said to himself, going towards the drawing-room. "I'll have a talk with the lady herself." He entered the room, and was thunderstruck. Lisa ... no, Akulina, dear, olive-skinned Akulina, not in her *sarafan*, but in a white morning-gown, was sitting at the window reading his letter; she was so absorbed that she did not hear him come in. Alexei could not stiffle a joyful exclamation. Lisa started, raised her head, cried out, and tried to run away. He tried to hold her back by force. "Akulina! Akulina!" Lisa tried to get away from him.... "*Mais laissez-moi donc, Monsieur! Mais êtes-vous fou?*" she kept saying, in the midst of her struggles. "Akulina! Akulina, my beloved!" he repeated over and over again, showering kisses on her hands. Miss Jackson who was a witness of this scene, knew not what to think. Just then the door opened, and Grigori Ivanovich entered.

"Aha!" he cried. "I see you've taken things into your own hands...."

The reader will relieve me of the superfluous task of describing the end of the story.

1830

END OF THE TALES OF I. P. BELKIN

THE QUEEN OF SPADES

*The Queen of Spades
Stands for Secret Enmity.*

Latest Book of Dreams

I

On a cold winter day
They would gather and play,
Smoking,

And many a stake
Those youngsters would make,
Joking.

Of the stakes that they won
They chalked up every one
Paying,

And so, many a day
They would squander away,
Playing.

Card-playing was going on in the quarters of Narumov, an officer in the Horse Guards. The long winter night passed imperceptibly; it was five in the morning when they sat down to supper. Those who had won, plied their forks eagerly; the rest sat in front of their empty plates with an air of abstraction. But champagne was set on the table, the talk became lively, and all took part in it.

"How did you get on, Surin?" asked the host.

"Lost as usual. It must be admitted that I am unlucky. I play for low stakes, I never get excited, always keep my head, and yet I lose all the time."

"And are you never tempted? Don't you ever long to raise the stakes on a card? Your firmness amazes me."

"Look at Hermann!" said one of the guests, pointing to a young officer from an engineer regiment. "Never picked up a card his whole life, never doubled a stake, and sits beside us till five o'clock, watching our play!"

"I take a great interest in cards," said Hermann, "but I am not in a position to sacrifice what is necessary in the hope of gaining what is superfluous."

"Hermann's a Teuton, and therefore cautious—that's all!" remarked Tomsky. "Now, my grandmother, Countess Anna Fedotovna—she's an enigma, if there ever was one."

"What? What's that?" cried the guests.

"I can't understand," continued Tomsky, "how it is that my grandmother never gambles."

"What is there remarkable about an eighty-year-old woman not wanting to gamble?" said Narumov.

"D'you mean to say you don't know anything about her?"

"Nothing whatsoever. Upon my word!"

"Then let me tell you."

"You must know that my grandmother, sixty years ago, visited Paris, and was all the fashion there. People followed her about to have a look at la Venus Moscovite; Richelieu paid her court, and my grandmother vows that her cruelty almost drove him to suicide.

"In those days ladies used to play faro. One day, while playing cards at court, she incurred a debt of honour for a great sum of money to the Duc d'Orleans. When she got home, my grandmother, while removing the patches off her face, and slipping out of her hooped skirt, recounted her losses to my grandfather, and ordered him to pay up.

"My late grandfather, as far as I can remember, was a kind of steward to my grandmother. He feared her like the plague; but when he heard of such appalling losses he flew into a rage, took up the abacus and proved to her that they had spent half a million during the last six months, that they had no Moscow or Saratov estates in the neighbourhood of Paris, and flatly refused to pay. My grandmother gave him a box on the ears, and banished him from her bedroom, as a token of her disfavour.

"The next day she sent for her husband, hoping that the domestic chastisement would have had its effect on him, but she found him adamant. For the first time in their married life she condescended to argument and explanations. She tried to shame him by pointing out condescendingly that there were debts and debts, and that there was a difference between a prince and a coachmaker. Useless! My grandfather rebelled. He said no, and that his 'no' was final. My grandmother was at her wits' end.

"Among her intimates was a very remarkable individual. You have heard of Comte St. Germain, of whom such extraordinary tales are told. You know he gave himself out to be the Eternal Jew, the discoverer of the elixir of life and the philosopher's stone, and so on. People laughed at him as a charlatan, and Casanova wrote in his memoirs that he was a spy; despite his mysterious reputation, however, St. Germain had a most respectable appearance and knew how to make himself agreeable in society. My grandmother loves him to distraction to this day, and will not allow him to be spoken of disrespectfully. She knew St. Germain had a great amount of money at his disposal, and, deciding to have recourse to his aid, sent him a note asking him to come to her at once.

"The old eccentric responded to her summons immediately and found my grandmother overcome with grief. She painted in the darkest colours her husband's cruelty, and ended by declaring that her only hope was in St. Germain's friendship and chivalry.

"St. Germain pondered. 'I could let you have this sum,' he said, 'but I know you would never have any peace until you had paid me back, and I should not like to cause you fresh cares. There is another means—you can win it back.'

"'But my dear Count,' replied my grandmother, 'I tell you we have no money at all.' 'You will not need money,' said the Count. 'Be so kind as to hear me out.' And he told her a secret which any one of us would pay dear to know....'"

The youthful gamblers redoubled their attention. Tomsky lit his pipe, inhaled the smoke, and continued:

"That same night my grandmother appeared at Versailles, *au jeu de la Reine*. The Duc d'Orleans dealt. My grandmother gave some slight apology for not having brought the money for her debt, inventing a little story in her justification, and began playing against him. She selected three cards, which she played one after another—all three proved to be winning cards, and my grandmother won back the whole of her debt."

"A mere fluke!" said one of the guests.

"A fairy-tale," said Hermann.

"Perhaps the cards were marked," put in another.

"Hardly," replied Tomsky with dignity.

"What!" said Narumov. "You have a grandmother who can play three winning cards running, and you have not yet been able to discover the secret of these cabalistics!"

"It's not so simple, devil take it!" replied Tomsky. "She had four sons, of whom one was my father. All four were desperate gamblers, and she did not disclose her secret to any of them, although this would have been no bad thing for them—nor for me either, for that matter. But this is what my uncle, Count Ivan Ilyich, told me, on his word of honour. The late Chaplitsky, that same Chaplitsky who died in poverty, having squandered millions, once lost about three hundred thousand rubles in his youth—to Zorich, I think. He was in despair. My grandmother, who was always very hard on the vagaries of young men, for some reason took pity on Chaplitsky. She named three cards to him, which he was to play in succession, but extorted from him the promise, on his word of honour, never to gamble any more. Chaplitsky went to the rooms of his fortunate opponent, and they sat down to the card-table. Chaplitsky staked fifty thousand on the first card and won; then he doubled and redoubled the stake, and won back his losses, with a generous margin...."

"But it's time to go to bed—it's a quarter to six." Indeed it was getting light already—the young men finished what was in their glasses and dispersed.

Nikolai Gogol (1809-1852). A major writer, founder of the critical realist trend in Russian literature. Pushkin had a very high opinion of Gogol's talent. "Here is real merriment, sincere and unconstrained, without any affectation or priggishness. And what poetry in places, what emotionality!" wrote Pushkin in his review of Gogol's book of stories *Evenings Near the Village of Dikanka*. A lithograph. 1834

Denis Davydov (1784-1839). A poet and a Hussar famed for his audacity and courage. Pushkin thought him a very attractive, unusual personality. Water-colours. 1836

Pushkin. Water-colours by P. Sokolov

Natalia Pushkina, *née* Goncharova (1812-1863). The poet's wife. Her beauty
was greatly admired by her contemporaries. In his poem "Madonna" addressed
to his fiancee Pushkin wrote:

Through Heaven's grace I'm filled with sweet elation:
My wish is granted—you are mine, Madonna,
Of purest loveliness the purest incarnation.

Water-colours by A. Bryullov

Tsarskoye Selo, the "Tsar's Village" near St. Petersburg. In 1831, Pushkin rented a villa there for the summer. He loved taking walks in the company of his wife "in the resplendent gardens", which had remained dear to his heart from his school days, when he lived in Tsarskoye Selo.

Oils by Martynov. 1820s

II

— Il paraît que monsieur est décidément pour les suivantes.
— Que voulez-vous, madame? Elles sont plus fraîches.

SOCIETY TALK

The old Countess was sitting in her dressing-room in front of her mirror. Three serving-maids hovered around her. One held a pot of rouge, another a box of hairpins, and the third a high cap with flame-coloured ribbons. The Countess, who had not the slightest pretensions to beauty, which had long faded, nevertheless preserved all the habits of her youth, adhering strictly to the fashions of the 1770s, and spending as much time and energy over her toilet as she had done sixty years before. Seated before a tambour at the window was a young lady, the Countess' companion.

"Good morning, Grand'maman!" said a young officer who had just come into the room. "*Bonjour, Mademoiselle Lise.* I have come to ask a favour of you, Grand'maman."

"What is it, Paul?"

"Permit me to introduce a friend of mine to you, and to bring him to your ball on Friday."

"Bring him straight to the ball, you can introduce him to me there. Were you at the ***'s yesterday?"

"Oh, yes! It was very gay. We danced till five. Eletskaya was exquisite."

"Eh, my dear! What can you see in her? You should have seen her grandmother, the Princess Darya Petrovna! She must be very old now, I suppose—the Princess Darya Petrovna."

"Old?" replied Tomsky absently. "She's been dead these seven years."

The young lady at the window raised her head and made a sign to the young man. He remembered that the death of her contemporaries was always kept from the old Countess, and bit his lip. But the Countess received this information, which was news to her, with the utmost indifference.

"Dead!" she repeated. "And I did not know! We became maids of honour at the same time, and when we were presented, the Empress...."

And the Countess told her story to her grandson for the hundredth time.

"Well, Paul," she said, after a pause. "Now help me to get up. Lise, where's my snuff-box?"

And the Countess retired behind a screen, accompanied by her maids, to finish her toilet. Tomsky remained with the young lady.

"Whom do you wish to introduce to her?" asked Lisaveta Ivanovna in low tones.

"Narumov. Do you know him?"

"No. Is he a military or a civilian?"

"Military."

"An engineer?"

"No. A cavalryman. What made you think he was an engineer?"

The girl gave a short laugh, but answered not a word.

"Paul!" cried the Countess from behind the screen. "Send me a new novel, but not a modern one, if you please."

"What do you mean, Grand'maman?"

"I mean a novel in which the hero strangles neither his father nor his mother, and in which there are no drowned bodies. I have a perfect horror of drowned bodies!"

"There are no such novels nowadays. Unless, of course, you would like a Russian novel."

"Are there any Russian novels? Send me one, Sir, by all
means, send me one!"

"I must say good-bye to you, Grand'maman. I am pressed
for time. Good-bye, Lisaveta Ivanovna. What made you think
Narumov was an engineer?"

And Tomsky went out of the dressing-room.

Lisaveta Ivanovna remained alone—she turned from her
embroidery and began looking out of the window. Very soon
a young officer made his appearance round the corner on the
other side of the street. A blush covered her cheeks; she took up
her work again, bending her head low over the canvas. Just then
the Countess reappeared, fully dressed.

"Order the carriage, Lisanka," she said. "We'll go for a
drive."

Lise rose from the embroidery frame and began putting
away her work.

"Are you deaf, Child?" cried the Countess. "Order the carriage instantly!"

"Yes, Grand'maman," said the girl softly, and went quickly
into the entrance hall.

A servant entered with some books for the Countess from
Prince Pavel Alexandrovich.

"Very good. Give him my thanks," said the Countess.
"Lise! Lise! Where are you going?"

"To dress."

"There's plenty of time, Child! Stay where you are! Open
the first volume. Read to me. . . ."

The girl picked up the book and read a few lines.

"Louder!" said the Countess. "What's the matter with you,
my dear? Have you lost your voice? Wait a minute—give me a
footstool. Nearer, can't you?"

Lisaveta Ivanovna read two more pages. The Countess
yawned.

"Put the book down," she said. "A lot of nonsense! Send it
back to Prince Pavel with my thanks. Well, where's the carriage?"

"The carriage is ready," said Lisaveta Ivanovna, glancing
out of the window.

"And why aren't you dressed?" said the Countess. "You
always keep me waiting. It's intolerable, my dear!"

Lise ran to her room. Before two minutes had passed the

Countess began ringing her bell with all her might. The three maids came running in at one door, and the footman at the other.

"Can't you come when you're called?" exclaimed the Countess. "Tell Lisaveta Ivanovna I'm waiting for her."

Lisaveta Ivanovna came in, in her cloak and hat.

"At last!" said the Countess. "How you're dressed up! What for, I wonder? Whom do you want to conquer? What's the weather like? It seems to be windy."

"Not at all, Your Highness. It's very still weather," replied the footman.

"You always say the first thing that comes into your head. Open the *fortochka*.* There, I knew there was a wind, and a very cold one, too! Send away the carriage. We're not going, Lise. You needn't have dressed yourself up."

"And this is my life!" thought Lisaveta Ivanovna.

Indeed, Lisaveta Ivanovna was a most unhappy creature. The bread of charity is bitter, said Dante, and the steps to a stranger's house are steep, and who knows that bitterness so well as a poor girl dependent on an aristocratic old dame? The Countess did not really have a bad disposition, but she was capricious, like all women who have once been the spoilt darlings of society, and she was stingy, completely absorbed in her cold selfishness, like all old people who, having expended their tenderer emotions during a long lifetime, feel that they do not belong to the present. She participated in all the vanities of high society, dragging herself to balls, where, seated in a corner, rouged and dressed according to the fashion of ancient days, she was the hideous and essential ornament of the ball-room; newly-arrived guests went up to her and bowed low, as though in obedience to an established ritual, after which nobody took any notice of her. In her own home she received the whole town, observing the strictest etiquette, though she did not recognise any of her guests. Her innumerable house-hold, growing fat and grey in her hall and in the servants' quarters, did whatever they liked and vied with one another in plundering the dying old woman. Lisaveta Ivanovna was a domestic martyr. She poured out tea and was scolded for the waste of sugar; she read novels aloud and was held guilty for

---

* Small ventilation pane in window.—*Tr.*

all the author's shortcomings; she accompanied the old lady on her drives, and had to answer for the weather and the state of the road. She was allotted a salary which she never received in full; and was expected to be dressed like everyone else, which is to say like very few. In society she played the most pitiable role. Everyone knew her and no one took any notice of her; at balls, she only danced when a *vis-à-vis* was needed, and the ladies took her arm whenever they had to retire in order to set to rights some detail of their toilet. Sensitive and therefore fully alive to her position, she was always on the lookout for a deliverer. But the young men, vain and calculating, did not honour her with their attention, although Lisaveta Ivanovna was infinitely more attractive than the cold, arrogant maidens upon whom they danced attendance. How many times, noiselessly departing from the dull, luxurious drawing-room, did she retire to weep in her humble chamber, with its wall-papered screen, its chest of drawers, its little mirror and painted bedstead, in which a tallow candle in a brass candlestick burned dimly!

Once—a day or two after the evening described in the beginning of this tale, and a week before the scene just enacted— Lisaveta Ivanovna, seated before her tambour at the window, happened to glance into the street, and caught sight of a young man in the uniform of an engineer regiment standing motionless, his eyes fixed on her window. She lowered her head and resumed her work; five minutes later she looked out again—the young officer was still there. Not being in the habit of flirting with passing officers, she stopped looking out of the window and went on stitching for another two hours or so without raising her head. Dinner was served. Rising, she began to put away her tambour and, glancing out of the window, observed that the officer was still there. This struck her as somewhat strange. After dinner she went to the window with uneasy feelings, but the officer was no longer there—and she forgot about him....

Two days later, while going out with the Countess to get into the carriage, she saw him again. He was standing right at the porch, his beaver collar turned up to hide his face—a pair of black eyes gleamed from beneath his cap. Lisaveta Ivanovna was alarmed, she knew not why, and seated herself in the carriage with inexplicable trepidation.

As soon as she returned home she ran to the window—the officer was standing in his former place, his eyes fixed on her; she moved away, tortured by curiosity and an agitation which was quite new to her.

From that time, not a day passed without the young man appearing beneath the windows of their house at a certain hour. A curious relationship sprang up between them. While seated at her work she would feel his approach and raise her head, her glance resting on him for a longer space of time every day. The young man seemed to be beholden to her for this; with the keen sight of youth, she saw the instant blush which covered his pale cheeks whenever their eyes met. A week later, and she was greeting him with a smile....

When Tomsky asked permission to introduce his friend to the Countess, the poor girl's heart began to beat. But when she learned that Narumov was not an engineer but a horse-guards-man she regretted that, by her indiscreet question, she had given away her secret to the volatile Tomsky.

Hermann was the son of a Russianised German who had left him a very small fortune. Firmly convinced of the necessity of consolidating his independence, Hermann did not even touch the interest from it, and lived exclusively on his pay, never allowing himself the slightest indulgences. He was, however, reserved and ambitious, and his comrades seldom had occasion to laugh at his excessive thriftiness. He was a man of strong passions and a fiery imagination, but his firmness of character saved him from the usual errors of youth. Thus, while by nature a gambler, he never played cards, calculating that his fortune was not such as to allow him (to use his own words) *to sacrifice the necessary in the hope of gaining the superfluous*, and yet he would sit beside the card-tables all night long, following with feverish excitement the vicissitudes of the game.

The story of the three cards affected his imagination powerfully, and he could not get it out of his head all night. "Supposing," he said to himself, roaming the streets of Petersburg the next night, "supposing the old Countess were to reveal her secret to me? Supposing she were to tell me the names of those three infallible cards? Why should I not try my luck? Present myself to her, get into her favour—perhaps become her lover ... but all this would take time, and she is eighty-seven, she might die next week, the day after tomorrow! And the story itself—is

it to be believed? No! Caution, moderation and diligence—
these are my three faithful cards, with these I will treble my
fortune, increase it seven-fold, achieve tranquillity and independence."

Thus meditating, he found himself in one of the principal
streets of Petersburg, before a house of ancient architecture.
The street was thronged with carriages, which were still rolling
up one after another to the brilliantly lighted porch. The slender
foot of some young belle, a jackboot with jingling spurs, the
striped stocking and the slipper of an ambassador, were thrust
in rapid succession from the carriage doors. Furred mantles and
cloaks flashed past the majestic footman. Hermann came to a
standstill.

"Whose house is this?" Hermann asked the gendarme at
the corner.

"The Countess'," replied the latter.

Hermann was thrown into trepidation. The marvellous story
again rose before the eye of his fancy. He began walking up and
down in front of the house, thinking of its mistress and her
miraculous power. It was late when he returned to his humble
dwelling; he lay awake a long time, and when sleep overcame
him he dreamt of cards, the baize-covered table, heaps of notes,
piles of golden coins. He staked one card after another, firmly
doubled the stakes, won repeatedly, scraped the gold towards
him, pocketed the notes. He awoke late, sighing for the loss of
his fantastic riches, and once more went to roam the city, once
more found himself in front of the Countess' mansion. It was
as if some mysterious force had drawn him to it. He stood still
and looked up at the windows. Behind one of them he saw a
dark head bent either over a book or work. The head was lifted.
Hermann saw a youthful face and black eyes. This moment
decided his fate.

III

*Vous m'écrivez, mon ange, des
lettres de quatre pages plus vite
que je ne puis les lire.*

Correspondence

Hardly had Lisaveta Ivanovna taken off her cloak and hat, when the Countess sent for her and ordered the carriage to be brought round again. And so they went out of the house to get into it. Just at the moment when two footmen were half-lifting, half-pushing the old dame through the carriage door, Lisaveta Ivanovna saw her engineer standing close to the wheels. He seized her hand; she was almost stupefied with terror; the young man vanished—a letter remained in her hand. She hid it inside her glove and neither saw nor heard anything during the whole drive. It was the Countess' habit to fire off question after question when in the carriage—Who's that, just gone by? What bridge is that? What's written on that sign? This time Lisaveta Ivanovna answered at random, and her meaningless remarks angered the Countess.

"What's come over you, my dear? Don't you hear me, or is it that you don't understand what I say?... I don't lisp, thank the Lord, and I am still in possession of my wits!"

Lisaveta Ivanovna in very truth was not listening. As soon as she got back she hastened to her room and drew the missive out of her glove—it was unsealed. Lisaveta Ivanovna ran her eye over it. The letter contained professions of love: it was tender and respectful, copied word-for-word from a German novel. But Lisaveta Ivanovna, who did not know German, was enchanted with the letter.

The letter she had received nevertheless caused her excessive agitation. It was the first time she had entered upon secret, intimate relations with a young man. His audacity appalled her. She reproached herself with indiscreet behaviour, and could not make up her mind what to do. Should she stop sitting at the window and cool the officer's desire for further pursuit by displaying indifference? Ought she to send him back his letter, or, perhaps, answer it coldly and decisively? There was no one for her to consult—she had neither friends nor counsellors. Lisaveta Ivanovna made up her mind to reply.

She sat down at her little writing-table, got out pen and paper, and fell to musing. She began her letter several times, tearing it up each time—her words seemed to her either too indulgent, or too severe. At last she succeeded in writing a few lines with which she was satisfied: "I am confident," she wrote, "that your intentions are honourable and that you would not wish to insult me by a thoughtless act; but our acquaintance must not begin in this wise. I return you your letter and trust that in future I shall have no cause to complain of unmerited disrespect."

The next day, as soon as she saw Hermann approaching, Lisaveta Ivanovna rose from her tambour, went into the adjoining room, opened the *fortochka* and tossed her letter out of the window, relying on the young officer's dexterity. Hermann ran to the spot where the letter had fallen, picked it up and entered the shop of a pastry cook. Breaking the seal, he found his own letter and the reply of Lisaveta Ivanovna. It was what he had expected and he went home deeply absorbed in his intrigue.

Three days after this, a sharp-eyed girl from a milliner's shop brought Lisaveta Ivanovna a note.

Lisaveta Ivanovna opened it anxiously, fearing it might be a dun, when she suddenly recognised Hermann's handwriting.

"You've made a mistake, Child," she said. "This note is not for me."

"It is, it is! It's for you," answered the bold girl, not troubling to conceal a sly smile. "Be so good as to read it."

Lisaveta Ivanovna ran her eye hastily over the note. Hermann demanded a rendez-vous.

"You must be mistaken, my girl," said Lisaveta Ivanovna, alarmed both by the precipitancy of the demand, and the means employed by Hermann. "This letter is probably not intended for me." And she tore it into fragments.

"If it's not for you then why did you tear it up?" said the shop-girl. "I could have given it back to the person who sent it."

"I would ask you not to bring me any more notes, in the future, Child," said Lisaveta Ivanovna, flushing at the girl's remark. "And tell the person who sent you that he ought to be ashamed of himself. . .."

But Hermann did not desist from his efforts. Lisaveta Ivanovna received letters from him daily, through various channels. They were no longer translated from German. Hermann wrote them under the inspiration of passion, and used language which was natural to him—his letters expressed both his unwavering desire and the chaos of his unbridled imagination. Lisaveta Ivanovna no longer attempted to return them to him, she revelled in them; she began answering them, and her notes became longer and more tender with every day. At last she threw the following letter out of the window to him:

"There is a ball at the Embassy tonight. The Countess will be there. We shall be there till two o'clock. This would be your chance to see me alone. As soon as the Countess leaves, her servants are sure to go away; there will be only the doorman in the porch, and he usually goes into his own little room. Come at half past eleven. Go straight upstairs. If you find anyone in the hall, ask for the Countess. They'll tell you she isn't at home, and there will be nothing for you to do, but go. But you will probably meet no one. The maids stay in their own room, all together. From the hall, turn to the left and go straight on till you get to the Countess' bedroom. There you will see a screen in front of two little doors. The one on the right leads to the study, where the Countess never goes. The one on the left leads to a passage, from which there is a narrow spiral staircase to my room."

Hermann awaited the appointed time, like a tiger ready to pounce. By ten o'clock he had already taken up his position in

front of the Countess' house. The weather was atrocious, the
wind howled and snow fell in moist flakes. The lamps burned
dimly, the streets were deserted. Every now and then a cabby
drove his lean hack by, in the hope of picking up a belated wayfarer. Hermann had nothing on over his frock-coat, but was
conscious neither of wind nor snow. At last the Countess'
carriage was brought round. Hermann saw the footmen come
out, supporting on either side the bowed form of the old woman
in her sable cloak, and her youthful companion slip by after her,
in her thin wrap, with flowers in her hair. The carriage door
slammed. The carriage rolled heavily over the loose snow. The
doorman closed the front door. The windows went dark. Hermann began walking up and down in front of the deserted
mansion. When he got to a street lamp he glanced at his
watch—it was twenty minutes past eleven. He stood in the light
of the lamp, his eyes fixed on the hands of his watch, waiting
for the remaining minutes to pass. Precisely at half past eleven
he stepped on to the Countess' porch and into the brightly lit
entrance. The doorman was not there. Hermann ran up the
stairs, opened the door into the hall, and saw a serving-man
asleep beneath a lamp, in an ancient, greasy arm-chair. Hermann
passed him with a light, firm tread. The ball-room and drawing-
room were dark. The lamp in the hall shed a dim light on them.
Hermann entered the bedroom. A gilded lamp swung in front
of an iconostasis filled with ancient icons. Arm-chairs upholstered
in faded damask, and downstuffed sofas, with the gilt wearing
off in patches, stood in mournful symmetry along the walls,
which were hung with Chinese wallpaper. There were two por-
traits painted in Paris by Madame Lebrun on the walls. One
was the likeness of a man of some forty years, rosy-cheeked
and stout, in a bright-green uniform with a star on his breast;
the other showed a young belle with an aquiline nose, her
powdered locks, brushed up from the temples, adorned with a
rose. In every corner could be seen porcelain shepherdesses,
clocks made by the skilled hand of Leroy, ornamental boxes,
tops, fans, and various toys invented for the amusement of
ladies in the end of the previous century, along with Mont-
golfier's balloon, and Mesmer's magnetism. Hermann went
behind the screen. There, stood a small iron bedstead; on the
right was the door of the study, on the left the door into the
passage. Hermann opened it, and saw the narrow spiral stair-

case leading to the poor young lady's room. But he turned back and entered the dark study.

The hours passed slowly. All was quiet. The clock in the drawing-room struck midnight. Clocks in all the other rooms chimed in one after the other. And all was quiet again. Hermann stood leaning against the cold stove. He was quite calm; his heart beat regularly, like that of one who has resolved upon what is dangerous, but inevitable. The clocks struck one, and then two—and he heard the distant sound of carriage wheels. He was thrown into a state of agitation. The carriage drove up and came to a stop. He could hear the clatter of the steps being let down. There were sounds of bustle in the house. People came running, voices were heard, and the house lit up. Three elderly lady's maids hastened into the bedroom, and the Countess, more dead than alive, entered and sank into the high-backed arm-chair. Hermann peeped through a crack in the door. Lisaveta Ivanovna passed close to him. He could hear her hurried footsteps ascending her staircase. He felt something like a pang of remorse, but it died down at once. He stood as if turned to stone.

The Countess began undressing in front of the mirror. Her maids unpinned her rose-trimmed cap, removed the powdered wig from her grey, closely cropped head. Pins fell from her in showers. The yellow dress embroidered in silver dropped to her swollen feet. Hermann was a witness of the horrid secrets of her toilet. At last the Countess was clad in nothing but a night-gown and night-cap—in this attire, more appropriate to her age, she was not so sinister and hideous.

Like all old people, the Countess suffered from insomnia. When her maids had undressed her she sat down near the window in the high-backed arm-chair and dismissed them. The candles were carried out, and once more the only light in the room came from the icon lamp. Her face a bilious yellow, her drooping lips twitching, the Countess swayed from left to right in her chair. Utter absence of thought could be seen in her dim eyes. Looking at her, one might have supposed that the terrible old woman swayed from side to side, not of her own accord, but under the influence of some concealed galvanic force.

Suddenly an indescribable change came over her death-like countenance. Her lips ceased their twitching, and a light came into her eyes. A strange man stood before the Countess.

"Do not be afraid, for God's sake, do not be afraid!" he was saying in low, clear tones. "I have no intention of harming you—I have come to beg a single favour of you."

The old woman gazed at him in silence, but seemed not to have heard him. Hermann, supposing her to be deaf, bent right over her ear and repeated his words. The old woman was as silent as ever.

"You can make me happy for life," continued Hermann, "and it will cost you nothing. I know that you are able to guess three cards to be played in succession...."

Hermann broke off. Evidently the Countess understood what was wanted of her, and was searching for words to answer him with.

"It was only a jest," she said at last. "I swear to you! It was a jest!"

"This is no jesting matter," replied Hermann sternly. "Remember Chaplitsky whom you helped to win back his losses."

The Countess was visibly embarrassed. Some powerful emotion showed itself on her face, but very soon she sank back into her former apathy.

"Can you name me these three infallible cards?" continued Hermann.

The Countess remained silent. Hermann continued:

"For whom are you treasuring your secret? For your grandchildren? They are rich, as it is; they do not understand the value of money. Your three cards will not help a spendthrift. He who allows a father's legacy to slip through his fingers will die in poverty, despite any diabolical efforts. I am no spendthrift. I know the value of money. Your three cards will not be wasted on me. Come, now!..."

He ceased speaking, and waited anxiously for her reply. The Countess remained silent. Hermann fell on his knees.

"If your heart ever knew the feeling of love," he said, "if you remember its ecstasies, if you have only once smiled to hear the crying of a new-born son, if anything human ever beat in your bosom, I appeal to you as wife, mistress, mother, by all that is sacred in life, do not refuse my request! Reveal your secret to me! Perchance it may be linked with some terrible sin, with the forfeiture of eternal bliss, a pact with the devil. Bethink yourself that you are old, you have not long to live, I am ready to take your sins on myself. Only reveal to me your secret.

Bethink yourself that the happiness of a human being is in your hands. That not only I, but my children, grandchildren and great-grandchildren will bless your memory, and hold it sacred...."

The old woman did not say a word.

Hermann rose.

"Old witch!" he said, clenching his teeth. "Then I will make you answer me!"

With these words he drew a pistol from his pocket.

At the sight of the pistol the Countess again showed signs of powerful emotion. She jerked back her head and raised her hand, as if to ward off a shot.... Then she fell against the back of her chair ... and remained motionless.

"Come, you are not a child!" said Hermann, taking her hand. "I ask you for the last time—do you intend to tell me what these three cards are? Yes or no?"

The Countess made no answer. Hermann saw that she was dead.

IV

7 Mai 18...

Homme sans mœurs et sans religion!

Correspondence

Lisaveta Ivanovna was seated in her room, still in her ball dress, absorbed in profound meditation. As soon as she got home she hastily dismissed her drowsy maid, who offered her services reluctantly, and said she would undress herself. Then she went up to her own room with a fluttering heart, hoping to find Hermann there, and desiring not to find him. She saw at a glance that he was not there, and thanked her stars for the obstacle in the way of their rendez-vous. She sat down without taking off her clothes and began to go over in her mind all the circumstances which had carried her so far in such a short space of time. Three weeks had not yet elapsed since the day she had first seen the young man beneath her window—and she was already corresponding with him, while he had wrung from her the promise of a nocturnal rendez-vous. If she knew his name, it was only because some of his letters had been signed. She had never spoken to him, never heard his voice, never heard anything about him—till this very evening. And strange to say, at the ball, Tomsky, vexed with the youthful Princess Pauline—

for flirting with someone else for a change—wished to revenge himself and show his indifference. He invited Lisaveta Ivanovna to dance with him, and went through the endless mazes of the mazurka with her. He had jested the whole time about her partiality for engineers, assuring her that he knew a great deal more than she could possibly imagine, and some of his jests so nearly hit the mark that Lisaveta Ivanovna could not help thinking, more than once, that he knew her secret.

"Who told you all this?" she asked him, laughing.

"A friend of a certain person whom you know," replied Tomsky. "A most remarkable man."

"And who is this remarkable person?"

"His name is Hermann."

Lisaveta Ivanovna made no reply, but her hands and feet turned cold as ice.

"This Hermann," continued Tomsky, "is a most romantic individual. He has the profile of a Napoleon, and the soul of a Mephistopheles. I believe he has at least three crimes on his conscience. How pale you are!..."

"My head aches.... What did that, what's his name—Hermann—tell you?"

"Hermann is greatly displeased with his friend. He says he would have acted quite differently, himself.... I'm inclined to think that Hermann has an eye on you himself, for he listens with great interest to the enamoured exclamations of his friend."

"But where can he have seen me?"

"At church, perhaps, or out driving.... God knows—perhaps in your room, while you were asleep. Anything may be expected of him."

Three ladies came up to them with the question: "*oubli ou regret?*" and the conversation, of such agonising interest for Lisaveta Ivanovna, had to be interrupted.

The lady whom Tomsky chose was the Princess herself. During one round of the ball-room and a turn in front of her chair they had come to an understanding, and by the time Tomsky got back to his place he was no longer interested either in Hermann or in Lisaveta Ivanovna. She was longing to revive the interrupted conversation; but the mazurka came to an end, and soon after the old Countess took her departure.

Tomsky's words had been nothing but ball-room small talk, but they had sunk deep into the soul of the romantic girl. The portrait sketched by Tomsky coincided with the image she had herself formed, and this type, which the latest novels have made a commonplace, at once alarmed and captivated her imagination. She sat with her bare arms folded, her head, with the flowers still in her hair, drooping over her half-exposed breast. . . . Suddenly the door opened and Hermann entered. She felt a profound thrill. . . .

"Where have you been?" she asked in a frightened whisper.

"In the old Countess' bedroom," replied Hermann. "I've just come from her. The Countess is dead."

"Dear God! What d'you mean?"

"And it seems," continued Hermann, "that it was I who caused her death."

Lisaveta Ivanovna glanced at him, and Tomsky's words echoed in her heart: that man has at least three crimes on his conscience. Hermann seated himself on the window-sill next to her and told her all.

Lisaveta Ivanovna heard him with horror. And so it was not love that had inspired all those passionate letters, those ardent requests, that audacious, stubborn pursuit! Money—that was what his soul thirsted after. It was not she who could quench his desires and make him happy. The poor companion had been nothing but the blind accomplice of a criminal, the murderer of her old benefactress. She wept bitterly, in her belated, anguished repentance. Hermann looked at her in silence—he, too, felt a pang, but it was not the poor girl's tears, nor the exquisite beauty of her grief which stirred his hard heart. He felt no remorse at the thought of the old woman who was dead. Only one thing appalled him—the irretrievable loss of the secret which he had hoped would enrich him.

"You are a monster," said Lisaveta Ivanovna at last.

"I did not desire her death," replied Hermann. "My pistol was not loaded."

They were both silent.

Day began to break. Lisaveta Ivanovna extinguished the dying candle—a pale light crept into the room. She dried her eyes, which were red with weeping, and raised them to Hermann's face: he was sitting on the window-sill with his arms crossed, frowning ominously. In this pose he strikingly resembled a portrait of Napoleon. Even Lisaveta Ivanovna was impressed by the likeness.

"How are you to get out of the house?" she said, after a pause. "I had intended to take you by a concealed stairway, but we should have to go past her bedroom, and I am afraid."

"Tell me how I can find this concealed stairway. I will go."

Lisaveta Ivanovna rose, went to her chest of drawers and took out a key which she handed to Hermann, giving him full instruction. Hermann pressed her cold, passive hand, kissed the top of her bent head, and went away.

He descended the spiral staircase and once more entered the bedroom of the old Countess. The dead old woman sat there as if turned to stone; there was an expression of profound calm on her features. Hermann stood before her, gazed long at her, as if desirous of confirming to himself the appalling truth. At last he went into the study, felt for the papered door in the wall, and began descending a dark staircase, a prey to the strangest sensations. By this very staircase, he told himself, sixty years ago into this very bedroom, at this very hour, in a long embroidered coat, his hair brushed *à l'oiseau royal*, his three-cornered hat pressed to his heart, may have stolen a young fortunate, now long mouldering in the grave, while the heart of his aged mistress had this day ceased to beat....

At the foot of the staircase Hermann found a door, which he unlocked with the same key, and emerged in a passage leading right through the house to the street.

V

The late Baroness von V. appeared
to me in a dream tonight.
She was attired in white and said to me:
"Greetings, Mr. Privy Councillor."

Swedenborg

Three days after the fatal night Hermann went to the monastery, where a service was to be held over the remains of the deceased Countess. While he felt no remorse he could not, however, quite silence the voice of conscience, which told him: it is you who murdered the old woman. He had little true faith, but many superstitious beliefs. He believed that the dead Countess might have an injurious influence on his life—and resolved to attend her funeral in order to beg her forgiveness.

The church was full. Hermann could hardly push his way through the crowd of mourners. The coffin stood on a rich bier beneath a velvet pall. The dead woman lay with hands folded on her breast, clad in a lace cap and white satin dress. Around the coffin stood her household—the servants in black liveries, with crested ribbons on their shoulders, holding candles, the relatives—her children, grandchildren and great-grandchildren —in deep mourning. No one wept; tears would have been *une affectation.* The Countess had been so old that her death caused no surprise to anyone, and her relatives had long regarded her as one who had outlived her time. A youthful priest preached the funeral sermon. He described in simple and touching phrases the peaceful end of the pious lady, for whom the long years had been a calm affecting preparation for a Christian death. "The angel of death," said the preacher, "found her awake, in the midst of holy meditations, awaiting the midnight bridegroom." The service was accomplished with mournful propriety. The relatives went first to bid farewell to the body. After them, the innumerable guests, who had come to pay obeisance to her who had so long been a participator in their vain festivities, moved towards the coffin. Then came the members of the household. And finally there approached an ancient serving-maid, who was the same age as her mistress. Two youthful serving-maids held her up by her arms. She had no strength to bow down to the ground, and, alone of them all, shed a few tears as she kissed the cold hand of her late mistress. After her, Hermann ventured to approach the coffin. He bowed to the ground, prostrating himself for a few moments on the cold paving-stones, strewn with branches of fir. Then he rose, as white as the corpse itself, ascended the steps of the bier, and bent down.... It seemed to him that the dead woman looked at him quizzically, and winked. Retreating hastily, he missed the step, and fell flat on the ground. He was picked up. At that very moment Lisaveta Ivanovna was carried out to the porch of the church in a swoon. This incident disturbed for a few moments the solemnity of the gloomy ritual. A hollow murmur arose from the crowd and a lean courtier, a near relation to the deceased, whispered in the ear of an Englishman standing beside him that the young officer was her son, to which the Englishman replied with a dry: "Oh?"

Hermann was in a state of excessive agitation all day. He dined in a lonely tavern and, contrary to his custom, drank a great deal, in the hope of drowning his anxiety. But the wine only inflamed his imagination still more. As soon as he got home he threw himself down on his bed in his clothes, and fell sound asleep.

When he woke up it was night; the moon lit up his room. He glanced at his watch—it was a quarter to three. He no longer wanted to sleep, and sat up in bed, thinking about the old Countess' funeral.

Just then someone in the street looked at him through the window, and immediately stepped back. Hermann paid no attention to this. A minute later he heard the front door being opened. He thought it was his orderly, drunk as usual, returning from his nocturnal revelries. But he heard unfamiliar footsteps: someone approached with softly shuffling slippers. The door of his room opened and a woman in a white dress entered. Hermann took her for his old nurse and wondered what could have brought her there at such a time. But the white woman glided forward, and was suddenly quite close to him—and Hermann recognised the Countess.

"I have come to you against my will," she said in firm tones. "I have been bidden to fulfil your request. A Three, a Seven and an Ace in succession are your winning cards, but only on condition that you do not stake more than one card a day, and after that never again play your whole life long. I forgive you my death, on condition that you marry my protégée Lisaveta Ivanovna...."

With these words she turned softly towards the door, and shuffled out. Hermann heard the door in the porch bang, and saw someone peer through the window into his room again.

It was a long time before he could recover his senses. He went into the next room. The orderly was asleep on the floor. Hermann roused him with great difficulty. He was drunk as usual, and Hermann could get nothing out of him. The door to the porch was bolted. Hermann went back to his room, lit a candle and wrote an account of the vision he had seen.

VI

"Attendez!"
"How dare you tell me *attendez?*"
"I said '*attendez-vous*', Your Excellency."

Two fixed ideas cannot exist simultaneously in our moral nature, any more than two bodies can occupy one and the same place in the physical world. The Three, the Seven, the Ace soon blurred the image of the dead old woman in Hermann's imagination. The Three, the Seven, the Ace were continually in his mind, and hovered on his lips. When he caught sight of a young girl he said: "How graceful she is—a regular Three of Hearts!" When asked what the time was, he answered five minutes to the Seven. Every paunchy man he came across reminded him of the Ace. The Three, the Seven, the Ace haunted his dreams, assuming all sorts of forms. The Three blossomed out before his eyes in the image of an enormous flower, the Seven was represented by Gothic portals, the Ace by a huge spider. All his thoughts were merged in a single one—to profit by the secret which had cost him so dear. He began thinking of retiring and travelling. He longed to wrench the treasure from enchanted Fortune in the public gambling salons of Paris. Chance relieved him of these cares.

At that time there was a society of wealthy gamblers in Moscow presided over by the renowned Chekalinsky, whose whole life had been spent playing cards, and who had accumulated millions, winning promissory notes, and losing ready cash. His experience and wisdom had earned him the confidence of his comrades, and his hospitality, famous chef, kindliness and cheerfulness had gained him the esteem of the public. He came to Petersburg. The young men flocked to him, neglecting balls for card-playing and preferring the seductions of faro to the sweets of courting. Narumov brought Hermann to his house.

They passed through a suite of resplendent rooms lined with respectful menservants. A few generals and privy councillors were playing whist. Young men sprawled on the damask sofas, eating ices and smoking pipes. The host was keeping the bank at a long table in the drawing-room, around which crowded some twenty gamblers. He was a man of about sixty of the most genteel appearance. His hair was a silvery grey; his plump, fresh-coloured countenance expressed good humour; his eyes shone, lit up by a continual smile. Narumov introduced Hermann to him. Chekalinsky pressed his hand cordially, asked him not to stand upon ceremony, and went on playing.

The game was a long one. There were over thirty cards on the table. Chekalinsky paused after every deal in order to give the players time to look over their hands, jotted down losses, lent a courteous ear to all demands, and still more courteously smoothed back the corner of a card bent over by a careless hand. At last the game came to an end. Chekalinsky shuffled the cards and prepared to begin another.

"I would like to stake a card, if you please," said Hermann, stretching out his hand from behind a fat gentleman at the card-table. Chekalinsky smiled and bowed silently, in token of submissive consent. Narumov laughingly congratulated Hermann on the breaking of his long fast, and wished him good luck.

"I am ready!" said Hermann, chalking in the sum above his card.

"What's that?" asked the holder of the bank, screwing up his eyes. "I am not sure that I read your sum right."

"Forty-seven thousand," replied Hermann.

At the sound of these words all heads were turned immediately, and all eyes were fixed on Hermann.

"He's gone mad," thought Narumov.

"Allow me to remark," said Chekalinsky, with his habitual smile, "that your stake is high. No one has ever staked more than two hundred and seventy-five *simple* here."

"Well?" replied Hermann. "Will you play?"

Chekalinsky bowed with his usual air of submission.

"I only wished to inform you," he said, "that, since I am honoured with the confidence of my friends, I am obliged to play for cash only. For my part, I am, of course, willing to rely on your word, but for form's sake and to avoid misunderstanding I would ask you to place your money on the table."

Hermann took a bank-note from his pocket and handed it to Chekalinsky, who, glancing rapidly at it, placed it on Hermann's card.

He began dealing. On the right lay a nine, on the left a three.

"Mine!" said Hermann, showing his card.

A murmur rose from the players. Chekalinsky frowned, but the smile returned immediately to his face.

"Shall I give it you now?" he asked Hermann.

"If it's no trouble."

Chekalinsky drew a bundle of bank-notes from his pocket, and counted out the required sum. Hermann took his winnings and retired from the table. Narumov was almost beside himself. Hermann drank a glass of lemonade and went home.

On the evening of the next day he repaired to Chekalinsky's again. The host was dealing. Hermann went up to the table; the other players immediately made room for him. Chekalinsky bowed to him urbanely.

Hermann waited for a fresh deal, and laid down a card, on which he placed his forty-seven thousand, and his winnings of the previous night.

Chekalinsky began dealing. A knave was on the right, a seven on the left.

Hermann turned up a seven.

Everyone gasped. Chekalinsky was visibly disconcerted. He counted out ninety-four thousand in notes and handed them to Hermann. Hermann received them with the utmost sang-froid and immediately withdrew.

On the following evening Hermann was again at the table. Everyone was expecting him. The generals and privy councillors abandoned their rubber of whist to watch the unusual play. The young officers sprang up from the sofas. All the menservants were gathered in the drawing-room. Everyone pressed round Hermann. The other players did not put down their stakes, but waited eagerly to see how the game would go. Hermann stood at the table, ready to play against the pale, but ever-smiling Chekalinsky. Each unsealed a new pack of cards. Chekalinsky shuffled. Hermann cut and laid down his card, covering it with a heap of bank-notes. It was like a duel. Profound silence reigned in the room.

Chekalinsky began to deal with an unsteady hand. On the right he turned up a queen, on the left, an ace.

"The ace wins," said Hermann, and showed his card.

"Your queen is covered," said Chekalinsky urbanely.

Hermann started: it was true—instead of an ace there lay the Queen of Spades. He could hardly believe his eyes, and wondered how he could have made such a blunder.

And all of a sudden it seemed to him that the Queen of Spades was narrowing her eyes and laughing at him. He was struck by an extraordinary likeness.

"The old woman!" he cried in horror.

Chekalinsky drew his winnings towards him. Hermann stood motionless. When he went away from the table everyone started talking loudly. "What a game!" exclaimed the players. Chekalinsky again shuffled the cards: the game went on as usual.

CONCLUSION

Hermann has gone mad. He is in ward Number 17 of the Obukhov Hospital, and never answers when he is spoken to, only muttering over and over again with extraordinary rapidity: "Three, seven, ace ... three, seven, queen!..."

Lisaveta Ivanovna married a very well-bred young man; he works in a government office and is the possessor of a considerable fortune. He is the son of the old Countess' former steward. Lisaveta Ivanovna is bringing up an impoverished female relative.

Tomsky has been promoted to a captaincy and is going to marry the Princess Pauline.

1833

THE CAPTAIN'S DAUGHTER

Guard your honour in the days of your youth.

Proverb

Chapter One

SERGEANT OF THE GUARDS

"In the Guards, he would have been
a captain soon."
"What matter! Let him share the
soldier's bread."
"Aye, and the soldier's task! 'Tis
truly said."
"Who is his father?"

*Knyazhnin**

My father, Andrei Petrovich Grinev, served under Count
Minikh in his youth, and retired with the rank of brevet-major
in 17.... He then went to live on his Simbirsk estate, and there
married Avdotya Vasilyevna Y., the daughter of an impoverished
gentleman of those parts. Nine children were born of the
marriage. All my brothers and sisters died in infancy.

While I was still in my mother's womb I was entered in the
Semenov regiment as a sergeant, through the kindness of
Prince B., Major of the Guards, and our near kinsman. If the
hopes of my parents had been disappointed by my mother's
giving birth to a daughter, my father would have reported the
death of the defaulting sergeant, and there the matter would
have ended. I was considered on leave till my schooling should
be completed. In those days education was not what it now is.
At the age of five I was handed over to the care of Savelich,
a groom, promoted for sobriety to be my tutor. Under his tu-
ition I learned to read and write my native tongue by the age of
twelve, and was a competent judge of the points of a hound. My
father then engaged a French tutor for me, one Monsieur
Beaupré, who was sent for from Moscow, with the year's
supply of wine and olive oil. Savelich was greatly displeased by

* From the comedy *The Braggart* by Yakov Knyazhnin (1742-1791).

his arrival. "The child has been washed and groomed and fed up till now, thank God!" he grumbled. "Why should they waste money on a Monseer, as if we had not enough people of our own?"

In his native land Beaupré had been a barber, then he had served in the Prussian army, and subsequently travelled to Russia, *pour être "outchitel"*,* the meaning of which word was not very clear to him. He was a good-humoured fellow, though excessively flighty and dissolute. His chief weakness was a passion for the fair sex, and his advances frequently won for him bruises over which he groaned for days. Moreover (to borrow his own phrase), he was no "foe to the bottle", in other words he was prone to indulge in a drop too much. Since, however, wine was only served in our house at dinner, and then only a wine glass to each diner, while the teacher was usually passed over, Monsieur Beaupré very quickly accustomed himself to Russian cordials, and soon came to prefer them even to the wines of his own country, regarding them as a great deal better for the digestion. He and I were soon on the best of terms, and although he had undertaken to teach me "French, German, and all other subjects", he found it very much easier to pick up a smattering of Russian from me, and each of us was content to mind his own business. We got on capitally. I could not have desired a better mentor. But fate soon separated us, as I will now relate.

Palashka, the fat, pock-marked laundry-maid, and the one-eyed cow-woman Akulka, made a compact to throw themselves at the feet of my mother, pleading their sinful weakness, and complaining of Monseer, who had taken advantage of their inexperience. My mother took a serious view of such matters, and complained to my father. My father acted with promptitude, and sent for the French canaille. He was informed that Monseer was giving me a lesson. My father went to my room, where he found Monsieur Beaupré on the bed, sleeping the sleep of the just. I was occupied about my own affairs. I ought to mention that a large map had been ordered from Moscow for my benefit. It hung uselessly on the wall, and the width and good quality of the paper on which it was printed had long been a temptation to me. I decided to use it for making a kite, and took advantage

---

* *Teacher* (transliteration from the Russian)—*Tr.*

of Beaupré's slumbers to embark upon this undertaking. My
father came into the room just at the moment when I was
fabricating a tail by attaching a wisp of bast to the Cape of
Good Hope. He pulled my ear by way of recognition of my
geographical studies, and then strode up to Monsieur Beaupré,
whom he waked without the slightest compunction, and
showered him with reproaches. Beaupré, much perturbed, tried
to rise, but could not—the unfortunate Frenchman was dead
drunk. A single punishment had to suffice for all his offences.
My father lifted him from the bed by his coat-collar, pushed
him out of the room, and drove him from the house that very
day, to the indescribable delight of Savelich. And thus my education came to an end.

I grew up an ignoramus, amusing myself with carrier-pigeons,
and playing leap-frog with the boys on the estate. In this way
I reached my sixteenth year. And from this moment my life
underwent a change.

One day in autumn my mother was stewing berries in honey
in the drawing-room, and I stood by, looking at the boiling
scum and licking my lips. My father was seated at the window
reading the Court Calendar, a publication we received annually.
This volume always exercised a powerful effect on him. He never
read it without the liveliest concern, and the perusal of it invariably aroused his spleen. My mother, who knew by heart all his
ways and habits, used to thrust the obnoxious volume into some
remote hiding-place, so that several months would sometimes
pass without his eyes falling on the Court Calendar. When he
did happen to light upon it, however, he would not let it out of
his hands for hours on end. And so my father was reading the
Court Calendar, from time to time shrugging his shoulders and
muttering under his breath: "Lieutenant-General—he was a
sergeant in my regiment. And now, Cavalier of the two highest
Russian orders—it seems only yesterday that he and I—" At
last, flinging the Court Calendar on the sofa, he plunged into
deep meditation, a symptom which boded little good for the
household.

Suddenly he turned to my mother: "Avdotya Vasilyevna, how
old is Petrusha?"

"Why, he's turned sixteen," replied my mother. "Petrusha
was born the year Aunt Nastasya Gerasimovna lost the sight
of her eye...."

"Good!" interrupted my father. "It's time for him to serve. He's been hanging round the women's quarters and the dove-cotes long enough."

The thought of the imminent parting with me so overwhelmed my mother that she dropped the spoon into the vat, and tears rolled down her cheeks. For myself I was indescribably elated. The thought of military service was identified in my mind with the idea of freedom and the delights of life in Petersburg. I fancied myself an officer of the Guards, a situation which I considered the height of human bliss.

My father was not fond either of altering his intentions or postponing their execution. The day for my departure was appointed. On the eve my father told us that he intended to give me a letter for my future superior officer, and demanded pen and ink.

"Don't forget to give my regards to Prince B., too," said my mother. "You can say I hope he will not cease to extend his kindness to Petrusha."

"Nonsense!" replied my father, frowning. "Why should I write to Prince B.?"

"Why, you said you were going to write a letter to Petrusha's commander."

"Well, and what if I did?"

"Well, Prince B. will be his superior officer. Petrusha's entered in the Semenov regiment, isn't he?"

"Entered! What's it to me if he's entered? Petrusha's not going to Petersburg. What would he learn from serving in Petersburg? Nothing but dissipation and extravagance. Let him serve in the army, carry a knapsack, and smell powder, let him be a soldier, not a mere fop. Entered in the Guards! Where's his passport? Give it to me!"

My mother found my passport, which she kept put away in a chest, together with my christening-robe, and handed it to my father with a trembling hand. My father scanned it, placed it on the table in front of him, and began writing his letter.

I was devoured with curiosity. Where was I to be sent, if not to Petersburg? I never took my eyes off my father's quill, as it travelled slowly over the page. At last he came to an end, sealed up the letter and my passport in an envelope, took off his spectacles and called me to him, with the words: "Here's a letter for

Alexandra Smirnova, *née* Rosset (1809-1882), a lady in
waiting. A great friend of Pushkin's, who admired her
independent mind.
A miniature of the 1820s

St. Petersburg. Nevsky Prospekt. A view of Kazan Cathedral. Pushkin mentions its "colossal granite columns" in his poem dedicated to the memory of Field-Marshal Mikhail Kutuzov.
A lithograph. 1830s

St. Petersburg. Nevsky Prospekt. A view of the Imperial
Public Library.
A lithograph. 1830s

A group of Russian authors in St. Petersburg's Summer Gardens: (left to right) Krylov, Pushkin, Zhukovsky and Gnedich. This picture by Chernetsov (1832) is a study from nature for a large documentary canvas "Parade in Tsaritsin Lug"

Andrei Karlovich R., my old companion and friend. You will
go to Orenburg to serve under him."

And so all my hopes of brilliant future were brought to the
ground! Instead of the pleasures of Petersburg, there awaited
me the tedium of life in some remote, god-forsaken spot.
Military service, which only a moment ago had been the subject
of my enthusiastic dreams, now appeared to me in the light of a
severe trial. But protests would have been of no avail. The next
morning the travelling sleigh was brought round to the front
porch; my trunk, a casket equipped with all the appurtenances
for tea-making and bundles containing fresh rolls and pies,
farewell symbols of domestic indulgence, were put into it. My
father and mother gave me their parental blessing. My father
said to me: "Good-bye, Pyotr. Serve faithfully him to whom
you pledge allegiance; obey your superiors; do not seek their
good graces; do not offer your services unasked; do not refuse
services asked of you; and remember the proverb: 'Keep your
coat clean while it is still new, and guard your honour in the
days of your youth.'" My mother adjured me, with tears, to
take care of my health, at the same time bidding Savelich to look
after the child. They made me wear a coat of tanned hareskin, and
over it a cloth coat lined with fox-fur. Weeping profusely, I took
my place in the sleigh beside Savelich, and started on my journey.

By nightfall we arrived at the town of Simbirsk, where we were
to stay till the next day in order to make certain necessary pur-
chases, a task entrusted to Savelich. We put up at an inn. Early
the next morning Savelich set off for the shops. Tired of looking
out of the window at the dirty street, I began a tour of all the
rooms. In the billiard-room I saw a tall gentleman, of about
thirty-five years of age, with a drooping black moustache; he
wore a dressing-gown and held a billiard-cue in his hand and a
pipe between his teeth. He was playing with the marker, who
drank a glass of vodka whenever he won, and had to go on all
fours under the table every time he lost. I stood and watched
the game. The longer they played, the more frequently the
marker had to go on all fours, till at last he stayed under the
billiard-table for good. The gentleman uttered a few oaths by
way of a funeral oration and invited me to play a game with
him. As I did not know how to play, I refused. He appeared to
find something exceedingly strange in this, regarding me almost
with pity. But we soon got into conversation. I learned that his

name was Ivan Ivanovich Zurin, that he was a captain of the Hussars, was in Simbirsk for recruiting purposes, and was staying at the inn. Zurin asked me to take pot-luck with him, soldier-fashion. I willingly agreed. We sat down to table. Zurin drank a great deal, and kept filling my glass, saying I must get used to military service. He told me funny stories of army life, which made me almost choke with laughter, and we rose from our meal the best of friends. He now offered to teach me to play billiards. "It is absolutely essential for us soldiers. For instance, you come to some little place on the march. What is there for you to do? You can't beat Jews all the time. There's nothing for it but to go to an inn and get up a game of billiards. And for that you must know how to play." I was completely convinced by his argument, and applied myself to the study with the utmost diligence. Zurin encouraged me loudly, professing his astonishment at the rapidity of my progress. After a few trial games he suggested that we play for very low stakes, not for the sake of gain, but so as not to play for nothing, than which, according to him, there could be no worse habit. To this also I agreed, and Zurin ordered punch, and persuaded me to try it, again saying that I must get used to military life. And what would life in the army be without punch? I obeyed him. In the meantime we went on with our game. With every sip I took, I became more valiant. My balls flew off the table continually, I lost my temper, abused the marker for not knowing how to score, kept putting up the stakes, in a word, behaved like a boy escaped from authority. The hours flew by unnoticed. Zurin glanced at his watch and, putting down his cue, announced that I had lost a hundred rubles to him. This somewhat upset me. Savelich had my money. I began to apologize. Zurin broke through my apologies: "Never mind that! Don't let it trouble you in the least! I can wait, and in the meantime we will go and visit Mademoiselle Arinushka."

What would you have? I ended up the day as foolishly as I had begun it. We supped at Mademoiselle Arinushka's. Zurin continually refilled my glass, repeating that I must get used to the service. When I tried to rise I found I could hardly stand; Zurin escorted me back to the inn at midnight.

Savelich met us in the entry. He gasped when he saw the unmistakable signs of my zeal for the service. "What have you been doing, Sir?" he said in piteous tones. "Where could you have got so tipsy? My God, my God! Was there ever such wickedness?"

"Silence, you old grumbler!" I said thickly. "You must be drunk! Go to bed ... and put me to bed."

I woke up the next morning with a headache and vague recollections of the events of the day before. My meditations were interrupted by Savelich, bringing me a cup of tea. "You've begun carousing early, Pyotr Andreich," he said, shaking his head. "And who do you take after? Neither your father nor your grandfather were drunkards, I believe, and your mother never touched anything in her life but *kvass*.* And who is to blame for it all? That accursed Monseer. Always pestering the housekeeper: 'Madame, *je vous prie*, vodka.' Here's a fine *je vous prie* for you! He certainly taught you a thing or two, the hound! Why did they have to hire an infidel for you? Hadn't the master enough servants of his own!"

I was ashamed. Turning aside, I said: "Go away, Savelich, I don't want any tea." But there was no getting rid of Savelich when he started moralising. "You see what drinking leads to, Pyotr Andreich. Your head aches, you can't eat. A man who drinks is good for nothing.... Have a drink of cucumber-brine and honey, or best of all sober yourself on half a glass of vodka. Shall I order it?"

Just then a boy came in with a note for me from I. I. Zurin. I opened it and read the following lines:

> "Dear Pyotr Andreyevich, kindly send by the boy the hundred rubles you lost to me last night. I am in urgent need of money.
>
> "Your faithful servant,
> "Ivan Zurin."

There was no help for it. Assuming an air of indifference I turned to Savelich, who "kept my purse, and ordered my affairs,"** and bade him give the boy a hundred rubles. "What? What for?" asked Savelich in astonishment. "I owe it him,"

---

* A fermented drink made from bread.—*Tr.*
** A line from the poem *A Message to My Servants* by Denis Fonvizin (1745-1792).

I replied as coolly as I could. "Owe it!" echoed Savelich, his astonishment growing. "When did you contrive to get into debt, Sir? There must be something wrong here. Say what you like, Sir, I shall not give the money."

I told myself that if I did not get the upper hand of the obstinate old fellow at this critical moment, it would be difficult for me in future to shake off his tutelage, so I said, with a haughty glance at him: "I'm your master and you are my servant. The money belongs to me. I lost it because I chose to. And I would counsel you not to try to be clever, but to do as you are bid."

Savelich was so overwhelmed by my words that he could only throw out his hands helplessly. "Don't stand there gaping!" I shouted angrily. Savelich burst into tears. "Why, Pyotr Andreich, Master," he said in a shaking voice, "don't make me die of grief! Light of my eyes, heed me, an old man! Write and tell that scoundrel you were only joking, and we don't possess such a sum. A hundred rubles! Merciful heavens! Tell him your parents have strictly forbidden you to gamble for anything higher than nuts . . . ."

"That'll do," I said sternly. "Hand over the money, or I'll turn you out!"

Savelich cast me a look of profound sorrow and went for the money. I was sorry for the old man, but I was determined to make a stand and prove that I was no longer a child. The money was dispatched to Zurin. Savelich hastened to take me away from the accursed inn. He came and told me that the horses were ready. It was with an unquiet conscience and silent remorse that I left Simbirsk, without taking leave of my teacher, whom I never expected to meet again.

Chapter Two

THE WAYFARER

> Distant land,
> Unknown to me!
> I went not forth to seek thee,
> My good steed did not bear me to thee.
>
> Brave lad that I was,
> 'Twas the recklessness of youth,
> The madness of strong drink,
> That brought me to thee.
>
> *Old Song*

My reflections on the way were not very pleasant. My loss was a considerable one for those times. In my heart I could not but admit that my conduct at the Simbirsk inn had been foolish, and I felt I had treated Savelich ill. All this tormented me. The old man sat morosely on the box-seat, his back to me, quite silent but for an occasional grunt. I was determined to make my peace with him but did not know how to set about it. At last I said: "Come now, Savelich! Enough—let us make it up! I was wrong—I see myself that I was wrong. I played the fool yesterday, and I shouldn't have spoken harshly to you. I promise to behave better, and obey you in the future. Come now, don't be angry—let us make it up!"

"Oh, Pyotr Andreich, Master!" he replied heaving a deep sigh. "It's myself I'm angry with—it was all my fault. I should never have left you all alone at the inn! Oh well—I couldn't resist the temptation, and I took it into my head to go and visit my old friend, the sexton's wife. There you are—a visit to friends, in gaol sometimes ends. It's terrible! How can I show myself to my master and mistress? What will they say when they hear that their child drinks and gambles?"

In order to console the unhappy Savelich I promised never to spend a single kopek in future without his consent. Gradually he calmed down, although every now and then he still murmured to himself, shaking his head, "A hundred rubles! That's no joke!"

I was approaching my destination. All around stretched the dreary plain, broken up in places by mounds and ravines. Snow lay over all. The sun was sinking in the west. The sleigh was gliding over a narrow path, or, to be exact, the tracks left by peasants' sleighs. All of a sudden the driver began casting anxious glances in one direction, and at last taking off his cap and turning to me, he said: "We'd better turn back, Sir!"

"What for?"

"The weather's treacherous—the wind is beginning to rise. See how it's blowing the newly-fallen snow about."

"What does that matter?"

"Look over there." (The driver pointed to the east with his whip.)

"I see nothing but the white steppe and the clear sky."

"Over there—that cloud!"

Now I could make out a small white cloud right on the horizon, which I had taken for a distant hill. The driver explained to me that this cloud portended a storm.

I had heard of the blizzards in these parts, and knew that whole caravans of sleighs had been snowed under by them. Savelich was for heeding the driver and counselled me to return. But I did not consider the wind very strong, and hoped we should have time to get as far as the next posting-station, so I told the driver to whip up his horses.

He drove rapidly ahead glancing ever and anon towards the east. The horses galloped with a will. The wind grew ever more violent. The little cloud grew, rising ponderously, till it gradually covered the entire heavens. A fine snow began to fall, and suddenly the air was filled with big flakes. The wind howled, the blizzard was upon us. In less than a minute the dark sky had become one with the ocean of snow. All landmarks vanished. "There you are, Master!" yelled the driver. "The blizzard— we're in for it!"

I peered out from under the hood—nothing but gloom and whirlwind. The wind was howling with such expressive ferocity that it seemed to be a living creature. Savelich and I were soon covered with snow; the horses went at a foot-pace, and halted.

"Why don't you go on?" I asked the driver impatiently. "What's the good?" he replied, clambering down from the box-seat. "I don't even know where we are—no road, and pitch-dark." I began scolding him, but Savelich took his side. "Why didn't you heed him?" he said angrily. "We ought to have gone back to the inn, had some hot tea, stayed there overnight, till the storm passed, and then started on our journey again. We're in no particular hurry, are we? It's not as if we were going to a wedding." Savelich was right. We were in a strait. The snow was falling faster and faster. An immense drift had formed beside the sleigh. The horses stood with drooping heads, every now and then starting nervously. The driver walked around, adjusting the harness for the sake of doing something. Savelich grumbled to himself; I looked all round, hoping to discern some slight sign of life or of a road, but could see nothing but the whirling of the blizzard. And then my eyes suddenly fell on a black object. "Hey, driver!" I shouted. "Look! What's the black thing over there?" The driver gazed in the direction I pointed out. "Lord knows, Master," he said, getting back to his seat on the driver's box. "It doesn't look like a sleigh or a tree, and it seems to be moving. It must be either a wolf or a man."

I bade him drive towards the unknown object, which was now moving in our direction. In a minute or two we pulled up beside a man. "Hey, good man!" shouted the driver. "Do you know where the road is?"

"The road is here; I am standing on firm ground," replied the wayfarer, "but what's the good of that?"

"Listen, fellow," I said to him. "Do you know these parts? Couldn't you show us the way to a place where we could spend the night?"

"I know these parts," replied the wayfarer, "I ought to—I've been the length and breadth of them on foot and on horseback, time and again. But look at the weather! It's easy to get lost here. You'd better stay where you are and wait—the storm is bound to pass and then the sky will clear and we shall be able to find our way by the stars."

His composure instilled fresh hope in me. I had already decided, resigning myself to the will of God, to spend the night in the midst of the steppe, when suddenly the wayfarer hoisted himself with surprising agility on to the box-seat, saying to our driver: "Thank God, there's a house not far off. Turn to the right and drive straight ahead."

"Why should I turn to the right?" asked the driver, resentfully. "I see no road! It's easy to say 'drive on!' Another man's horses, another man's sleigh, drive as you will, you won't have to pay!" I thought the driver was right. "Why do you say there's a house not far off?" I asked. "Because the wind is blowing from that direction, and I can smell smoke," replied the traveller. "That means there must be a village somewhere near." His ingenuity and the acuteness of his senses amazed me. I bade the driver go on. The horses plodded with difficulty through the deep snow. The sleigh progressed slowly, pushing through snowdrifts, almost falling into gullies, lurching perilously from side to side, like a ship tossing on a stormy sea. Savelich kept falling against me, grunting. I let down the straw blind, wrapped my fur-coat closer round me, and dozed off, lulled by the whistling of the storm and the slow motion of the carriage.

I had a dream which I have never been able to forget, and which I still regard as almost prophetic, taken in connection with the strange circumstances of my life. The reader will forgive me, probably knowing from experience how easily a man gives way to superstition, however much he may despise it.

I was in that bodily and spiritual condition in which reality, yielding to dreams, merges with them in the vague images which haunt the first stage of slumber. It seemed to me that the storm was still raging, and we were still roaming over the snowy steppe.... Suddenly I saw before me a gate, and drove into the yard in front of our manor-house. My first thought was that my father would be angry with me for my enforced return to my parents' roof, regarding this as deliberate defiance of his will. I leaped out of the sleigh in my agitation and saw my mother coming to meet me with an air of profound grief. "Hush!" she said to me. "Your father is very ill—he is at death's door—he wishes to take leave of you." Overcome by terror I followed her. I found myself in a dimly-lit room; around the bed stood men and women with mournful faces. I went softly up to it; my mother lifted a corner of the curtain, saying: "Andrei Petrovich, Petrusha has come; he heard of your illness and turned back; give him your blessing." I knelt down and gazed at the sick man. But what did I see? Instead of my father there lay on the bed a peasant with a black beard, who looked at me cheerfully.

Pavel Nashchokin (1800-1854). A Moscow nobleman who squandered a huge fortune in revelry. An original, passionate nature, he was Pushkin's closest friend in 1830s. Water-colours. 1836

Vissarion Belinsky (1811-1842). A critic and publicist, the founder of scientific literary criticism in Russia, the author of several brilliant critical articles analysing Pushkin's work. Water-colours. 1820s

Natalia Pushkina, *née* Goncharova, Pushkin's wife.
Water-colours by V. Gau. 1843

Pushkin. An engraving by T. Right. 1837

Mikhail Lermontov (1814-1841). A great Russian poet, who responded to Pushkin's death with a wrathful poem, for which he was banished to the Caucasus

I turned to my mother in bewilderment. "What does this mean?"
I asked her. "That is not my father. Why should I ask a peasant
to give me his blessing?" "No matter, Petrusha," replied my
mother. "He will take your father's place at your wedding. Kiss
his hand and let him give you his blessing...." I would not consent to this. Then the peasant jumped out of bed, seized a hatchet
from somewhere behind him, and began brandishing it in all
directions. I tried to run away ... but could not; the room
filled with dead bodies! I stumbled over corpses and my feet
slipped in pools of blood.... The frightful peasant called out
to me in friendly tones: "Don't be afraid, come here and let me
give you my blessing." I was seized by terror and bewilderment.... At that moment I woke up; the horses were standing;
Savelich was tugging at my sleeve, saying: "Get out, Sir—we've
arrived."

"Arrived? Where?" I asked, rubbing my eyes. "At the inn.
By God's mercy we happened to stumble against the fence.
Get out, Sir, quick, and come in to the warm."

I got out of the sleigh. The storm was still raging but with
less force. All around was pitch-dark. The innkeeper met us in
the doorway, sheltering a lantern beneath the skirts of his coat,
and led me into a small room, cramped but fairly clean; its only
illumination was a rushlight. Hanging on the wall were a rifle
and a high-crowned Cossack cap.

The innkeeper, a Yaik Cossack, was a man of some sixty
years, well-preserved and agile. Savelich came after me with the
box of tea-things and called for a light, so that he could start
making tea, which had never before seemed to me so desirable.
The innkeeper went to make his arrangements.

"Where's our guide?" I asked Savelich.

"Here, Your Honour," came from overhead. I looked up at
a ledge high against the wall and caught sight of a black beard
and a pair of gleaming eyes. "Cold, brother?" I said. "How can
I help being cold, in this thin, ragged coat?" he replied. "I did
have a sheepskin, but to tell the truth I pawned it last night at
the tavern—I didn't think the frost was so keen." Just then the
innkeeper came in with a boiling samovar. I offered our guide
a cup of tea, and he clambered down from the ledge. His
appearance seemed to me remarkable. He was evidently about
forty years old, of middle height, lean and broad-shouldered.
His black beard was streaked with grey, and his great eyes

were full of life and in constant motion. The expression of his face was at the same time attractive and roguish. His hair was cut in the Cossack fashion; he wore a torn sheepskin and Tatar breeches. I handed him a cup of tea; he took a sip and made a wry face. "Do me a favour, Your Honour, tell them to bring me a glass of vodka; tea is no drink for a Cossack." I complied with his request readily. The innkeeper took a bottle and a glass from the cupboard, and approaching him, looked into his face: "Oho!" he said, "so you're in our parts again! What brings you here?" My guide winked meaningfully and answered in riddles: "I flew about the vegetable plot and pecked at hemp-seed. Granny threw a stone at me, but she missed me! Well, and how about your folk?"

"Our folk?" echoed the innkeeper, taking up the allegorical vein. "Time to ring for vespers, but the priest's wife won't let us: the priest's away, and the devil's at large." "Silence, old man!" said my tramp. "If there is rain, there'll be mushrooms, and if there are mushrooms, there'll be baskets for them. And now" (he winked again) "keep your axe in your belt, the woodman's near. Your Honour's health!" Saying this, he picked up his glass, crossed himself, and gulped down the contents. Then he bowed to me and clambered back to his resting-place.

At that time I could make nothing of this thief's gibberish, but later I divined that they had been talking about the affair of the Yaik troops, recently subjugated after their mutiny in 1772. Savelich listened to all this with an air of profound dissatisfaction. He glanced suspiciously from the innkeeper to our guide. The inn, or, as the local name was, the *umyet*, was situated away from the road, in the midst of the steppe, remote from human habitation, and might well be a robbers' den. But we had no choice. There could be no thought of continuing our journey. Savelich's discomfort entertained me greatly. As for me, I decided to spend the night where I was and stretched myself out on a bench. Savelich got on to the stove-ledge to sleep. The innkeeper lay on the floor. Very soon the whole room was snoring, and I slept like a log.

Waking up rather late the next morning, I saw that the storm had abated. The sun was shining. Snow lay in a dazzling carpet over the boundless steppe. The horses were harnessed. I settled with the innkeeper whose charges were so moderate that even

Savelich did not protest or try to bargain as he usually did, and the suspicions of the night before were completely banished from his mind. I called our guide, and thanked him for his help, telling Savelich to give him fifty kopeks for drink. Savelich frowned. "Fifty kopeks for vodka!" he said. "What for? For being so kind as to allow us to drive him to an inn? As you like, Sir, but we haven't got any fifty kopeks to throw away. If you give everyone money for drink you'll soon come to want yourself." I could not argue with Savelich. All the money, as I had promised it should be, was in his charge. But I was vexed not to be able to show my gratitude to a man who had saved me, if not from disaster, at any rate from a highly disagreeable situation. "Very well," I said calmly. "If you don't want to give him fifty kopeks, let him have something of mine to wear. He's too lightly clad. Give him my hareskin coat."

"Why Pyotr Andreich, Master!" said Savelich. "What would he do with it? He'd sell it for drink, the dog, at the next tavern."

"It's nothing to do with you, old fellow, whether I sell it for drink or not," said my tramp. "His Honour has a mind to give me the coat off his back: it is his pleasure, and you are a bondsman, it is your duty to obey, not argue."

"Have you no shame, you rogue?" cried Savelich angrily. "You can see the child understands nothing, and you're ready to rob him, just because he's such a simpleton. What d'you want with a gentleman's coat? You wouldn't be able to squeeze your accursed shoulders into it."

"Stop arguing," I said to my old tutor, "and go and fetch my coat."

"Dear God!" groaned my Savelich. "The hareskin coat is almost new! And to think that it goes to a drunken tramp!"

But the hareskin coat was produced. The *muzhik* tried it on then and there. The coat, which I myself had also outgrown, really was a little tight for him. But he managed to get it on with only a little splitting at the seams. Savelich almost howled when he heard the stitches tearing. The tramp was excessively delighted with my present. He accompanied me to the sleigh and said, bowing low: "Thank you, Your Honour! May the Lord reward you for your goodness. I will never forget your kindness." He went his way, and I journeyed on, paying no attention to Savelich's vexation, and soon forgetting yesterday's blizzard, my guide, and the hareskin coat.

When I got to Orenburg I went straight to the General. I saw a man of great height, already bent with age. His long hair was completely white. His old and faded uniform made him look like a warrior of the time of Anna Ioanovna, and he spoke with a strong German accent. I handed him my father's letter. On hearing his name he glanced up at me quickly. "Mein Gott!" he said. "It seems only yesterday that Andrei Petrovich was your age, and look at you, a fine young fellow! Ah, how time flies!" he tore open the envelope and began reading the letter under his breath, making a running commentary on the contents. "'My dear Andrei Karlovich, I hope Your Honour'— dear me, how very ceremonious we are! Ach, he ought to be ashamed of himself! Discipline before all, of course, but is that the way to write to an old Kamerad?... 'Your Honour has not forgotten' ... h'm ... 'and when the late Field-Marshal Min ... campaign ... and Karolinka....' Ach, Bruder! He still remembers our old pranks.... 'And now to business ... am sending you my young rascal'... h'm.... 'Handle him with hedgehog gauntlets'.... Hedgehog gauntlets?" he repeated, turning to me. "What does that mean? Is it a Russian saying?"

"It means," I replied with an innocent air, "you must treat me kindly, not be too strict, give me plenty of liberty, handle me with hedgehog gauntlets."

"H'm, I see ... 'and don't give him too much liberty' ... no, 'hedgehog gauntlets' evidently doesn't mean what you say.... 'Herewith his passport....' Where? Oh, here it is! 'Let the Semenov regiment know....' Good ... good ... it shall be done.... 'I venture to embrace you, without reference to rank, as your old comrade and friend' ... ah, at last ... and so on, and so on. Well, Sir," he said, after he had finished reading the letter and put away my passport—"It shall be done. You will receive officer's rank in the X. regiment, and so as to waste no time you will proceed tomorrow to the Belogorsk fortress, where you will serve under Captain Mironov, a worthy and honourable man. There you will see real service, and learn discipline. There is nothing for you to do in Orenburg; idleness is bad for young man. And today, I shall be happy to see you at dinner."

From bad to worse! I asked myself: what good it had done me to be made a sergeant of the Guards in my mother's womb?

To what had it brought me? To a regiment in a remote fortress on the borders of the Kirghiz-Kaisa steppe! I dined with Andrei Karlovich—we were three, he, his old aide-de-camp and myself. The strictest German economy prevailed at his table, and I am not sure that the fear of having to invite another guest to his bachelor meals had nothing to do with my hasty dispatch to the garrison. The next day I bade the General farewell and set off for my destination.

Chapter Three

THE FORTRESS

> In our fortress, bleak and bare,
> Bread and water is our fare.
> But if our foes come seeking cheer,
> We will feast them, never fear!
> With powder and bullet, with shot and
> shell,
> We will feast them, and feast them well.
>
> *Soldiers' Song*

"People of the old school, Sir!"

The Dunce by Denis Fonvizin

The Belogorsk fortress was situated at a distance of forty *versts* from Orenburg. The road lay along the steep bank of the Yaik.* The river was not yet frozen over, and its leaden current showed dark and dreary between the monotonous snow-covered banks. On either side stretched the Kirghiz steppe. I was plunged in meditation, for the greater part melancholy. Garrison life held few attractions for me. I tried to imagine what Captain Mironov, my future superior officer, would be like, and formed a picture of a severe, bad-tempered old man, oblivious to all but the service, and ready to arrest me and put me on bread and water for the most trivial offence. The dusk was beginning to fall. We were driving at a fair speed. "Is it far to the fortress?" I asked my driver. "Not very," he replied. "It's just coming into sight, yonder." I looked all around me, expecting to see formidable bastions, turrets, and ramparts; but I could see nothing but a huddle of wooden buildings surrounded by a log fence. On one side of the road were three or four haystacks, half-covered with snow, on the other a tumble-down mill with idly drooping bark sails. "Where's the fortress?" I asked in surprise.

---

* *Yaik* — the old name of the river Ural.

"There it is," replied the driver, pointing to the hamlet into which we were turning at that moment. At the gate I saw an ancient iron cannon; the streets were narrow and crooked; the houses low and most of them had straw thatches. I ordered the driver to go on to the commandant's office, and a minute later the sleigh drew up before a small wooden house, standing on high ground, next to a wooden church.

Nobody came to meet me. I went into the porch and opened the door into the passage. An invalided soldier was perched on a table putting a blue patch on the elbow of a green uniform. I told him to announce my arrival. "You can go in, Sir," he replied. "They're at home." I went into a clean little room, furnished in the old-fashioned style. In one corner was a crockery cupboard, on the wall hung an officer's diploma, framed and glazed; next to it were crude pictures representing the storming of Kistrin* and Ochakov**, "The Choice of a Bride", and "The Cat's Funeral". At the window sat an old lady in a wadded jacket with a kerchief on her head. She was winding wool which a one-eyed ancient in officer's uniform held up for her around his outstretched hands. "What can I do for you, Sir?" asked the old woman going on with her occupation. I replied that I had come to serve in the army and considered it my duty to report to the captain, and here I turned to the one-eyed old man, whom I took for the commandant. But the mistress of the house interrupted the speech I had prepared beforehand. "Ivan Kuzmich is out," she said. "He has gone to visit Father Gerasim; but it is no matter, Sir. I am his wife, and you are very welcome. Take a seat, Sir." She called a servant-girl, whom she told to go for the sergeant. The old man observed me inquisitively from his solitary eye. "May I venture to enquire what regiment you were in?" he asked. I satisfied his curiosity. "And may I ask," he continued, "what caused you to leave the Guards for a garrison?" I replied that such had been the will of my superiors. "For conduct unworthy of an officer of the Guards I presume," continued my importunate interrogator. "Enough of your prattle," said the captain's lady, "can't you see the young man is tired from his journey—let him alone! (Hold your hands up, do!) And you, Sir," she went on, addressing me,

---

* The Prussian fortress besieged by the Russian troops in 1758.
** The Turkish fortress captured by the Russian troops in 1797.

"don't grieve at having been packed off to this out-of-the-way spot. You're not the first, you won't be the last. You won't mind it, after you get used to it. It's over four years since Alexei Ivanovich Shvabrin was transferred to us for manslaughter. The Lord knows what made him do it; you see, he and some lieutenant went to the outskirts of the town, and took their swords with them, and started prodding at each other; and Alexei Ivanovich ran the lieutenant through the body, and that in the presence of two witnesses. Can't be helped! It might happen to anyone."

Just then the sergeant, a stalwart young Cossack, entered the room. "Maximich," said the old lady, "find quarters for the officer, clean ones." "Yes, Vasilissa Yegorovna," replied the sergeant. "Shall I quarter His Honour on Ivan Polezhaev?" "No, no, Maximich," said the captain's lady. "It's crowded enough there as it is, but Polezhaev is my friend, and understands that we are his superiors. Take the officer ... what's your name, Sir? Pyotr Andreich. Take Pyotr Andreich to Semen Kuzov. He let his horse into my vegetable garden, the rascal! Well, Maximich, is everything in order?"

"All is quiet, thank God!" replied the Cossack. "Except that Corporal Prokhorov had a quarrel with Ustinya Negulina in the bath-house, about a tub of hot water."

"Ivan Ignatich!" said the captain's lady, now addressing the one-eyed old man. "Speak to Prokhorov and Ustinya, find out which of them is in the wrong. Punish them both, anyhow. Well, Maximich, off with you! Pyotr Andreich, Maximich will show you your quarters."

I bowed myself out. The sergeant led me to a hut on the high bank of the river, at the very edge of the territory belonging to the fortress. Half the house was occupied by Semen Kuzov and his family, the other half was allotted to me. It consisted of one room, divided by a partition, and was quite clean. Savelich began to unpack while I looked out of the narrow window. Before me lay the dismal steppe. Almost opposite were a few huts, and chickens wandered up and down the street. An old woman holding a tub stood in her doorway calling to some pigs, which responded with friendly grunts. And in this place I was condemned to pass my youth! I was overcome with melancholy; I turned away from the window and went to bed without supper, despite the remonstrances of Savelich, who kept repeating ruefully: "God Almighty! He won't eat! What will the mistress say if her child falls ill?"

The next morning, just as I was beginning to dress, the door opened and a young officer, rather short of stature, swarthy-complexioned, anything but handsome, though with a lively expression, entered the room. "Pardon," he said in French, "for coming to make your acquaintance so unceremoniously. I heard of your arrival yesterday; I was so overcome by the desire to see a human face at last, that I could not wait. You will understand that when you have been here a short time." I guessed that this was the officer transferred from the Guards for a duel. We struck up an acquaintance then and there. Shvabrin, who seemed exceedingly intelligent, was a witty and entertaining talker. He gave me a spirited description of the commandant and his family, and of the society and surroundings to which my fate had led me. I was laughing heartily, when the soldier whom I had seen the day before patching a uniform in the commandant's passage, came in and invited me in the name of Vasilissa Yegorovna to have dinner with them. Shvabrin offered to take me there.

As we approached the commandant's house we saw about twenty old men drawn up at attention on the square, all wearing their hair in long pigtails, and with three-cornered hats on their heads. In front of them stood the commandant, a tall, agile old man, in a night cap and dressing-gown. Catching sight of Shvabrin and myself he stepped towards us, addressed a few kind words to me, and went on drilling his men. We would have liked to stop and watch, but he asked us to go to Vasilissa Yegorovna, promising to follow soon himself. "There's nothing for you to see here," he added.

Vasilissa Yegorovna received us with simple cordiality, and treated me as an old acquaintance. The invalided soldier was helping the servant-girl to lay the table. "My Ivan Kuzmich is taking a long time over his drilling today," said the commandant's lady. "Palasha, call the master to dinner. And where's Masha?" At this a round-faced, rosy girl of about eighteen, with flaxen hair combed smoothly behind her glowing ears, came into the room. I did not take to her at first glance. I regarded her with a prejudiced eye. Shvabrin had described Masha, the captain's daughter, as a kind of simpleton. She sat down in a corner and began sewing. In the meantime the cabbage-soup was brought in. Vasilissa Yegorovna, not seeing her husband, sent Palasha out for him again. "Tell the master his guests are waiting, the soup is getting cold. The drilling can wait—God knows, he'll have plenty of time to shout at the men later." Soon after the captain appeared, accompanied by the one-eyed ancient. "What's this, Sir? Dinner's on the table long ago, and you can't be called away." "Now listen, Vasilissa Yegorovna," replied Ivan Kuzmich, "I was busy—I was drilling my old boys."

"Tut-ṭut!" said his lady. "What's the good of drilling them? They'll never learn, and you don't know much about it yourself. You had much better stay at home and say your prayers. Come to the table, dear guests."

We sat down to table. Vasilissa ·Yegorovna never stopped talking for a moment, showering questions at me—who were my parents? Were they still alive? Where did they live, and how much money they had? Learning that my father had three hundred serfs, she exclaimed:

"Fancy that! How rich some people are! And all we have is one servant-girl—Palasha. But thank God we don't do so badly. Our only grief is Masha—the girl is ready for marriage, and what is her dowry? A comb, a broom, and a silver coin (God save the mark!). If an honest man asks for her, well and good, otherwise the girl must be an old maid all her life." I glanced at Marya Ivanovna; her face was crimson, and tears were actually dropping into her plate. I felt sorry for her, and hastened to change the conversation. "I have heard," I said, somewhat irrelevantly, "that the Bashkirs intend to attack your fortress." "And where did you hear that, Sir, if I may ask?" enquired Ivan Kuzmich. "I was told in Orenburg," I replied. "Nonsense!" said the commandant. "All has been quiet here for a long time. The Bashkirs are intimidated, and the Kirghiz have had their lesson. They're hardly likely to give us any trouble, and if they do, I'll give them a shaking up they won't forget for ten years."

"Doesn't it frighten you to be living in a fortress exposed to such danger?" I continued, turning to Vasilissa Yegorovna. "I'm used to it, good Sir," she replied. "Twenty years ago when we were transferred from the regiment here, God alone knows how frightened I was of those heathens! Whenever I saw their lynx-fur caps, or heard their yells, my heart seemed to stop, it

did indeed, Sir! But I'm so used to them now, I wouldn't move
a step if someone were to come and tell us that the ruffians were
prowling around the fortress."

"Vasilissa Yegorovna is a very brave woman," remarked
Shvabrin sententiously. "Ivan Kuzmich can testify to that."

"Why, yes," said Ivan Kuzmich. "She's not one of your faint-
hearted wenches."

"And Marya Ivanovna?" asked I. "Is she as brave as you
are?"

"Masha brave?" replied her mother. "No, Masha is a coward.
She still can't get used to the sound of rifle-shooting; it makes
her all a-tremble. When Ivan Kuzmich ordered salvos of can-
non-fire on my name-day, two years ago, she almost died of
fear, my pet. Since then we don't fire from the accursed cannon."

We all rose from the table. The captain and his lady went to
their room for a nap; and I went to Shvabrin's room, and spent
the whole evening with him.

Chapter Four

THE DUEL

> Stand up, good Sir, and I will do my best
> To run my trusty rapier through your breast.
>
> *Knyazhnin**

A few weeks passed, and my life in the Belogorsk fortress had become not merely bearable, but actually pleasant. I was received in the home of the commandant like one of the family. The commandant and his lady were most worthy persons. Ivan Kuzmich, a soldier's son who had become an officer, was an uneducated, simple man, but extremely honest and kind. His wife ruled him, and this suited his easy-going disposition. Vasilissa Yegorovna regarded the service as a branch of her housekeeping, and ruled the fortress just as she ruled her home. Marya Ivanovna soon stopped being shy of me. We made friends. I found her to be a girl possessed of both sense and feeling. I grew imperceptibly attached to the kindly family, even to Ivan Ignatich, the one-eyed garrison lieutenant who, Shvabrin insinuated, was in illicit relations with the mistress of the house. There were not the slightest grounds for such a supposition, but this did not trouble Shvabrin.

In due time I received an officer's rank. My duties were not onerous. In this god-forsaken fortress there were neither reviews, drilling nor sentry watches. Every now and then the commandant took it into his head to drill his soldiers; but he had never been able to teach all of them to distinguish right from left, though a good many, for fear of making a mistake, crossed themselves every time they had to turn. Shvabrin had a few

---

* From Yakov Knyazhnin's comedy *The Eccentrics*.

French books. I began reading, and developed literary aspirations. In the mornings I read, tried my hand at translation, and sometimes even composed verse. I dined at the commandant's almost every day, and I usually spent the rest of the day there; Father Gerasim and his wife Akulina Pamfilovna, the prime gossip of the whole district, sometimes came there in the evening. Shvabrin, of course, I saw every day; but his conversation became more and more distasteful to me as time went on. His incessant jokes about the commandant's family, and especially his derisive remarks about Marya Ivanovna, displeased me intensely. There was no other society in the fortress, and I desired no other.

Despite the prophecies, the Bashkirs showed no signs of unrest. Tranquillity prevailed in the neighbourhood of our fortress. But our peace was disturbed by unexpected internal hostilities.

I have already said that I had begun writing myself. My efforts were quite fair for those times, and Alexander Petrovich Sumarokov,* some years later, praised them cordially. Once I succeeded in writing a poem with which I was satisfied. It is well known that authors frequently seek an indulgent listener, under the pretence of asking advice. And so, having finished composing a lyric, I took it to Shvabrin, who was the only person in the fortress capable of appreciating poetry. After a few introductory phrases I drew my note-book out of my pocket, and read him the following verses:

> *My amorous thoughts I fain would shun,*
> *The lovely Masha I would flee,*
> *When she is gone, my dearest one,*
> *Then, only then, my thoughts are free.*

> *But oh, those eyes to me so dear,*
> *They give me peace, nor day, nor night,*
> *They shine before me, ever near,*
> *I perish in their fatal light.*

> *Now, Masha, witness of my grief,*
> *Pity my sufferings, I implore thee,*

---

* An 18th century writer, a representative of Russian classicism (1718-1777).

> *For thou alone canst bring relief*
> *To him who lies enchained before thee.**

"What d'you think of it?" I asked Shvabrin, expecting praise as my rightful due. To my intense annoyance, however, Shvabrin usually so indulgent, firmly declared that my song was bad.

"But why?" I asked, concealing my annoyance.

"Because," he replied, "such verses are worthy of my teacher, Vasili Kirillich Tredyakovsky,** and strongly remind me of his love poems."

With this, he took the note-book from me and began ruthlessly criticising every line and every word, holding me up to biting ridicule. Unable to bear any more, I tore the book from his hands and said I would never again show him my verses. Shvabrin laughed at this threat, too. "Let's see if you keep your word," he said. "A poet must have a listener, just as Ivan Kuzmich must have his glass or two of vodka before dinner. And who is this Masha for whom you declare such a tender passion, and who causes you such delightful agonies? Surely not Marya Ivanovna?"

"It's none of your business who it is!" I replied, frowning. "I want neither your opinion, nor your surmises."

"Oho! A touchy poet and a discreet lover!" continued Shvabrin, with whom I was beginning to feel more and more provoked. "But hearken to my friendly counsel—if you want to succeed, I advise you not to confine yourself to mere warblings."

"What do you mean by that, Sir? Be so kind as to explain yourself!"

"Willingly. I mean that if you wish Masha Mironova to visit you in the twilight, you must offer her a pair of ear-rings, and not tender verses."

My blood boiled. "And what makes you have such a low opinion of her?" I asked, hardly able to contain my indignation.

"Because," he replied, with a diabolical sneer, "I know her morals and habits from experience."

"You lie, you scoundrel!" I shouted, enraged. "You lie shamelessly!"

---

* This poem was taken from the book *A New and Full Collection of Russia's Songs* compiled by Nikolai Novikov, an 18th century enlightener.

** An 18th century poet and translator, who championed Russian prosody, and whose verses were frequently made mock of by his contemporaries.

Shvabrin turned pale. "I can't let that pass," he said, clutching my hand. "You will give me satisfaction."

"Gladly! Whenever you like!" I answered, greatly relieved. At that moment I was ready to tear him to pieces.

I went at once to look for Ivan Ignatich, whom I found with a needle in his hand—at the behest of the commandant's lady he was threading mushrooms on a string to dry them for the winter. "Ah, Pyotr Andreich!" he said, on catching sight of me. "Come in! What good wind brings you here? What is your business, if I may ask?" I explained to him briefly that I had quarrelled with Alexei Ivanovich, and that I wanted him to be my second. Ivan Ignatich heard me out attentively, blinking at me from his solitary eye. "You are good enough to inform me," he said, "that you intend to run Alexei Ivanovich through the body, and that you desire me to be a witness of this. Is that your meaning, may I ask?"

"Yes, Sir!"

"Bless my soul, Pyotr Andreich! What are you thinking about? You have quarrelled with Alexei Ivanich. What then? Words never broke any bones. He swears at you—you swear back at him; he strikes you in the face, you strike him on the ear, and so it goes, and you separate; and we will see to it that you make it up. For surely no good can come of running your sword through your neighbour. All very well if you kill him! I don't care about Alexei Ivanich—I never liked him. But supposing he is the one to run his sword through *you*! What then? Who'll be the fool then, I venture to enquire?"

The arguments of the reasonable lieutenant failed to shake me. I adhered to my intention. "Just as you like," said Ivan Ignatich. "Do as seems best to you. But why should I look on? What for? Do you think I've never seen people fighting? I've fought against the Turks and the Swedes—I've seen enough fighting in my day."

I explained to him as best I might the duties of a second, but Ivan Ignatich could not understand what I was talking about. "As you will, Sir," he said. "But the only part for me to take in this affair would be to go to Ivan Kuzmich and report to him, in duty bound, that a bad deed, contrary to the interests of the state, is being planned in the fortress, and to ask the commandant to be so good as to take the proper measures...."

Thoroughly alarmed, I implored Ivan Ignatich not to tell the commandant. I managed with the utmost difficulty to dissuade him, but at last he gave me his word and I decided to leave him alone.

I spent the evening as usual at the commandant's house. I tried to appear cheerful and nonchalant, so as to give no grounds for suspicions, and avoid tiresome questions, but I cannot lay claim to that indifference of which those in my position are wont to boast. I was in a tender and sentimental mood that evening. Marya Ivanovna had never seemed so attractive to me. The thought that this was perhaps the last time I should see her lent her a touch of pathos in my eyes. Shvabrin was there, too. I drew him aside and told him of my conversation with Ivan Ignatich. "What do we need seconds for?" he said coldly. "We can dispense with them." We agreed to fight behind the haystacks not far from the fortress, and to be there at seven o'clock the next morning. We seemed to be conversing so amicably that Ivan Ignatich, in his delight, let the cat out of the bag. "That's right," he said, with a pleased air. "A bad peace is better than a good quarrel, a whole skin is better than honour."

"What's that, Ivan Ignatich?" asked the commandant's lady who was sitting in a corner telling fortunes with a pack of cards. "I didn't hear what you said."

Ivan Ignatich, seeing signs of dissatisfaction in my face, and remembering his promise, was confused, and did not know how to answer her. Shvabrin hastened to his aid.

"Ivan Ignatich is glad to see us such good friends again," he said.

"And who have you been quarrelling with, Sir?"

"Pyotr Andreich and I had quite a serious dispute."

"What about?"

"Oh, a mere trifle! A song, Vasilissa Yegorovna."

"A song? That's not worth quarrelling over. How did it come about?"

"It was like this: Pyotr Andreich wrote a song a little while ago, and sang it in front of me, and I hummed my favourite couplet:

> *Captain's daughter, stay at home!*
> *In the moonlight do not roam.**

---

* A line from one of the songs included in the *Collection of Russian Folk Songs* compiled by Ivan Pratch, an 18th century composer and folklorist.

Emelyan Pugachev (1744-1775). The leader of a peasant rebellion in Russia in 1770s. Pushkin was so interested in the person of Pugachev that he not only studied all the available archive materials, but even made a trip to the gubernias which had taken part in the rebellion and talked to eye-witnesses. The result was his novel *The Captain's Daughter* and a historical treatise "The History of Pugachev's Rebellion". This engraving of 1834 was used to illustrate the first edition of "The History of Pugachev's Rebellion"

Catherine the Second (1729-1796). Russian Empress who
ascended the throne in 1762. The visual image of Catherine
the Second strolling in the park of Tsarskoye Selo in "a white
morning gown, night-cap and quilted jacket" and with a "white
dog of the English breed" that occurs in *The Captain's Daughter*
was probably suggested by this engraving from the picture of
Borovikovsky, 1827

And there was discord between us. Pyotr Andreich was just going to get really angry, but he remembered in time that everybody has the right to sing whatever he likes. And the matter ended there."

Shvabrin's impudence drove me almost mad with rage, but no one but myself understood his gross insinuations; at any rate no one paid any heed to them. The mention of songs led to a discussion of poets, the commandant observing that they were all dissipated fellows and drunkards, and giving me the friendly advice to let versemaking alone, as an occupation alien to the service, and leading to no good.

The presence of Shvabrin had become intolerable to me. I soon got up and said good-bye to the commandant and his family. Arrived at my quarters I examined my sword, tried its point, and went to bed, instructing Savelich to wake me soon after six.

At the appointed hour next morning I was behind the haystacks, awaiting my adversary. He did not keep me long. "We may be caught," he said, "we must hurry." We took off our tunics, and stood in our undervests, our swords bared. All of a sudden Ivan Ignatich and four or five garrison soldiers appeared from behind a haystack. He requested us to go to the commandant. We submitted with bad grace. The soldiers surrounded us and we set off for the fortress behind Ivan Ignatich, who led us in triumph, strutting pompously ahead.

We entered the house of the commandant. Ivan Ignatich opened a door, announcing solemnly: "I've brought them!" We were met by Vasilissa Yegorovna. "Ah, Sirs, Sirs! What is all this? What? Planning murder in our fortress! Ivan Kuzmich! Have them arrested immediately! Pyotr Andreich! Alexei Ivanich! Hand over your swords, hand them over this minute! Palasha, take those swords to the closet. Pyotr Andreich! I never expected this from you! Aren't you ashamed? Alexei Ivanich is different—he was transferred from the Guards for killing a man, he doesn't believe in God. But you, you! Do you want to be like him?"

Ivan Kuzmich thoroughly agreed with his wife and said again and again: "I tell you—Vasilissa Yegorovna is right. Duels are expressly prohibited in Military Regulations." In the meantime Palasha took our swords away from us and put them in the closet. I could not help laughing. Shvabrin maintained his dignity. "With all due respect to you," he said coldly, addressing Vasilissa Yegorovna, "I cannot refrain from remarking that it is not for you to constitute yourself our judge. Leave that to Ivan Kuzmich, it's his affair." "Sir, Sir," the commandant's wife chided him, "are not husband and wife one flesh and one spirit? Ivan Kuzmich! Why don't you do something? Put them under arrest in different rooms and keep them on bread and water till the devil goes out of them! And let Father Gerasim impose a penance on them—to implore God to forgive them and express repentance for their sin in public."

Ivan Kuzmich could not make up his mind what to do. Marya Ivanovna was excessively pale. Little by little the tempest abated. The commandant's lady calmed down, and made us kiss each other. Palasha brought us back our swords. We left the house apparently reconciled. Ivan Ignatich accompanied us. "You ought to be ashamed of yourself," I said to him angrily, "informing on us to the commandant after giving me your word you would not!" "As God is my judge, I didn't tell Ivan Kuzmich," he replied. "Vasilissa Yegorovna wormed it all out of me. She arranged everything without the commandant's knowledge. But the Lord be thanked that it all ended the way it did." With this he went home and Shvabrin and I were alone. "Our quarrel cannot end like this," I said. "Of course not," replied Shvabrin. "You will answer for your insolence with your blood; but they will probably keep a watch on us now. We must keep up a pretence of friendship for a few days. Good-bye!" And we parted as if nothing whatever had happened.

Returning to the commandant's house I sat down next to Marya Ivanovna, as usual. Ivan Kuzmich was not at home; Vasilissa Yegorovna was busy with her housework. We spoke in low tones. Marya Ivanovna reproached me in tender accents for the anxiety they had all felt on account of my quarrel with Shvabrin. "I almost fainted," she said, "when they told me you intended to fight with swords. How strange men are! For a single word, which they would probably forget in a week's time, they are ready to kill each other and sacrifice not only their own lives, but their consciences and the welfare of those who.... But I feel sure you were not the one who began it. It must have been Alexei Ivanich's fault."

"What makes you think that, Marya Ivanovna?"

"I don't know ... he's always sneering. I don't like Alexei

Ivanich. I don't like him; and yet, strange to say, I should be very sorry if I knew he disliked me! It would make me excessively uneasy."

"And what do you think, Marya Ivanovna—does he like you?"

Marya Ivanovna blushed.

"I think he does," she faltered.

"And why do you think that?"

"Because he proposed to me."

"Proposed to you? He proposed to you? When?"

"Last year. A month or two before you came here."

"And you didn't accept him?"

"As you see. Alexei Ivanich is a very clever man, of course, and comes of a good family, and has property. But when I think of having to stand up at the altar with him, and kiss him in front of everybody.... Not for the world, not for anything in the world!"

Marya Ivanovna's words opened my eyes and explained a great deal to me. I now understood the persistent malevolence with which Shvabrin invariably spoke of her. He must have noticed our mutual feelings and endeavoured to make mischief between us. The words which had given rise to our quarrel now appeared to me still more base when, in addition to gross ribaldry, I saw in them deliberate calumny. The desire to punish the insolent slanderer grew ever stronger within me, and I waited impatiently for an opportunity.

I had not long to wait. The very next day, as I was sitting over an elegy, nibbling the end of my quill in the search for rhymes, Shvabrin tapped on the wall beneath my window. I flung down the pen, picked up my sword and went out to him. "Why put it off any longer?" said Shvabrin to me. "Nobody is spying on us. Let's go to the river. Nobody will interfere with us there." We set off in silence. Descending by a winding path, we came to a halt on the bank of the river and unsheathed our swords. Shvabrin was the better swordsman, but I was stronger and bolder, and Monsieur Beaupré, who had served in the army at one time, had given me a few lessons in fencing, which I now profited by. Shvabrin had not expected to find so formidable an opponent in me. For a long time neither of us could injure the other; at last, noticing that Shvabrin was beginning to weaken, I attacked him with renewed vigour and almost forced him into the water. Suddenly I heard my name called in a loud voice. I looked round and caught sight of Savelich, running towards me down the hilly path. At the same moment I felt a sharp thrust in my chest, beneath the right shoulder; I fell to the ground unconscious.

Chapter Five

LOVE

Thou art too young to wed, Pretty One!
Ask your father, ask your mother, Pretty One!
Ask your father and your mother, ask your
kinsmen.
Wait till you get wisdom, Pretty One,
Wisdom, and a dowry, Pretty One!

Folk-Song

Find a better than I, and you'll forget me,
Find a worse—and you'll remember me.

Folk-Song

When I regained consciousness it was some time before I could remember what had happened. I was lying on a bed in a strange room, feeling very weak. By the bed stood Savelich with a candle in his hand. Somebody was carefully unwinding the bandages around my chest and shoulder. My thoughts gradually cleared. I remembered the duel and guessed that I was wounded. Just then the door creaked. "How is he?" whispered a voice which sent a tremor through me. "Just the same," replied Savelich with a sigh. "Unconscious all the time, and it's five days now." I wanted to turn in bed, but could not. "Where am I? Who is it?" I said, making a tremendous effort. Marya Ivanovna approached the bed and bent over me. "How do you feel?" she said. "God be thanked," I replied in a weak voice. "Is it you, Marya Ivanovna? Tell me..." I lacked the strength to go on, and broke off in the middle of the sentence. Savelich gasped. His face expressed the most lively joy. "He has come to his senses! Thanks be to Thee, Oh Lord!" he kept repeating. "Oh, Pyotr Andreich, how you frightened me, Sir! Only think—five days!" Marya Ivanovna interrupted him. "Don't talk to him too much, Savelich," she said. "He's still weak." She went out, closing the door quietly behind her. My thoughts were in a turmoil. So I was in the commandant's house. Marya Ivanovna had been to see me. I tried to put some questions to Savelich, but the old man shook his head and stopped his ears. I closed my eyes in vexation and soon found oblivion in slumber.

On waking I called for Savelich, but instead of him I beheld Marya Ivanovna at my side, who greeted me in her angelic voice. I could never hope to express in words the sweetness of the emotions which took possession of me at that moment. I seized her hand, clinging to it and bathing it in tears of rapture. Masha did not pull it away ... and suddenly her lips brushed against my cheek, in a kiss of innocent fervour. A flame ran through my whole being. "Dear, good Marya Ivanovna," I said to her, "be my wife, consent to make me a happy man for life!" She regained her self-possession. "Calm yourself, for heaven's sake," she said, taking away her hand. "You are not out of danger yet. Your wound might reopen. Take care of yourself, if only for my sake." With these words she went out of the room, leaving me in an ecstasy of delight. Happiness brought me back to life. She will be mine! She loves me! My whole being was filled with this thought.

From this moment I began gradually to recover. I was attended by the regimental barber, there being no other physician in the regiment, and thank heavens he did not try any experiments on me. Youth and nature hastened my recovery. The commandant's entire family looked after me. Marya Ivanovna hardly left my side. Naturally I seized the first opportunity to return to my interrupted declaration of love, and this time Marya Ivanovna heard me out with greater patience. She admitted her own feelings for me without coyness, saying that her parents would naturally be glad of her happiness. "But think it over well," she added. "Might not your own parents prove an obstacle?"

I pondered. I had no doubt of my mother's tenderness, but knowing the disposition and views of my father, I felt that he would not be particularly moved by the recital of my love, which he would probably regard as a young man's whim. I frankly admitted this to Marya Ivanovna, resolving, nevertheless, to write to my sire using all the eloquence at my disposal, and asking for his parental blessing. I showed the letter to Marya Ivanovna, who found it so convincing and touching that she

could not doubt of its persuasive powers, and surrendered herself to the emotions of her tender heart with all the trustfulness
of youth and love.

I made it up with Shvabrin on one of the first days after my
recovery. Ivan Kuzmich reproved me for the duel, saying: "Oh,
Pyotr Andreich! I ought to put you under arrest, but you have
been punished enough. Alexei Ivanich is under guard in the
baker's shop however, and Vasilissa Yegorovna has his sword
under lock and key. Let him think over his sins and repent."
Too happy to be able to bear anyone ill-will, I interceded for
Shvabrin, and the kind-hearted commandant, after taking counsel of his wife, resolved to set him at liberty. Shvabrin came to
see me; he expressed profound regret for what had passed between us, admitted that it had all been his fault, and asked me
to forget the past. It was not in my nature to harbour resent-
ment and I sincerely forgave him, both for the wrong he had
done me and the wound he had inflicted on me. Ascribing his
slander to the effects of wounded vanity and rejected love, I
magnanimously forgave my unfortunate rival.

I soon recovered completely and was able to go back to my
own quarters. I awaited impatiently a reply to my letter,
scarcely daring to hope, and endeavouring to stifle my forebodings. I had not yet said anything about my feelings to
Vasilissa Yegorovna and her husband, but I was aware that my
proposal could hardly come as a surprise to them. Neither
Marya Ivanovna nor myself took any pains to conceal our feelings from them, and we confidently anticipated their consent.

At last Savelich came to me one morning with a letter in his
hand. I seized it eagerly. The address was in my father's hand.
This in itself prepared me for something portentous for it was
usually my mother who wrote to me, while he added a few lines
at the end of her letters. For some time, unable to bring myself
to break the seal, I studied the solemn inscription: "To my Son
Pyotr Andreich Grinev, Orenburg Gubernia, Belogorsk Fortress", endeavouring to guess from the handwriting at the state
of mind in which the epistle had been indited; at last I broke
the seal, and the very first lines showed me that it was all over
with us. The contents of the letter were as follows:

"My Son, Pyotr! Your letter, in which you request
our parental blessing and consent to your marriage

with Marya Ivanovna, daughter of Mironov, was received by us on the 15th of this month, and not only have I no intention of giving either my blessing or my consent, but I mean to take you in hand and punish you for your pranks as if you were still a mere boy, despite your officer's rank, for you have shown that you are as yet unworthy to wear the sword bestowed upon you for the protection of your country, and not for duels with hot-heads like yourself. I shall write instantly to Andrei Karlovich, requesting him to transfer you from the Belogorsk fortress to some still more remote spot, where you will forget all this nonsense. When your mother heard of your duel and that you were wounded, she fell ill with grief, and has kept her bed ever since. What is to become of you? I pray God that you will improve, though I scarcely venture to hope for His great mercy.

"Your Father A. G."

The perusal of this letter aroused varying emotions in me. The harsh expressions, so unsparingly used by my father, wounded me deeply. The disrespectful manner in which he referred to Marya Ivanovna seemed to me both unseemly and unwarranted. The idea of being transferred from the Belogorsk fortress appalled me, but the news of my mother's illness grieved me most of all. I was indignant with Savelich, never doubting that my parents had learned of the duel from him. Pacing backwards and forwards in my narrow room I came to a halt in front of him, and said, looking daggers at him: "And so, not satisfied with being the cause of a wound which has kept me at death's door a whole month, you wish to kill my mother, too." Savelich was thunderstruck. "Why, Master," he said, almost sobbing. "What is this you say to me? *I* the cause of your wound? The dear Lord knows I was running to shelter yourself with my body from the sword of Alexei Ivanovich! My accursed years prevented me! And what have I done to your mother?" "What have you done?" I said. "Who asked you to write and inform on me? Have you been set over me as a spy?" "I write and inform on you?" exclaimed Savelich, weeping. "God Almighty! Be so kind as to read what the master wrote to me, and you will see how I informed on you." With this he drew a letter from his pocket, and I read the following:

"You ought to be ashamed, you dog, for not telling me about my son Pyotr, in spite of my strict injunctions, and for leaving strangers to inform me of his pranks. Is that the way you fulfil your duty and the will of your master? I'll send you to look after the pigs, you dog, for concealing the truth and conniving with one so young. On receipt of this letter I order you to write to me immediately as to his health, which, I am told, is improving; and to tell me where he was wounded, and if he is being properly looked after."

It was evident that Savelich had done me no wrong and that I ought not to have insulted him with my reproaches and suspicions. I begged his pardon, but the old man was inconsolable. "This is what I have come to," he moaned. "These are the favours I have merited from my masters! I'm a dog and a swineherd, and now I'm the cause of your wound! No, Pyotr Andreich, my young master, not I, but that accursed Monseer is to blame; it was he who taught you to thrust with iron spits, and stamp on the ground, as if thrusting and stamping could save you from a wicked man! Why did they hire a Monseer, wasting all that money for nothing!"

Who could have taken the trouble to inform my father about myself and my conduct? The General? He scarcely seemed interested enough in me for that; and Ivan Kuzmich had not found it necessary to report the duel. I was lost in surmises. My suspicions lit on Shvabrin. He alone could have anything to gain by giving information which might lead to my removal from the fortress and a break with the commandant's family. I went to tell Marya Ivanovna all about it. She met me in the porch. "What's the matter with you?" she cried, seeing my face. "How pale you are!" "All is over!" I said and handed her my father's letter. It was now she who turned pale. After reading the letter through she gave it back to me with trembling fingers, saying in a trembling voice: "It was not to be, you see.... Your parents do not wish to have me in their family. God's will be done! God knows what is good for us better than we do ourselves. It can't be helped, Pyotr Andreich—so long as you are happy...." "It shall not be so!" I exclaimed, grasping her hand. "You love me; I am ready for anything. Come, we will throw

ourselves at the feet of your parents; they are simple folk, their
hearts have not been hardened by pride. They will give us their
blessing; we will be married ... and then, in time, I am quite
sure we will be able to conciliate my father; my mother will be
on our side; and he will forgive me." "No, Pyotr Andreich,"
replied Masha. "I will not marry you without your parents'
blessing. Without their blessing there can be no happiness for
you. We must submit to the will of God. If you find your destined
bride, if· you love another, God's blessing be on you, Pyotr
Andreich; I will pray for you both...." Here she burst into
tears and left me; I had an impulse to follow her into the house,
but feeling that I was in no state to control my emotion I went
home.

I was seated in my room, deep in thought, when Savelich
interrupted my meditations. "Here, Sir," he said, handing me
a sheet of paper covered with writing. "See if I inform on my
master, and wish to set father and son at loggerheads." I took
the sheet from his hands. It was Savelich's reply to the letter
received by him. I give it word for word:

> "Esteemed Andrei Petrovich, my merciful master!
> "I have received your gracious letter in which you
> are pleased to be angry with me, your slave, saying I
> ought to be ashamed of disobeying my master's orders.
> But I am no dog, I am your loyal servant, I do obey
> my master's orders and have always served you faith-
> fully, and my hair has gone grey in your service. I did
> not write to you about Pyotr Andreich's wound, for
> fear of alarming you needlessly; and I now hear that
> the mistress, our dear Avdotya Vasilyevna, has taken
> to her bed in her alarm, and I will pray to God for her
> recovery. Pyotr Andreich was wounded beneath the
> right shoulder, in his chest, just under the bone, the
> wound was one and a half inches deep, and he lay in
> the house of the commandant, where we brought him
> from the river-bank, and he was attended by Stepan
> Paramonov, the barber. And now, thank God, Pyotr
> Andreich is well again, and I can write nothing about
> him but what is good. I hear his superior officers are
> pleased with him. And Vasilissa Yegorovna treats him
> like her own son. And if he has got himself into a

scrape—you can't put an old head on young shoulders.
Even a horse sometimes stumbles though it has four
legs. You are pleased to say that you will send me for
a swineherd, you are my master, and can do with me
what seems good to you. Receive the humble greetings
of

"Your faithful serf Arkhip Savelyev."

I could not repress an occasional smile, while perusing the
good old man's epistle. I was in no state to answer my father
myself, and it seemed to me that Savelich's letter was sufficient
to calm my mother's anxiety.

From this moment my situation altered. Marya Ivanovna
hardly ever spoke to me, and tried to keep out of my way as
much as possible. The commandant's house had lost all charm
for me. I gradually got used to sitting at home alone. At first
Vasilissa Yegorovna reproached me for this, but seeing my
determination, she left me in peace. Ivan Kuzmich I only saw in
the course of my duties. I seldom met Shvabrin and then
reluctantly, for I thought I observed in him a secret dislike of
myself, which confirmed me in my suspicions. My life became
intolerable to me. I sank into a state of melancholy brooding,
which was nourished by loneliness and inactivity. My love
blazed up in solitude, and became an ever-increasing burden to
me. I lost all interest in reading and literary composition. I fell
into dejection. I feared I should either go mad or take to drink.
And then an unexpected occurrence, which influenced the whole
of my life, gave me a powerful and beneficent shock.

Chapter Six

PUGACHEV AND HIS MEN

> Hearken, young men,
> To what we old ones have to tell you.*
>
> *Old Song*

Before entering upon a description of the strange events of which I was a witness, I feel bound to say a few words as to the situation in the Orenburg Gubernia towards the end of the year 1773.

This extensive and wealthy gubernia was the home of a number of half-savage peoples who had only recently acknowledged the sway of the Russian tsars. Their incessant risings, their inability to accustom themselves to laws and to civil life, their recklessness and cruelty, demanded perpetual surveillance on the part of the government to keep them in subjection. Fortresses were erected in places regarded as suitable, and chiefly manned by Cossacks who had long dwelt on the banks of the Yaik. But the Yaik Cossacks whose function it was to guard the peace and security of these regions, had themselves become restless subjects and source of danger to the government. In 1772 there was a rising in their principal citadel, caused by the severe measures which Major-General Traubenberg employed to reduce the troops to proper subjection. The result of this rising was the atrocious murder of Traubenberg, and arbitrary changes in the Cossack administration, and, finally, the crushing of the mutiny by savage reprisals and punishments.

---

* From the song about the capture of Kazan by Tsar Ivan the Terrible (from Nikolai Novikov's collection).

These events had occurred some little time before my arrival at the Belogorsk fortress. All was quiet by then, or at least had the appearance of being so; the authorities gave too easy credence to the supposed repentance of the cunning rebels, who nurtured their rancour in secret, only awaiting an opportunity to start fresh disorders.

I will resume my narrative.

One evening (it was at the beginning of October 1773), I was alone in my room listening to the howling of the autumn wind and watching through the window the clouds scudding past the moon. Someone came to call me to the commandant. I went to his house immediately. There I found Shvabrin, Ivan Ignatich and the Cossack sergeant. Neither Vasilissa Yegorovna nor Marya Ivanovna was in the room. The commandant greeted me with a preoccupied air. He then locked the door, caused us all to be seated, except the sergeant who took up his stand at the door, drew a sheet of paper from his pocket and said: "I have important news for you, gentlemen! Hear what the General writes." With this he put on his spectacles and read the following letter aloud:

> "To Captain Mironov, Commandant of the Belogorsk Fortress.
>
> *Strictly confidential!*

"I hereby inform you that the Don Cossack and Sectarian, Emelyan Pugachev, having escaped from detention, and had the unpardonable insolence to call himself by the name of the late Emperor Peter III, has rallied around him a lawless band, roused discontent in the Yaik villages and already captured and laid waste to several fortresses, committing robbery and murder everywhere. Therefore, Captain, on receipt of the present, you will immediately take the necessary measures for resistance to the above-named criminal and pretender, and, if possible, for his destruction, should he attack the fortress entrusted to your charge."

"Take the necessary measures!" repeated the commandant removing his spectacles and folding up the letter. "Easier said than done! The villain is evidently strong; and we have only a hundred and thirty men, not counting Cossacks, who are not to be relied upon, no offence meant to you, Maximich!" (The sergeant chuckled.) "But it cannot be helped, gentlemen! Be exemplary in the performance of your duties, form sentry-guards, and night watches. In case of attack lock the gates and rouse the soldiers. You, Maximich, keep a sharp watch on your Cossacks. Examine the cannon and have it thoroughly cleaned. And above all keep all this secret, so that no one in the fortress finds out about it beforehand."

Having issued these orders, Ivan Kuzmich dismissed us. Shvabrin and I left the house together, discussing what we had just heard. "How d'you think it will all end?" I asked him. "God knows," he replied. "We'll see. So far I see nothing particular in it. Of course, if...." Here he fell into a reverie, whistling a French tune abstractedly.

Despite all our precautions, the news of Pugachev's appearance spread over the fortress. Much as Ivan Kuzmich respected his wife, nothing on earth would have induced him to tell her a secret communicated to him in the line of service. On receiving the General's letter he had managed skilfully to get rid of Vasilissa Yegorovna, telling her that Father Gerasim had had wonderful news from Orenburg, which he was keeping a great secret. This made Vasilissa Yegorovna decide to go and see the priest's wife at once, taking Masha with her, on the advice of Ivan Kuzmich, so that the girl should not be lonely all by herself.

Ivan Kuzmich, now sole master of his own house, instantly sent for us, locking Palasha into the closet, to make certain that she would not overhear us.

Vasilissa Yegorovna, returning home without having been able to get anything out of the priest's wife, discovered that Ivan Kuzmich had held council of war in her absence, during which Palasha had been locked up. Realising that her husband had played a trick on her, she questioned him closely. But Ivan Kuzmich was prepared for such an attack. Not in the least perturbed, he gave cheery answers to the inquisitive partner of his life: "I tell you, my dear, our women took it into their heads to heat the stoves with straw; and since this might lead to a disaster, I gave strict orders for them not to use straw to heat their stoves with in future, but only dead branches and underbrush." "And why did you have to lock up Palasha?" asked his lady. "Why had the poor girl to sit in the closet till we

returned?" Ivan Kuzmich, who was unprepared for this question, muttered something inarticulate. Vasilissa Yegorovna saw
through her husband's duplicity, but, aware that she would not
be able to get anything out of him, desisted from her questions,
and changed the subject to the salted cucumbers which Akulina
Pamfilovna prepared in some quite special fashion. Vasilissa
Yegorovna could not sleep all night, and could not imagine
what it was that her husband knew that must not be divulged
to her.

The next morning, coming home from church, she noticed
Ivan Ignatich taking from the barrel of the gun rags, pebbles,
chips, old bones and all manner of rubbish thrust into it by the
children. "What can these military preparations mean?" the
commandant's wife asked herself. "Can it be they are expecting
an attack by the Kirghiz? Surely Ivan Kuzmich would not
conceal such a trifle from me?" She hailed Ivan Ignatich with
the firm intention of worming out of him the secret which was
torturing her feminine curiosity.

Vasilissa Yegorovna began by passing a few remarks of a
domestic nature, like a magistrate starting an interrogation
with casual questions, so as to put the subject off his guard.
Then, after a moment's pause, she sighed deeply and said, shaking her head: "My God, my God! What news! What will
come of it?"

"Have no anxiety, Madam," replied Ivan Ignatich. "God is
merciful. We have plenty of soldiers and sufficient powder, and
I have cleaned the cannon. Let us hope we shall be able to beat
off Pugachev. If the Lord is merciful we shall not be devoured."

"And who is this Pugachev?" asked Vasilissa Yegorovna.
Ivan Ignatich bit his tongue, seeing that he had given himself
away. But it was too late. Vasilissa Yegorovna forced him to tell
her all, promising not to say a word to anyone.

Vasilissa Yegorovna kept her promise and said not a word to
anyone, except to the priest's wife, and then only because the
latter's cow was at large in the steppe, and might be seized by
the ruffians.

Soon everyone was talking about Pugachev. All sorts of
rumours were afloat. The commandant sent the Cossack sergeant to find out all he could in the neighbouring villages and
fortresses. Maximich returned in two days, declaring that he
had seen numbers of campfires in the steppe about sixty *versts*

from the fortress, and had heard from the Bashkirs that vast forces were on the march. He could not however say anything for certain, having been afraid to venture further.

Extraordinary agitation was noticeable among the Cossacks in the fortress; they formed groups in all the streets, talking in low voices, and dispersing whenever a dragoon or garrison soldier came in sight. Spies were sent among them. Yulai, a converted Kalmyk, brought important information to the commandant. According to Yulai the sergeant's reports were false— on his return the cunning Cossack had told his own comrades that he had been in the camp of the rebels, and had even presented himself to their leader, who had let him kiss his hand and held a long conversation with him. The commandant immediately put the sergeant in the guard-room, and appointed Yulai in his place. This news was received by the Cossacks with evident dissatisfaction. They expressed their discontent loudly and Ivan Ignatich, while carrying out the commandant's instructions, heard with his own ears how they declared: "It'll be your turn next, Garrison Rat!" The commandant had meant to cross-examine the prisoner the same day, but the sergeant escaped from the guard-room, no doubt assisted in this by sympathisers.

A fresh occurrence increased the commandant's anxiety. A Bashkir was caught bearing incendiary leaflets. After this the commandant again decided to summon his officers, and again attempted to send Vasilissa Yegorovna away under some convenient pretext. But Ivan Kuzmich, being the most straightforward and truthful man in the world, could find no other way but the one he had already used.

"Listen, Vasilissa Yegorovna," he said, clearing his throat. "They say Father Gerasim has had news from the town...." "Enough of your lies, Ivan Kuzmich," interrupted Vasilissa Yegorovna. "You know very well you only want to call a council of war and talk about Emelyan Pugachev while I'm away; I'm not to be taken in so easily this time." Ivan Kuzmich opened his eyes wide. "Well, my dear," he said, "since you already know, then stay, if you like; we'll talk in front of you." "That's better, my dear," she replied. "You're no good at deception. Send for the officers."

We assembled again. Ivan Kuzmich read aloud, in his wife's presence, Pugachev's manifesto, which had evidently been written by some semi-literate Cossack. The ruffian declared his intention of coming immediately to our fortress, invited the Cossacks and soldiers to join his band, and counselled the officers not to resist, on pain of death. The appeal was written in coarse but forcible phrases, and was calculated to have a dangerous effect on the minds of simple folk.

"The scoundrel!" exclaimed the commandant's wife. "That he should dare to make proposals to us! We are to go out to meet him and place our banners at his feet! Oh, the cur! Doesn't he know that we have been in the service forty years, and have seen a thing or two? Surely there are no commanders who would listen to the ruffian."

"You'd think not," replied Ivan Kuzmich, "but they say the villain has captured a number of fortresses."

"Evidently he really is powerful," remarked Shvabrin.

"We'll soon discover how strong he is," said the commandant. "Vasilissa Yegorovna, give me the key of the barn. Ivan Ignatich, bring that Bashkir here and tell Yulai to come with his whips."

"Wait a bit, Ivan Kuzmich," said Vasilissa Yegorovna, getting up. "Let me get Marya Ivanovna out of the house. She might hear yells and be alarmed. And to tell the truth I'm not very fond of these investigations myself. Good luck to you!"

In the old days torture was so firmly rooted in legal practice that the merciful decree for its abolition remained long invalid. It was considered that a criminal's admission of guilt was essential for his complete exposure—a consideration which was not merely groundless, but actually contrary to sound judicial reasoning, for if the prisoner's denial is not regarded as proof of innocence, still less can his admission be regarded as proof of guilt. To this day I sometimes meet with old judges who regret that the barbarous custom has been abolished. In those times, however, neither judges nor the accused questioned the necessity of torture. And so the commandant's order caused none of those present the least astonishment or uneasiness. Ivan Ignatich went for the Bashkir, who was locked up in the barn, the commandant's wife keeping the key, and a few minutes later the prisoner was brought into the passage. The commandant gave orders for him to be brought in.

The Bashkir, whose feet were shackled, stepped with difficulty over the threshold and removing his tall cap, stood in the doorway. My blood ran cold as I glanced at him. I shall never forget that man. He seemed to be a little over seventy. He had neither nose nor ears. His head was shaved; and there were only a few grey hairs sprouting from his chin. He was short of stature, emaciated and bent, but there was still a fiery gleam in his slits of eyes. "Oho!" said the commandant, recognising from these terrible tokens a rebel punished in 1741.* "I see you're an old wolf, you've been in our traps before. So it's not the first time you've rebelled, to judge by the way your head has been sliced clean. Come nearer. Now tell me who sent you here?"

The old Bashkir stared blankly at the commandant without uttering a word. "Why don't you speak?" continued Ivan Kuzmich. "Don't you understand Russian? Ask him in your own tongue, Yulai, who it was that sent him to our fortress."

Yulai repeated the commandant's question in the Tatar language. But the Bashkir looked at him with the same expression, and replied not a word.

"*Yakshi!*"** said the commandant. "You'll soon talk! Take off his ridiculous striped robe and lash his back, lads! Mind he gets it hot, Yulai!"

Two old soldiers began undressing the Bashkir. The unfortunate man's face expressed alarm. He looked all round, like some small animal caught by children. But when one of the soldiers placing the prisoner's two hands on his own shoulders raised him on to his back and Yulai picked up the whip and brandished it, the Bashkir uttered a feeble, imploring moan, bending his head, and opening his mouth, in which a short stump stirred instead of a tongue.

When I recollect that this happened in my own times and that I have lived to see the meek reign of the Emperor Alexander,*** I cannot forbear to wonder at the rapid progress of education, and the spread of humane sentiments. Young man, if these lines of mine chance to fall under your eyes, remember that the best

---

* The reference is to the revolt of the Bashkirs in 1740 brutally suppressed by the tsarist government.

** Very well!

*** The irony of the words "meek reign" becomes apparent when we remember the description of Alexander I given by Pushkin in a quatrain where he calls him "a weak and treacherous ruler... a bald dandy ... an idler basking, by a trick of fate, in the rays of glory".

and most enduring changes are those which come from the improvement of morals without violent upheavals.

All were thunderstruck. "Well," said the commandant, "I can see we shan't get anything worth hearing out of him. Take him back to the barn, Yulai. Now, gentlemen, there are some other things for us to discuss."

We were about to discuss our position, when Vasilissa Yegorovna burst into the room, panting, her face showing all the marks of excessive agitation.

"What's the matter with you?" asked the commandant in astonishment.

"Bad news, my dear!" replied Vasilissa Yegorovna. "Lower Lake fortress was taken this morning. Father Gerasim's servant has only just come from there. He saw it taken. The commandant and all the officers have been hanged. All the soldiers have been taken prisoner. The ruffians will be here before we know where we are."

I was astonished and shocked by the unexpected tidings. I was acquainted with the commandant of the Lower Lake fortress, a quiet, modest young man. Two months before he and his young wife had put up at the house of Ivan Kuzmich on their way from Orenburg. Lower Lake fortress was not more than twenty-five *versts* from our own fortress. At any moment now we might expect to be attacked by Pugachev. I conjured up a picture of Marya Ivanovna's fate, and my heart sank.

"Ivan Kuzmich!" I said to the commandant. "It is our duty to defend the fortress to the last drop of our blood; we all know that. But we must think of the security of the women. Send them to Orenburg, if the road is still open, or to some safer fortress further away, out of the reach of the ruffians."

Ivan Kuzmich turned to his wife, saying:

"Now listen, my dear, don't you think we really ought to send you away till we have coped with the rebels?"

"Nonsense!" she replied. "Where is the fortress that a bullet cannot find? Why isn't Belogorsk safe? Lord knows we've lived here twenty-two years. We've seen Bashkirs and Kirghiz— let us hope we will survive Pugachev, too!"

"Well then, my dear," returned Ivan Kuzmich. "Stay where you are if you believe in our fortress. But what shall we do with Masha? If we beat him off, or get succour, well and good. But if they take the fortress?"

"Why *then*..." Vasilissa Yegorovna faltered, checking herself with an air of extreme agitation.

"No, Vasilissa Yegorovna," continued the commandant, observing that his words had, perhaps for the first time in his life, been effective, "it won't do for Masha to stay. We'll send her to Orenburg, to her godmother. There they have troops and plenty of cannon, and the walls are of stone. And I would advise you to go with her. You're an old woman, but who knows what may happen to you if the fortress is taken by storm."

"So be it," said Vasilissa Yegorovna. "We will send Masha away. But don't dream of asking me to go, for I will not, I'm not going to part with you in my old age, and seek a lonely grave in a strange land. We have lived together, together we will die."

"So that is settled," said the commandant. "Well, let there be no delay. Go and prepare Masha for the journey. We'll send her off tomorrow at daybreak, and we'll give her a convoy, though we have no men to spare here. But where is Masha?"

"She's at Akulina Pamfilovna's," his wife told him. "She felt faint when she heard of the capture of Lower Lake fortress; I'm afraid she may be ill. Oh, Lord and Maker, to what have we come!"

Vasilissa Yegorovna went off to see about her daughter's departure. The discussion in the commandant's room was still going on, but I no longer took any part in it, or heard the others. Marya Ivanovna appeared at the supper-table, pale and red-eyed. We supped in silence and rose from table sooner than usual. Taking leave of the whole family, we went each to his quarters. But I had left my sword behind on purpose, and went back for it. I had a feeling that I should find Marya Ivanovna alone. And indeed she met me at the door and handed me my sword. "Good-bye, Pyotr Andreich," she said, weeping. "I am to go to Orenburg. May you live and be happy! Perhaps the Lord will bring us together again. If not...." Here she began to sob. I took her in my arms. "Good-bye, my love," I said. "Farewell, my beloved, my dear one! Whatever happens to me, believe that my last thought and my last prayer will be for you!" Masha sobbed, clinging to my breast. I kissed her passionately, and hastened out of the house.

Chapter Seven

ASSAULT

> Head of mine, soldier's head!
> Three and thirty years this head
> Has well and truly served.
> But O my head, you never earned,
> Nor wealth, nor joy,
> Nor a kindly word,
> Nor rank above the soldier's rank.
> All that you earned, O head of mine,
> Were two stout posts
> And a maple beam,
> And a silken noose.
>
> *Folk-Song**

I neither slept nor took off my clothes that night, since I intended to be at the fortress gates at dawn to see Marya Ivanovna pass, and say a last farewell to her. I was conscious of a great change in myself. My present agitation of mind was a great deal easier to bear than the dejection in which I had till now been immersed. With the pain of parting were bound up hopes which, though vague, were exceedingly sweet, the impatient expectation of danger, and emotions of noble ambition. The night passed imperceptibly. I was just going to venture out, when my door opened and a corporal appeared before me with the report that our Cossacks had left the fortress in the night, taking Yulai with them by force, and that unknown men were riding about in the vicinity. The thought that Marya Ivanovna would not be able to leave in time appalled me. Hastily giving the corporal a few instructions, I rushed over to the commandant's house.

Day was already breaking. I was speeding along the street when I heard my name called. I stopped. "Where are you off

---

* From the "*New and Full Collection of Russian Songs*", quoting the first lines from the song about the execution of a "boyar-prince" in Moscow, probably a commander of the Streltsy.

to?" said Ivan Ignatich, overtaking me. "Ivan Kuzmich is on the ramparts and sent me for you. Pugachev has come." "Has Marya Ivanovna gone?" I asked, with a beating heart. "She was too late," replied Ivan Ignatich. "The road to Orenburg is cut off. The fortress is surrounded. Things are bad, Pyotr Andreich!"

We went to the ramparts, a natural rising of the ground, reinforced by palings. All the inhabitants of the fortress were crowded there already. The soldiers were drawn up, their rifles shouldered. The cannon had been dragged up the day before. The commandant was walking up and down the ranks of his small forces. The nearness of danger seemed to have had a stimulating influence on the veteran warrior's spirits. A score of horsemen were riding over the steppe at no great distance from the fortress. They seemed to be Cossacks, but there were Bashkirs among them, easily recognisable by their tall lynx caps and quivers. The commandant reviewed his troops, addressing the soldiers as follows: "Well, my lads, today we must defend our beloved Empress, and show the whole world that we are brave and loyal subjects." The soldiers expressed their zeal loudly. Shvabrin stood next to me, gazing steadily at the foe. The horsemen in the steppe, observing the movements in the fortress, had formed a group and were evidently discussing the situation. The commandant ordered Ivan Ignatich to train the cannon on them, and touched off the fuse himself. The cannon-ball hummed and flew over their heads harmlessly. The horsemen, scattering, immediately galloped out of sight, and the steppe was deserted.

Just then Vasilissa Yegorovna, accompanied by Masha, who would not leave her, appeared on the ramparts. "Well?" asked the commandant's lady. "How is the battle going? Where is the enemy?" "The enemy is not far off," replied Ivan Kuzmich. "God grant that all will be well. Are you afraid, Masha?" "No, Papa," replied Marya Ivanovna. "I'm more afraid to stay alone in the house." Here she glanced at me and forced a smile to her lips. I involuntarily gripped the hilt of my sword, remembering that I had yesterday received it from her hand, as if for the defence of my beloved. My heart burned within me. I fancied myself her knight, and thirsted to show myself worthy of her trust, awaiting with impatience the decisive moment.

There now appeared a new crowd of horsemen from behind a rising about half a *verst* from the fortress, and soon the steppe bristled with men armed with spears and bows-and-arrows. Amongst them, on a white steed, rode a man in a crimson robe, an unsheathed sword in his hand. It was Pugachev himself. He stopped his horse, and was instantly surrounded. Four riders, evidently on his orders, galloped at full speed right up to the fortress. We recognised in them our own traitors. One of them held a sheet of paper over his head. Another bore the head of Yulai stuck on the end of his spear, which he shook off, throwing it to us over the palisade. The head of the unfortunate Kalmyk fell at the feet of the commandant. The traitors shouted: "Don't shoot! Come out to the tsar! The tsar is here!"

"I'll give you 'tsar'!" shouted Ivan Kuzmich. "Fire, lads!" Our soldiers fired a volley. The Cossack carrying the letter swayed in the saddle and fell off his horse. The others galloped back. I glanced at Marya Ivanovna. Horrified by the sight of the bloody head of Yulai, and stunned by the volley, she seemed half-dazed. The commandant called a corporal and ordered him to take the sheet of paper from the hands of the dead Cossack. The corporal rode out into the field and returned leading the dead man's horse by the bridle. He handed the letter to the commandant. Ivan Kuzmich read it through and tore it into fragments. But the rebels were evidently getting ready for action. Very soon bullets began whistling past our ears, and a few arrows lodged themselves in the ground near us, and in the palings. "Vasilissa Yegorovna!" said the commandant. "This is no place for women. Take Masha away. Look—the girl's more dead than alive."

Vasilissa Yegorovna, subdued by the bullets, glanced over the steppe, where great liveliness was observable. Then she turned to her husband, saying: "Ivan Kuzmich, we are in God's hands, living or dead. Give Masha your blessing. Masha, go to your father!"

Masha, pale and trembling, went up to Ivan Kuzmich, fell on her knees and bowed to the ground before him. The old commandant made the sign of the cross over her three times; then, helping her to rise to her feet, and kissing her, he said in altered tones: "Well, Masha, may you be happy! Pray to God; he will not forsake you. If you meet with a good man, God send you

love and counsel. Live with him as Vasilissa Yegorovna and I
have lived together. Good-bye, Masha! Vasilissa Yegorovna,
take her away as quick as you can." (Masha threw herself on
his shoulder and sobbed.) "Let us kiss, too," said the commandant's lady, weeping. "Good-bye, my Ivan Kuzmich. Forgive me if I have ever done anything to grieve you." "Good-bye,
my dear, good-bye!" said the commandant, embracing his old
wife. "Enough, now! Go home, go home! And if you have time,
dress Masha in a *sarafan*." Mother and daughter departed.
I gazed after Marya Ivanovna, who looked back and nodded
to me. Then Ivan Kuzmich turned to us, his whole attention
now given to the enemy. The rebels, who were riding up to their
leader, all at once began dismounting from their horses. "Stand
firm now," said the commandant. "They are going to attack."
At that moment there was an appalling screeching and yelling—
the rebels were running with all their might towards the fortress.
Our cannon was charged with case-shot. The commandant
allowed the attackers to come quite near, and suddenly fired the
cannon again. The charge fell into the very midst of the crowd.
The rebels scattered right and left, and retreated. Their leader
remained alone in front.... He waved his sword and seemed
to be persuading them eagerly.... The yelling and screeching,
which had subsided for a moment, began again immediately.
"Now, lads!" said the commandant. "Open the gates and beat
the drum. Forward, lads, follow me!"

The commandant, Ivan Ignatich, and myself, were on the
other side of the ramparts in no time. But the garrison, terrified,
did not budge. "Why do you stand there, lads?" shouted Ivan
Kuzmich. "If we must die, then die we must! Such is the
soldier's lot." Just then the rebels ran upon us, forcing their
way into the fortress. The sound of the drum ceased, the garrison
flung down their rifles. I was knocked down, but I got up again
and entered the fortress with the rebels. The commandant,
wounded in the head, stood in the midst of a group of the
ruffians, all demanding that he give up the keys. I tried to rush
to his assistance, but several sturdy Cossacks seized me and
bound me with their belts, saying: "You'll get it for opposing
the tsar!" We were dragged along the streets. The inhabitants
came out of their houses bearing bread and salt. The church bells
peeled out. Suddenly there were cries in the crowd that the tsar
was in the square waiting for the prisoners to be brought before

him to take the oath of allegiance. The people swarmed into the square, and we, too, were driven thither.

Pugachev was seated in an armchair in the porch of the commandant's house. He wore a red Cossack robe trimmed with braid. A tall sable cap with gilt tassels was tilted over his gleaming eyes. His face seemed familiar to me. The Cossack elders surrounded him. Father Gerasim stood in front of the porch, pale and trembling, a cross in his hands, and seemed to be silently imploring mercy for the future victims. A gallows was being hastily erected in the square. As we approached, the Bashkirs drove away the people, and brought us up to Pugachev. The sound of bells ceased; a profound silence ensued. "Which is the commandant?" asked the Pretender. Our sergeant stepped out of the crowd and pointed to Ivan Kuzmich. Pugachev cast a menacing glance at the old man and said to him: "How dared you resist me, your tsar?" The commandant, faint from his wound, mustered up his failing strength and replied in a firm voice: "You are not my tsar, you are a thief and a pretender—that's what you are! D'you hear me?" Pugachev frowned ominously and waved a white handkerchief. Several Cossacks seized the old captain and dragged him to the foot of the gallows. The mutilated Bashkir whom we had interrogated the day before was astride on its cross-beam. He had a rope in his hands, and a minute later I saw poor Ivan Kuzmich strung up in the air. Then Ivan Ignatich was brought before Pugachev. "Take the oath," Pugachev said to him, "the oath of allegiance to Tsar Pyotr Fyodorovich!" "You're not our tsar!" replied Ivan Ignatich, repeating his captain's words. "You're a thief and a pretender, old fellow!" Pugachev again waved his handkerchief, and the worthy lieutenant dangled beside the body of his superior officer.

Then came my turn. I looked boldly at Pugachev, quite ready to reiterate the words of my noble-hearted comrades. Then, to my indescribable astonishment, I saw Shvabrin amongst the rebel elders, in a Cossack robe, his hair cut Cossack fashion. Going up to Pugachev, he whispered a few words in his ear. "Hang him!" said Pugachev, not so much as glancing towards me. A noose was thrown over my head. I began saying a prayer, offering God my sincere repentance for all my sins, and imploring him to save all those dear to me. I was dragged up to the gallows. "Don't be afraid!" my murderers kept repeating, per-

haps really desirous of cheering me. Suddenly I heard a shriek.
"Wait, accursed ones! Wait!" The executioners stopped in their
preparations. I looked round—there was Savelich at the feet of
Pugachev. "Merciful Father!" cried my unfortunate tutor.
"Why do you wish the death of my master's child? Let him go—
they'll pay you ransom for him. And if you want to make an
example, tell them to hang me, an old man, instead!" Pugachev
gave a sign, and I was immediately unbound and released. "Our
tsar pardons you," they told me. I cannot say that I rejoiced at
the time in my deliverance, but neither will I say that I regretted
it. My emotions were in too great confusion. I was again brought
before the Pretender, and set on my knees in front of him.
Pugachev stretched out a sinewy hand to me. "Kiss his hand!
Kiss his hand!" came from all sides. But I would have preferred
the most savage execution to such grovelling abasement.
"Pyotr Andreich, Master!" whispered Savelich, who was standing nudging me in the back. "Don't be stubborn! What do you
care? Spit, and kiss the vill—, I mean kiss his hand." I did not
stir. Pugachev withdrew his hand, saying tauntingly: "His
Honour is probably crazed with joy. Stand him up!" I was raised
and set at liberty, and was now able to regard the continuation
of the appalling farce.

The inhabitants were taking the oath of allegiance, coming
up one at a time, kissing the crucifix, and bowing to the Pretender. The garrison soldiers were there. The regimental tailor,
armed with a pair of blunt scissors, cut off their pigtails. Giving
themselves a shake, they kissed the hand of Pugachev, who
pronounced their pardon and accepted them in his gang. All this
took about three hours. At last Pugachev rose from his chair and
went out of the porch, accompanied by his elders. A white horse
adorned with rich trappings was led up to him. Two Cossacks
took him beneath the armpits and hoisted him into the saddle.
He told Father Gerasim that he would dine with him. Just then
a woman's shriek was heard. Some of the bandits were dragging
Vasilissa Yegorovna, dishevelled, stark naked, into the porch.
One of them had already found time to don her padded jacket.
Others were dragging out featherbeds, chests, a tea-service,
household linen and all sorts of odds and ends. "Sirs!" shrieked
the unfortunate old woman. "Let me die in peace! Merciful
fathers, take me to Ivan Kuzmich!" Suddenly she looked up at
the gallows and recognised the body of her husband. "Scoun-

drels!" she shouted in a frenzy. "What have you done to him? Ivan Kuzmich, light of my eyes, valiant soldier! Prussian bayonets and the Turkish bullets did not touch you; you did not lose your life in honourable battle, but at the hand of a runaway thief!" "Stop the old hag's tongue," said Pugachev. At this a young Cossack struck her over the head with his sword, and she fell dead on the steps of the porch. Pugachev took his departure. The people flocked after him.

Chapter Eight

AN UNINVITED GUEST

An uninvited guest is
worse than a Tatar.

*Proverb**

The square was deserted. I stood where I was, unable to collect my thoughts, confused by a multitude of terrible impressions.

The thing that caused me the greatest anguish was my ignorance as to Marya Ivanovna's fate. Where was she? What had happened to her? Had she managed to hide? Was her hiding-place a safe one? Filled with anxious thoughts I went into the commandant's office ... all was devastation; chairs, tables, chests were broken; china in fragments; everything carried away. I ran up the little flight of stairs leading to the bedroom, and for the first time in my life entered Marya Ivanovna's chamber. There was her bed, ransacked by the bandits; her wardrobe was broken, and robbed of its contents. The lamp still smouldered before the empty icon stand. And the mirror hanging between the windows was unbroken. Where was the mistress of this humble, virginal cell? An appalling conjecture flashed through my mind: I imagined her in the hands of the bandits. My heart seemed to stand still.... I wept bitter tears, loudly calling on the name of my beloved. And then I heard a slight noise, and Palasha appeared from behind the wardrobe, pale and trembling.

---

* An old Russian proverb which originated during the Tatar Yoke (thirteenth-fifteenth centuries).

"Oh, Pyotr Andreich!" she said, with a gesture of despair.
"What a day! What horrors!"

"Where is Marya Ivanovna?" I asked impatiently. "What's
happened to Marya Ivanovna?"

"The young mistress is alive," replied Palasha. "She's hiding
in Akulina Pamfilovna's house."

"At the priest's!" I cried in horror. "My God—why, Pugachev is there!"

I rushed out of the room, and was in the street in a moment,
running headlong towards the priest's house, oblivious to all
around me. Shouts, laughter and singing came from the
house.... Pugachev was feasting with his comrades. Palasha
ran after me. I sent her to call Akulina Pamfilovna as quietly
as she could. A minute later the priest's wife was with me in the
porch, an empty bottle in her hands.

"For God's sake tell me where Marya Ivanovna is!" I exclaimed, in unspeakable agitation.

"She is lying on my bed, behind the partition, the poor little
thing," replied the priest's wife. "Oh, Pyotr Andreich, something terrible almost happened, but thank God, it passed over.
The villain had hardly sat down to his dinner when the poor
child woke up and moaned. My heart stood still. He heard.
'Who's that moaning, old woman?' he asked. I bowed low:
'My niece, Sire. She's sick, she's been in bed over a week.'
'And is your niece young?' 'Yes, Your Honour.' 'Then show me
your niece, old woman.' My heart began to beat, but there was
no help for it. 'Certainly, Your Honour; but the girl can't get
up and come to Your Honour.' 'Never mind, old woman, I'll
go and look at her myself.' And in he went, the accursed one,
behind the partition. And what d'you think? He drew back the
curtain, stared with his hawk's eyes—and that was all! God was
merciful. Believe me, my old man and I were preparing ourselves for a martyr's death. Fortunately my darling didn't
recognise him. Almighty God—what have we lived to see! Ah
me! Poor Ivan Kuzmich! Who would have believed it! And
Vasilissa Yegorovna! And Ivan Ignatich! What had he done?
How is it they spared you? And what d'you think of Alexei
Ivanich Shvabrin? Cutting his hair like a Cossack, and sitting
with them in our house, feasting! Isn't he artful? When I said
about my sick niece you should have seen how he looked at me,
as if he could see right through me. But he didn't give her away,

we must be grateful to him for that." Here the drunken cries of the guests were heard, and the voice of Father Gerasim among them. The guests were demanding vodka, and the master of the house called for his spouse. The priest's wife began bustling about. "Go home, Pyotr Andreich," she said. "This is no place for you. The ruffians are holding carousal. Don't throw yourself in their way while they're drunk. Farewell, Pyotr Andreich. What is to be, will be. Perhaps God will be mindful of us."

The priest's wife went in. Somewhat relieved, I went back to my quarters. Passing the square I saw several Bashkirs crowding round the gallows, and dragging boots from the dangling bodies. I suppressed my rage with difficulty, well aware of the uselessness of interference. The bandits were running all over the fortress, looting the officers' quarters. Everywhere could be heard the yells of the drunken rebels. I went home. Savelich met me in the doorway. "Thank God!" he cried, on sight of me. "I was beginning to think the ruffians had got you again. Well, Pyotr Andreich, Master, what do you think—they've stolen all our things, the scoundrels—clothes, linen, dishes, nothing is left! But what does that matter? Thank God they let you go with your life. Did you recognise the ataman, Sir?"

"No, I didn't. Who is he?"

"What, Sir! Have you forgotten the drunken sot who got your hareskin coat from you at the inn? Quite a new hareskin coat, and the beast split it when he tried it on."

I was lost in amazement. Indeed the likeness between Pugachev and my guide was striking. Now that it was established that Pugachev and he were one and the same individual, I understood the reason for the mercy extended to me. I could not but wonder at the strange chain of circumstances—a boy's coat given to a tramp had delivered me from the hangman's noose, and the drunkard roaming from one inn to another was now besieging fortresses and shaking the foundations of the state!

"Will you not have something to eat?" asked Savelich, true to his traditions. "There's nothing in the house, but I'll look about for something to cook for you."

Left to myself I fell to thinking. What was I to do? To remain in the fortress, beneath the sway of the miscreant, or to follow his band would be equally disgraceful to an officer. Duty demanded that I show myself in that place where my services

could still be of use to my native land in this hour of difficulty . . .
but love counselled me forcibly to remain near Marya Ivanovna,
and be her defender and protector. Although I foresaw a rapid
and inevitable change in the situation, I nevertheless could not
help shuddering at the thought of her perilous situation.

My meditations were interrupted by the arrival of one of the
Cossacks, who came running in with the announcement that
"the great tsar demands your presence". "Where is he?" I
asked, preparing to obey.

"In the commandant's house," replied the Cossack. "After
dinner our master went to the bath-house, and now he is repos-
ing. By all the signs, Your Excellency, he must be an important
person—he ate two roast sucking-pigs at dinner, and steamed
himself so hot that Taras Kurochkin couldn't stand it, and gave
the besom to Fomka Bikbaev, and could hardly restore himself
with cold water. Say what you will—he has very grand ways.
And they say in the bath-house he showed them the tsarist
emblems on his chest—the double eagle, as big as a five kopek
piece on one side, and on the other his own portrait."

I did not see fit to oppose the opinion of the Cossack and set
off with him for the commandant's house, speculating on the
coming interview with Pugachev and trying to guess how it would
end. The reader will easily suppose that I was not altogether at
my ease.

Dusk was beginning to fall by the time I got to the commandant's house. The gallows loomed black and terrible with
its dangling victims. The body of poor Vasilissa Yegorovna still
lay on the porch, in front of which two Cossacks stood on duty.
The Cossack who escorted me went in to report my arrival and
returning immediately, led me into the room where, the day
before, I had parted with Marya Ivanovna so tenderly.

I was confronted by a remarkable sight. At a table covered
with a white cloth and littered with bottles and glasses, sat
Pugachev, surrounded by some ten Cossack elders in tall caps
and coloured shirts, all excited by drink, their coarse faces
flushed and their eyes gleaming. The newly recruited traitors
Shvabrin and Maximich were not among them. "Ah, Your
Honour!" said Pugachev, on seeing me. "Welcome! Give us
your company! Pray be seated!" The revellers made room for
me. I sat down in silence at the end of the table. My neighbour,
a slim, good-looking young Cossack, poured me out a glass of

vodka, which, however, I did not touch. I looked at the company around me with curiosity. Pugachev was at the head of the table, his elbow on the cloth, his black beard spreading over his massive fist. His features, which were regular and pleasing enough, showed no signs of ferocity. He turned frequently to a man who seemed to be about fifty years of age, addressing him now as Count, now as Timofeich, now simply as Uncle. All treated one another as comrades, without showing any particular deference to their leader. The subjects of conversation were the morning's attack, the success of the riot, and future action. All boasted, offered their opinions, and contradicted Pugachev freely. At this strange military council it was decided to march on Orenburg—an audacious move which was all but crowned with disastrous success. The march was announced for the morrow. "And now, brothers," said Pugachev, "sing me my favourite song before we go to bed. Chumakov! You begin!" My neighbour struck up a dreary bargeman's chant in a reedy voice, and all joined in the chorus:

> *Cease your murmur, mother-forest green,*
> *Do not hinder me, brave lad, from thinking.*
> *For tomorrow morn I go for trial*
> *Before the dreadful judge, the tsar himself.*
> *And the tsar, our master, he will ask me:*
> *Tell me, peasant's son, and tell me truly,*
> *Who went with you, plundering and stealing?*
> *Were your comrades few, or were there many?*
> *I will answer thee, o righteous tsar,*
> *I will tell you truly, tell you all.*
> *Four in number only were my comrades:*
> *My first was the dark night,*
> *My second was my keen blade,*
> *And my third was my trusty steed.*
> *My fourth was my taut bow,*
> *My messengers were sharp arrows.*
> *Then the righteous tsar will speak again:*
> *Praise to thee, o valiant peasant's son.*
> *You knew how to rob and you know how to answer!*
> *And for that, my lad, I shall reward you*
> *With a mansion high in the open field,*
> *Two stout posts and a bar between.*

It would be impossible to describe the effect produced on me by this folk-song about the gallows, chanted by men doomed to die on the gallows themselves. Their forbidding countenances, tuneful voices, the doleful expression with which they sang words eloquent enough in themselves, all combined to create in me a feeling akin to awe.

The guests had another glass all round, and rose from the table, bidding Pugachev farewell. I made as if to follow them, but Pugachev called me to sit down, saying: "I want to speak to you." We remained alone.

For a few moments neither of us spoke. Pugachev gazed steadily at me, every now and then screwing up his left eye with a remarkable effect of rascality and mockery. At last he burst out laughing with such genuine merriment that I, too, began laughing, without knowing why.

"Well, Your Honour," he said. "Admit that you got a fright when my lads tossed the noose round your neck! I'll be bound you were terrified out of your wits! And you would have swung from the cross-beam, but for your servant. I recognised the old bear at once. You never thought that the man who showed you the way to the wayside inn was the great tsar himself, did you, Your Honour?" (With these words he assumed a pompous and mysterious air.) "You have sinned greatly against me," he continued, "but I spared you for your kindness in doing me a service at a time when I was forced to hide from my foes. But wait and see! I'll do more for you when I get back my realm. Do you promise to serve me loyally?"

The rascal's question, and his audacity amused me so greatly that I could not help smiling.

"What are you smiling at?" he asked, frowning. "Don't you believe then, that I am the great tsar? Answer me truly."

I was thrown into some consternation. I could not bring myself to acknowledge this tramp as my sovereign, that would have seemed to me unpardonable cowardice. To call him an impostor to his face would have meant my own undoing. And what I had been ready to do, in the first flash of indignation, at the foot of the gallows, in sight of the assembled people, now seemed to be useless bravado. I hesitated. Pugachev grimly awaited my reply. At last (and I still remember this moment with a certain complacency), the feeling of duty triumphed over human weakness. I replied to Pugachev: "Very well—I will tell you the whole truth. Ask yourself if I can acknowledge you as my sovereign! You are a reasonable man—you would see at once that I was not being sincere."

"Then who am I, in your opinion?"

"God knows who you are. But whoever you may be, you are playing a perilous game."

Pugachev cast a swift glance at me. "So you don't believe," he said, "that I am Tsar Pyotr Fyodorovich? Very good. But is it not always the bold man who wins in the end? Did not Grishka Otrepyev* reign in the days of old? Think of me what you like, but stay with me. What do you care who I am? What does the name matter? Serve me faithfully and truly, and I will make you a field-marshal and a prince. What say you to that?"

"No," I replied firmly. "I am a nobleman born. I have sworn allegiance to my Empress. I cannot serve you. If you indeed wish me well, then let me go to Orenburg."

Pugachev seemed to be thinking. "And if I let you go," he said, "do you at least promise not to take service against me?"

"How can I promise you that?" I answered. "You know yourself my will is not my own. If I am ordered to take up arms against you, I shall do so, and there is an end of it. You are now in authority yourself. You demand obedience of your subordinates. What would you think of me if I refused to serve when my service was required? My life is in your hands—if you let me go, I will say thank you, if you have me hanged, God be your judge. At least I have told you the truth."

My frankness amazed Pugachev. "Very well, then," he said, smiting me on the shoulder. "When I punish, I punish and when I pardon, I pardon. Go where you will, and do what you will. Come tomorrow to bid me farewell, and now go home and sleep, I am drowsy myself."

I left Pugachev and went out of the house. It was a still, frosty night. The moon and stars shone brightly, lighting up the square and the gallows. All was quiet and dark in the fortress. The only light came from the tavern, whence issued the shouts of delayed revellers. I looked towards the priest's house. The

---

* Grishka Otrepyev—a fugitive monk who posed as Prince Dmitry, son of Ivan the Terrible. A placeman of the Polish interventionists, this "False Dmitry" held the throne of Moscow for eleven months during the years 1605 and 1606.

shutters and gates were closed. Everything seemed to be quiet there.

When I got back to my quarters I found Savelich grieving over my absence. The news of my freedom caused him indescribable joy. "Thanks be to thee, O Maker!" he said, crossing himself. "We will leave the fortress at daybreak and go wherever seems best to us. I have prepared some food for you. Eat, Master, and then sleep till morning, secure in the mercy of the Lord."

I followed his advice and, supping with a hearty appetite, fell asleep on the bare floor, exhausted body and soul.

Chapter Nine

PARTING

> To learn to love thee was most sweet,
> O dearest of my heart.
> To lose thee was as sad as if
> With mine own soul to part.
>
> *Kheraskov**

I was awakened early in the morning by the sound of a drum, and went straight to the place of assembly. Pugachev's men were already getting into formation beside the gallows, from which yesterday's victims still swung. The Cossacks were on horseback, the soldiers armed with rifles. Banners waved. A few cannon, among which I recognised our own, had been hoisted on to gun-carriages. All the inhabitants were here, waiting for the Pretender to appear. A Cossack stood in front of the commandant's house, holding a magnificent white horse by the bridle. I looked for the body of the commandant's wife. It had been shifted slightly to one side and covered with sacking. At last Pugachev emerged from the porch. The people bared their heads, Pugachev stood in the porch and greeted them all. One of the elders handed him a bag full of copper coins which he began throwing among the crowd by the handful. The people rushed to pick up the coins, and not a few were maimed. Pugachev was surrounded by his principal accomplices, among whom was Shvabrin. Our eyes met. Reading the contempt in mine he turned away with unfeigned rancour and affected scorn. Pugachev, catching sight of me in the crowd, nodded to me and called me to him. "Listen to me," he said. "Go straight to Oren-burg and tell the governor and all the generals to expect me in

---

* From the song "Separation" by Mikhail Kheraskov (1733-1807).

a week. Advise them to receive me with child-like affection and
docility. Otherwise they will not escape a cruel death. A happy
journey, Your Honour!" Then he turned to the people and said,
pointing to Shvabrin, "Here's your new commander, lads!
Obey him in everything, he will answer for you and for the
fortress to me." These words struck horror to my heart. Shvabrin was in command of the fortress, Marya Ivanovna would
be left in his hands! Dear God, what would be her fate? Pugachev came down the steps of the porch. The horse was led up to
him. He leaped lightly into the saddle, before the Cossacks had
time to help him.

At that moment I saw my Savelich push his way through the
crowd and hand Pugachev a sheet of paper. I could not imagine
how this would end. "What is this?" asked Pugachev pompously.

"Read it, and you'll see," replied Savelich. Pugachev took the
paper and gazed long at it with a significant air. "You write
such a crabbed hand," he said at last. "Our illustrious eyes can
make nothing of what you have written. Where is my first
secretary?"

A youth in corporal's uniform ran swiftly up to Pugachev.
"Read it aloud," said the Pretender, giving him the paper. I was
exceedingly curious to learn what my tutor had taken it into
his head to write to Pugachev. The first secretary, spelling out
the words a syllable at a time, loudly read out the following:

"Two robes, one calico, the other striped silk, six rubles."

"What does this mean?" said Pugachev, frowning.

"Tell him to go on," replied Savelich calmly.

The first secretary continued:

"One uniform of fine green cloth, seven rubles.

"Trousers, white cloth, five rubles.

"Twelve holland shirts with cuffs, ten rubles.

"Chest containing tea-service, two rubles fifty kopeks."

"What's all this about?" burst out Pugachev. "What have
I to do with your tea chests and trousers and cuffs?"

Savelich, clearing his throat, began explaining. "Well, Sir,
you see it's a list of my master's property stolen by the ruffians."

"What ruffians?" thundered Pugachev.

"Excuse me, a slip of the tongue," said Savelich. "Not ruffians
then, but your lads ransacked the house and made free with our
property. Do not be angry—even a horse sometimes stumbles
though it has four legs. Tell him to go on reading."

"Go on," said Pugachev. The secretary continued:
"One cotton quilt, wadded, one taffeta quilt—four rubles.
"One coat of red cloth, lined with fox-fur—40 rubles.
"And one hareskin coat, given to Your Honour at the inn, 15 rubles."

"What's all this?" cried Pugachev, his eyes blazing.

I admit I was alarmed for my poor tutor. He was about to make further explanations, but Pugachev interrupted him. "How dare you come to me about such trifles?" he shouted, snatching the paper out of the secretary's hands, and flinging it in Savelich's face. "Foolish old man! They were robbed—what a misfortune! Why, you ought to pray for me and my lads for the rest of your life, for not hanging you and your master here with the others who refused to obey me. Hareskin coat! I'll give you hareskin coat! Don't you know I could have you flayed alive and your skin made into a coat?"

"As you will," replied Savelich. "But I am a bondsman, and have to answer for my master's property."

Pugachev was evidently in a generous mood. He turned away and rode off without another word. Shvabrin and the elders followed him. The band issued from the fortress in good order. The crowd surged out to watch Pugachev's departure. Savelich and I were left alone in the square. My tutor held his list in his hands, examining it with an air of profound regret.

Seeing the good terms I was on with Pugachev, he had thought to profit by the occasion. But his sage intentions had not been fulfilled. I meant to rebuke him for his misplaced zeal, but could not help laughing. "You may laugh, Sir," said Savelich. "But when we have to start housekeeping anew you will see if it is a laughing matter."

I hastened to the priest's house to see Marya Ivanovna. The priest's wife met me with mournful tidings. Marya Ivanovna had been seized with a violent fever in the night, and was now unconscious and delirious. The priest's wife led me to her room. I went softly up to the bed, and was amazed at the alteration in her countenance. She did not recognise me. I stood long at her bedside, hearing not a word of what Father Gerasim and his kindly wife were saying, in their efforts to console me. I was the prey of sombre thoughts. The situation of the poor, defenceless orphan, abandoned amidst ferocious rebels, and the thought of my own powerlessness filled me with horror. Shvabrin, above all Shvabrin, haunted my imagination. Vested in authority by the Pretender, made the ruler of the fortress in which the unfortunate girl, the innocent object of his detestation, was left, there was no knowing what he might do. And what was there that I could do? How could I give her aid—how deliver her out of the hands of the miscreant? There was only one way open to me—I resolved to go to Orenburg immediately, in order to hasten the deliverance of the Belogorsk fortress and do what I could to help effect this. I took leave of the priest and Akulina Pamfilovna, warmly recommending to her care the unhappy girl whom I regarded as my wife. I took the poor maiden's hand and kissed it, wetting it with my tears. "Farewell," said the priest's wife, as she accompanied me to the door. "Farewell, Pyotr Andreich, God grant we meet again in better times. Do not forget us and write frequently. Poor Marya Ivanovna—she has no other consoler or protector but you."

Stepping into the square I paused for a moment to look up at the gallows, bowed to it, left the territory of the fortress, and started along the road to Orenburg, accompanied by Savelich, who had been close at my heels all this time.

I was walking on, absorbed in thought, when I suddenly heard the sound of horses' hoofs behind me. Looking back I saw a Cossack galloping out of the fortress, leading a Bashkir horse by the bridle, and making signs to me from a distance. I stopped and very soon recognised our sergeant. Galloping up, he got off his own horse and said, putting the bridle of the other into my hand: "Your Honour! Our Master sends you this horse, and the coat off his back." (A sheepskin coat was fastened to the saddle.) "He also sent you—" here the sergeant paused, stumbling in his speech—"fifty kopeks, but I lost it on the way, for which I pray your forgiveness." Savelich shot a sidelong glance at him, muttering: "Lost it on the way? And what's that jingling inside your shirt? Shameless creature!" "Jingling inside my shirt?" repeated the sergeant with the utmost unconcern. "Bless you, old fellow—why, that's only a bridle, it isn't money." "Very good," I said, cutting the argument short, "thank him who sent you to me. And try to pick up the 50 kopeks you lost on your way back and get yourself a drink with it." "Thank you, Your Honour," he replied, turning back his horse. "I will always pray for you." With these words he galloped back, holding the front of his shirt with one hand, and in a minute was out of sight.

I put on the sheepskin and got into the saddle, making Save-lich get up behind me. "You see, Sir," said the old man, "it was a good thing I handed the rascal my petition! The thief was ashamed of himself. A long-legged Bashkir nag and a sheepskin don't come to the half of what the rascal stole from us, not counting what you were good enough to give him your-self. Still it will come in useful, and a tuft of hair from a mangy cur is better than nothing."

Yekaterina Karamzina, *née* Kolyvanova (1780-1851). The wife of the historian Karamzin. From his youth Pushkin was a frequent visitor at the Karamzins' house in St. Petersburg. He cherished the feeling of deferential respect for Karamzina.
Oils. 1840s

Konstantin Danzas (1801-1870). Pushkin's schoolmate and friend, his second at the fatal duel with Dantes. A drawing. 1840s

Pushkin's duel with Dantes on 27th January (8th February, New Style), 1837.
A picture by Naumov. 1884

Pushkin's grave in the cemetery of the Svyatogorsk Monastery.
A lithograph. 1837

Chapter Ten

THE SIEGE OF THE TOWN

> Stationing his troops upon the hills and meadows,
> Like a soaring eagle, he gazed upon the town.
> He had a rampart raised to hide his thunders,
> Which, when the night fell, would be carried down.
>
> *Kheraskov**

As we approached Orenburg we came upon a crowd of con-
victs with shaven skulls and features mutilated by the tongs of
the torturer. They were working in the vicinity of the fortifica-
tions under the surveillance of invalided soldiers from the
garrison. Some were carrying rubbish away from the moat in
carts, others digging with spades in the earth. Stone-masons
were ascending the ramparts with bricks and repairing the city
wall. We were stopped at the gates by sentries, who demanded
our passports. The sergeant, on learning that I was from the
Belogorsk fortress instantly led me to the house of the General.

I found the General in his garden, examining his apple-trees,
which were stripped by the blasts of autumn; with the aid of an
old gardener he was lovingly swathing their trunks in straw.
His countenance expressed calm, health, and good-humour.
He was delighted to see me and began enquiring into the
terrible events of which I had been a witness. I told him everything. The old man heard me out attentively, clipping off dry
branches the while. "Poor Mironov!" he said, when I had
finished my melancholy narrative. "What a pity! He was a
splendid officer. And Madam Mironova was a very kind woman,
and pickled mushrooms so nicely. And what about the captain's
daughter, Masha?" I replied that she had remained in the fort-

---

* From Kheraskov's epic poem *The Rossiada*, commemorating the
taking of Kazan by Ivan the Terrible in 1552.

ress under the care of the priest's wife. "That's too bad,"
remarked the General. "Very bad! The discipline of those
ruffians can by no means be relied upon. What will come of the
poor girl?" I replied that it was not far to the Belogorsk fortress,
and that I was confident His Excellency would not delay dis-
patching troops for the liberation of its unfortunate inhabitants.
The General shook his head dubiously. "We'll see, we'll see,"
he said. "There will be time to discuss that. I hope you will come
and have a cup of tea with me. I am holding a council of war
today. You can give us true information as to that scamp
Pugachev and the state of his troops. And now go and have
a rest."

I went to the quarters allotted me, where Savelich was
already busy making order, and settled down to wait with what
patience I could muster for the appointed time. The reader
will easily conceive that I did not fail to appear at the council
of war, which was destined to have such an influence on my fate.
At the appointed hour I was already at the General's house.

I found one of the city officials there before me, the director
of the customs' office, if I am not mistaken, a stout red-cheeked
ancient in a brocade robe. He began asking me about the fate
of Ivan Kuzmich, whom he called his old friend, continually
interrupting my narrative with questions and instructive remarks
which, while not revealing much knowledge of military science
did, however, show him to be endowed with intelligence and
quickness of apprehension. In the meanwhile the other persons
invited arrived. There was not a single military man among
them with the exception of the General himself. When all were
seated, and cups of tea handed round, the General gave an
extremely lucid and detailed exposition of the situation. "Now,
gentlemen," he continued, "it is for us to decide what means
must be employed against the rebels—*offensive*, or *defensive*?
Each of these methods has its advantages and disadvantages.
Offensive action offers more hope of the rapid destruction of
the enemy. Defensive action is more reliable and safe. We will,
therefore, take a vote in the proper way, that is to say, beginning
with the lowest rank present. Ensign!" he went on, turning to
me. "Be so good as to lay your opinion before us."

I rose and after giving a brief description of Pugachev and
his band went on to state that the Pretender would be unable
to withstand regular forces. My opinion was received by the

officials with evident disfavour. They saw in it the hotheaded-ness and audacity of youth. A murmur rose, and I clearly distinguished the word "puppy", uttered in undertones. The General turned to me, saying with a smile: "Ensign! The first votes at military councils are usually given in favour of offensive action; that's in the nature of things. We will now proceed with the voting. Let us have *your* opinion, Councillor!"

The old man in the brocade robe hastily finished his third cup of tea, considerably tinctured with rum, and replied to the General as follows: "I consider, Your Excellency, that we should act neither offensively, nor defensively."

"What, Councillor!" exclaimed the General in astonishment. "But there are no other methods—nothing but defensive, or offensive action...."

"We must use purchasing tactics, Your Honour."

"Ah, ha! Your opinion is extremely rational. Purchasing tactics are also permissible, and we will take advantage of your advice. We might offer—say, seventy rubles, even a hundred rubles from the secret fund, for the head of the rascal...."

"And then," interrupted the director of the customs, "those robbers will hand over their ataman to us, bound hand and foot, or I am a Kirghiz sheep and not a councillor!"

"We will think the proposition over and discuss it," replied the General. "It will, however, be necessary, in any case, to take military measures also. Gentlemen, let us have your votes in due order."

All the opinions given were in opposition to mine. All the officials referred to the unreliability of the troops, the uncer-tainty of success, the need for caution, and so on. All considered that it would be more reasonable to remain behind the sturdy stone walls under cover of the cannon than to trust to the for-tunes of war in the open field. At last the General, having heard everyone's opinion, knocked the ashes out of his pipe and uttered the following speech:

"Gentlemen! I must inform you that I myself am completely of the opinion of the ensign, for his opinion is based on all the rules of sound tactics, which are invariable on the side of offensive rather than defensive action."

Here he paused and began filling his pipe. My vanity triumphed. I cast an arrogant glance at the officials, who were whispering among themselves with an air of dissatisfaction and anxiety.

"But, gentlemen," continued the General, emitting, together with a profound sigh, a dense cloud of smoke, "I will not venture to take such vast responsibility on myself, when it is a matter of the safety of the provinces entrusted to me by Her Imperial Majesty, my most gracious Empress. I therefore adhere to the majority of votes, by which it has been decided that the most reasonable and safe measure would be to await a siege within the town, while beating off the enemy with the strength of our artillery and (should this be found possible) by sorties."

It was now the turn of the officials to look mockingly at me. The council dispersed. I could not but regret the weakness of the venerable warrior, who, against his own convictions, had resolved to adopt the opinion of ignorant and inexperienced men.

A few days after this famous council we learned that Pugachev, true to his word, was marching on Orenburg. I saw the rebel troops from the top of the city wall. It seemed to me that their numbers had increased enormously since the last attack, of which I had myself been a witness. They now had artillery, seized by Pugachev in the smaller fortresses already conquered by him. Remembering the decision of the council of war, I foresaw prolonged confinement within the walls of Orenburg, and was ready to cry with vexation.

I will not attempt to describe the siege of Orenburg, which belongs to historical rather than domestic annals. I will merely state, as briefly as possible, that this siege, owing to the carelessness of the local administration, proved disastrous for the inhabitants, who underwent famine and all manner of sufferings. It may easily be imagined that life in Orenburg was quite intolerable. All awaited dejectedly the consummation of their fate; all groaned at the high prices, which were indeed appalling. The inhabitants grew accustomed to cannon balls falling in their yards; even the assaults of Pugachev no longer evoked general curiosity. I nearly died of ennui. Time passed. I received no letters from the Belogorsk fortress. All roads were cut off. The separation from Marya Ivanovna was becoming unendurable to me. My ignorance of her fate tortured me. My only distraction consisted in riding. Thanks to Pugachev I had a good horse, with which I shared my scanty food, and on which I took daily rides beyond the town, to exchange shots with Pugachev's horsemen. In these engagements the advantage was usually on the side of the rebels, who were well fed, well supplied with drink, and well mounted. The lean cavalry of the town could not cope with them. Sometimes our famished infantry took the field, too, but the deep snow prevented them from doing much harm to the scattered rebel cavalry. Our guns thundered in vain from the top of the ramparts, and when they went into the battlefield they got stuck in the earth, and the horses were too exhausted to pull them out. Such was the pattern of our military activities, and this was what the Orenburg officials called caution and discretion.

On one occasion, when we had somehow managed to scatter and beat off a fairly dense enemy formation, I rode down a Cossack cut off from his comrades. I was just about to smite him with my Turkish sword, when he removed his cap, crying: "Pyotr Andreich! How do you fare!"

I looked at him and recognised the sergeant. I was indescribably delighted to see him. "Why, it's Maximich!" I said. "Are you long from Belogorsk?"

"Not long, Pyotr Andreich, Sir, I only got back yesterday. I have a note for you."

"Where is it?" I cried, flushing deeply.

"Here it is!" replied Maximich, thrusting his hand into the front of his shirt. "I promised Palasha I would get it to you somehow." He handed me a piece of folded paper, and galloped off. I unfolded it, and with feelings of the utmost agitation read the following lines:

> "It was the will of God to deprive me suddenly of my father and mother. I have neither relatives nor protectors left on the earth. I turn to you, knowing that you have always wished me well, and that you are ever ready to help those in need. I pray God this letter will fall into your hands. Maximich promised to give it to you. Palasha heard from Maximich that he often sees you during sorties, and that you take not the least care of yourself, never thinking of those who pray for you with tears. I was ill for a long time, and when I recovered, Alexei Ivanovich, who commands us in the place of my late father, compelled Father Gerasim to hand me over to him, threatening to report

him to Pugachev unless he complied. I am living in our old house, under guard. Alexei Ivanovich is trying to make me marry him. He says he saved my life, by not giving Akulina Pamfilovna away when she told the ruffians that I was her niece. But I would rather have died then, than become the wife of such a man as Alexei Ivanovich. He treats me with great cruelty, and says unless I change my mind and give my consent he will take me to the camp of the rebels, and then, he said, you will share the fate of Lizaveta Kharlova. I begged Alexei Ivanovich to give me time for thought. He agreed to wait another three days, and if I refuse to marry him in three days, he will show me no mercy. Dear Pyotr Andreich! You are my only protector. Defend an unfortunate girl! Ask the General and all the commanders to send us aid as soon as possible, and come yourself if you can. I remain the poor humble orphan

"Marya Mironova."

The perusal of this letter drove me almost out of my mind. I galloped back to the town, spurring my poor horse mercilessly. All the way I turned over plans for delivering the poor girl and could find none. Galloping into the town I went straight to the General, and rushed headlong into his presence. He was pacing up and down the room, smoking a meerschaum pipe. Seeing me he halted. My appearance no doubt amazed him and he enquired solicitously as to the cause of my impetuous arrival. "Your Excellency," I said, "I turn to you as to my own father. For God's sake do not refuse my entreaty—the happiness of my whole life is at stake."

"What is it, my friend?" asked the astonished veteran. "What can I do for you? Speak!"

"Your Excellency, command me to take a company and a few Cossacks and clear the Belogorsk fortress of the rebels!"

The General stared at me, no doubt thinking I had taken leave of my senses (in which he erred but little).

"What's that? Clear the Belogorsk fortress?" he said at last.

"I guarantee success," I replied eagerly. "Only let me go!"

"No, young man," he said, shaking his head. "At such a great distance the enemy would have no difficulty in cutting you off from communication with the main strategic point, and gaining complete victory over you. When communications are cut off...."

I feared that he was going to start a discussion of tactics, and hastened to interrupt him. "Captain Mironov's daughter has written me a letter," I said. "She asks for help. Shvabrin is trying to force her to marry him."

"Indeed? Oh, that Shvabrin is a veritable rascal! If he falls into my hands I will have him tried within twenty-four hours and we'll shoot him on the parapets of the fortress! But for the time we must exercise patience!"

"Patience!" I echoed frantically. "And in the meantime he will marry Marya Ivanovna!"

"Oh!" rejoined the General. "She might do worse. Better for her to be Shvabrin's wife for a time, he can look after her and when we shoot him, we will find her a bridegroom, God willing. Pretty widows do not languish long in a state of virginity, or rather, I would say, a young widow finds a husband more easily than a girl does."

"I would die rather than give her up to Shvabrin!" I cried in rage.

"Oh!" drawled the old man. "Now I understand! I see you are in love with Marya Ivanovna yourself. That quite alters matters. Poor fellow! Nevertheless I can by no means give you a company and Cossacks. Such an expedition would be most irrational. I cannot take the responsibility for it."

I hung my head, giving myself up to despair. Suddenly an idea flashed through my mind—the reader will learn from the following chapter, as old-fashioned novelists used to say, what this idea was.

Chapter Eleven

THE REBEL VILLAGE

> Tho' fierce by nature, the lion had eaten, then.
> "What signifies this visit to my den?"
> He asked politely.
>
> *A. Sumarokov**

I left the General and hastened back to my own quarters. Savelich met me with his usual remonstrances. "Going out skirmishing against drunken ruffians. Sir! Is this work for a gentleman? If anything should happen, you would have perished for nothing. If they were Turks or Swedes, now—but I'm ashamed to name the fellows you are fighting!"

I interrupted his speech by asking him how much money I possessed altogether. "Money you have," he replied with a satisfied air. "The rogues ransacked our property, but I managed to hide some away". And with these words he drew from his pocket a long, woven purse, full of silver. "Come, Savelich," I said, "give me the half of it, and keep the rest for yourself. I am going to the Belogorsk fortress."

"Pyotr Andreich, Master!" said my kind tutor in a broken voice. "For God's sake! How can you set off in these times, when the roads are thick with rebel bands? Take pity on your parents, if you have no pity for yourself! Why should you go? What for? Wait a little—the troops will come and catch the rascals. Then go wherever you like."

But my mind was made up. "It's too late to argue," I told the old man. "Go I must, and go I will. Do not grieve, Savelich. God is merciful, perhaps we shall meet again. Mind, be neither scrupulous nor overthrifty. Buy everything you require,

---

* The epigraph attributed to Sumarokov was actually written by Pushkin himself.

however high the price. This money I bequeath to you as a gift. If I am not back in three days...."

"What do you mean, Sir?" cried Savelich, interrupting me. "As if I would allow you to go alone! Do not dream of asking such a thing of me! Since you have resolved to go, I will go with you—on foot, if need be, but I will never abandon you. Can you believe I would stay here without you, safe behind stone walls? Do you think I am out of my mind? Say what you like, Master, but I shall not leave you."

I knew that it was no use trying to argue with Savelich, and allowed him to make preparations for the journey. Half an hour later I was seated on my good steed, with Savelich beside me on a lame and skinny nag presented to him by a townsman who was unable to feed it himself. We rode up to the city gates. The sentries let us pass. We left Orenburg behind us.

Dusk was beginning to fall. My way led past the village of Berda, now a Pugachev stronghold. The road was snowed-up, but the imprints of hoofs, daily renewed, were visible all over the steppe. I rode at a fast trot. Savelich could hardly keep me in sight, and shouted constantly: "A little slower, Sir, for God's sake! A little slower! My accursed nag cannot keep pace with your long-limbed brute! What's your hurry? Anyone might think we were going to a feast ... and we are only making for the gallows—mark my words! Pyotr Andreich.... Master.... Spare me! Great God, my master's child will perish!"

The lights of Berda soon came in sight. We rode up to a gully forming as it were a natural defence for the village. Savelich followed me all the time, never ceasing his piteous entreaties. I was hoping to skirt the village in safety, when suddenly I saw right in front of me in the dusk a group of about five peasants, armed with clubs; this was an outpost of Pugachev's camp. They called out to us. Not knowing the password I intended to ride on in silence, but they instantly surrounded me, one of them seizing my horse's bridle. Drawing my sword I struck the man over the head. His cap saved him, but he staggered and let go of the bridle. The others ran away in confusion. I took advantage of the moment's breathing-space, thrust the spurs into my horse's sides, and galloped off.

The darkness of approaching night might have delivered me from all danger, when suddenly, looking back, I saw that Savelich was no longer with me. The poor old fellow had not

been able to get away from the rebels on his lame nag. What was
to be done? Waiting a moment or two to assure myself that he
had been detained, I turned my horse's head and rode back to
his aid.

As I neared the edge of the gully I heard shouting in the
distance, amidst which I made out the voice of my Savelich.
I rode on faster and soon found myself once more amidst the
peasant guard which had halted me a few minutes before.
Savelich was surrounded. The men had dragged the old man
from his horse, and were about to bind him. Well pleased by my
arrival on the scene, they rushed at me shouting loudly, and in
a minute had dragged me off my horse. One of them, apparently
their leader, announced to us that he would take us to the tsar,
immediately. "And our tsar," he added, "can tell us whether
to hang you at once, or wait till daybreak." I offered no
resistance. Savelich followed my example, and the sentries bore
us off in triumph.

Climbing to the other side of the gully, we entered the village.
There were lights in all the huts. The air was filled with noise
and shouts. The street was full of people, but it was so dark that
nobody noticed us, or recognised me as an Orenburg officer.
We were led straight to a hut situated at the cross-roads. At its
gate were a few barrels of spirits and two cannon. "That's the
palace," said one of the peasants. "I'll go in and report your
arrival." He entered the hut. I glanced at Savelich. The old
man kept crossing himself, and muttering prayers. I had to wait
a long time, but at last the peasant came back and said to me:
"Go in. Our tsar told me to send the officer in."

I went into the hut, or the palace, as the peasants called it.
It was lit by two tallow candles, and the walls were papered
with tinfoil. Otherwise it was just an ordinary hut with benches,
a table, a hanging wash-stand, a towel on a nail, a pair of oven
prongs in the corner, and earthenware pots standing on the
broad stone-ledge. Pugachev was seated beneath the icons in
the corner, in a red robe, a tall cap, his arms akimbo.

Near him stood several of his principal associates all in
attitudes of exaggerated obsequiousness. It was clear that the
tidings of the arrival of an officer from Orenburg had been
received with the utmost curiosity by the rebels, and that they
intended to receive me in state. Pugachev recognised me instantly. His assumed solemnity vanished immediately. "Ah,

Your Honour!" he cried with animation. "How are you? And what brings you here?" I replied that I was travelling on my own affairs and that his people had detained me. "And what affairs?" he asked me. I did not know how to answer him. Pugachev, supposing that I was reluctant to speak before witnesses, turned to his comrades and bade them leave him. All but two obeyed, and these did not move. "You may say what you like in front of them," said Pugachev. "I have no secrets from them." I shot a sidelong glance at the Pretender's intimates. One of them, a puny, stooping ancient with a little grey beard, was remarkable only for a blue ribbon slung across his frieze coat. But I shall never forget the other till the day of my death. He was tall, stout, and broad-shouldered, and seemed to be about forty-five years old. His dense red beard, gleaming grey eyes, his nose, shorn of nostrils, the reddish spots on his brow and cheeks, lent a sinister expression to his broad, pock-marked countenance. He wore a red shirt, a Kirghiz robe, and Cossack riding breeches. The first (as I afterwards learned) was Beloborodov, a runaway corporal, the other was Afanasy Sokolov (nicknamed Khlopusha), a convict who had thrice escaped from Siberian mines. Despite the emotions dominating my mind, the company in which I so unexpectedly found myself impressed my imagination forcibly. But Pugachev brought me back to a sense of my situation by the question: "What is the business which has brought you from Orenburg? Speak."

A strange thought flitted through my mind. It seemed to me that providence, leading me a second time to Pugachev, had presented me with an opportunity for carrying out my intention. I resolved to make use of it and without stopping to consider over my decision, replied to Pugachev's question.

"I was on my way to Belogorsk fortress to save an orphan who is being maltreated there."

Pugachev's eyes gleamed. "Which of my people dares to maltreat an orphan?" he cried. "Be he as cunning as a fox, he will not escape justice! Speak—who is the villain?"

"Shvabrin!" I replied. "He is keeping in confinement the sick maid you saw at the priest's house, and is trying to force her to marry him."

"I will teach Shvabrin a lesson," said Pugachev menacingly. "He shall learn what it means to act without orders, and maltreat my people. He shall be hanged."

"Allow me to say a word," said Khlopusha in husky tones. "You were in a great hurry to appoint Shvabrin commandant of the fortress, and now you are in a hurry to hang him. You have already insulted the Cossacks by setting a nobleman over them. Do not frighten off the gentry by executing one of their number at the first accusation."

"There is no reason either to spare, or promote them," said the old man wearing the blue ribbon. "It would do no harm to hang Shvabrin. And it would not be amiss to interrogate this officer. What brings His Honour here? If he does not acknowledge you to be his emperor, then why does he seek justice at your hands? And if he does, what has he been doing all this time in Orenburg with your sworn foes? Let me have him taken to headquarters, and have the irons heated. Something tells me that His Honour has been sent to us by the Orenburg commanders."

The old rascal's logic seemed to me sufficiently convincing. My blood ran cold at the thought of the hands I was now in. Pugachev observed my uneasiness. "Well, Your Honour?" he said, winking at me. "I think my field-marshal is speaking sense. What say you?"

Pugachev's taunt gave me back my courage. I replied quietly that I was in his power and that he could do with me whatever he thought best.

"Good," said Pugachev. "Now tell me—what sort of state is your city in?"

"All is well there, thank God," I said.

"Well?" repeated Pugachev. "And the people dying of starvation!"

The Pretender spoke the truth. But I, faithful to my oath of allegiance, began assuring him that these were mere idle rumours and that there were plenty of supplies in Orenburg.

"You see," interposed the old man. "He is lying to your face. All fugitives without exception tell us that there is famine and plague in Orenburg, that they are eating carrion, and are glad when they can get that. And His Honour swears that there is plenty of everything. If you want to hang Shvabrin, then hang this brave lad on the same gallows, so that neither of them can be jealous."

The words of the detestable old man seemed to be having an effect on Pugachev. Fortunately Khlopusha began to remonstrate with his comrade. "That'll do, Naumich," he said. "And you would like to have everyone throttled or beheaded. You're a fine figure of a man, I must say. You look as if you could scarcely keep body and soul together. On the verge of the grave yourself, and yet you think of nothing but destroying others. Isn't there enough blood on your conscience?"

"And are you a saint, yourself?" retorted Beloborodov. "What makes you so tenderhearted all of a sudden?"

"I know I too am a sinner," replied Khlopusha, "and this hand" (here he clenched his bony fist and, pushing back his sleeve, exposed a hairy arm), "this hand has helped to shed much Christian blood. But I killed enemies, not guests; I kill my man at the cross-roads, or in the dark forest, not sitting at home, by his hearth; I kill with a club or an axe, not with old wives' gossip."

The old man turned away, muttering: "Slit-Nose!"

"What's that you're mumbling, old rat?" cried Khlopusha. "I'll give you Slit-Nose, you wait, your time will come! God willing, and you will smell the pincers too. In the meantime, mind I don't tear out your beard!"

"Gentlemen Generals!" announced Pugachev pompously. "No more squabbling! It would not matter if all the Orenburg dogs were to dangle from one gallows. But for *our* dogs to fight one another, does matter! Come on, make it up!"

Khlopusha and Beloborodov stared morosely at each other without a word. I perceived the necessity for changing the conversation, which threatened to end in the most disadvantageous manner for myself, and turning to Pugachev, said cheerfully: "Why, I almost forgot to thank you for the horse and sheepskin. But for you, I would never have got to the town, and would have frozen to death on the way."

My ruse proved successful. Pugachev was amused. "One good turn deserves another," he said, winking and screwing up his eyes. "Now tell me what the girl who Shvabrin has ill-treated is to you? Is she your sweetheart, by any chance? Eh?"

"She is my betrothed," I told him, seeing the favourable change in the weather, and not considering it necessary to conceal the truth.

"Your betrothed!" cried Pugachev. "Why didn't you say so before? We'll marry you, and feast at your wedding." Then,

turning to Beloborodov, he added: "Listen, Field-Marshal! His
Honour and I are old friends. Let us sit down to supper. Wisdom
comes with the morning. Tomorrow we'll decide what to do
with him."

I would gladly have refused the proffered honour, but there
was no help for it. Two young Cossack girls, the daughters of
the owner of the hut, put a white cloth on the table, and
brought bread, fishsoup, and some bottles of vodka and beer,
and once again I found myself sharing a meal with Pugachev
and his formidable comrades.

The orgy of which I was the involuntary spectator continued
far into the night. At last my companions succumbed to the
fumes of drink. Pugachev dosed in his chair; his companions
rose and made me a sign to leave him. I went out of the hut
with them. On the orders of Khlopusha, the sentries led me to
headquarters, where I found Savelich and where they locked us
up for the night. My tutor was so astounded by all that had
taken place, that he did not put a single question to me. Lying
down in the darkness, he sighed and groaned for a long time.
At last he began to snore, and I gave myself up to thoughts
which kept me awake the whole night.

The next morning Pugachev sent for me. I went to his hut.
At the gate was a sleigh to which three Tatar horses were harnessed. The street was crowded with people. I met Pugachev in
the entry. He was dressed for travelling, in a fur-lined coat and
Kirghiz cap. His companions of the evening before surrounded
him with an air of obsequiousness which was in forcible contrast
to what I had witnessed the evening before. Pugachev greeted
me cheerfully and made me get into his sleigh.

We took our seats. "To Belogorsk fortress!" said Pugachev
to the broad-shouldered Tatar, who stood up to drive the
three horses. My heart beat violently. The horses started, the
bell jingled, the sleigh flew over the snow.

"Stop! Stop!" sounded a voice which I knew all too well,
and I saw Savelich running to meet us. Pugachev gave the
order to stop. "Pyotr Andreich, Master!" cried Savelich. "Do
not leave me in my old age amongst those scoun—"

"Ah, old fellow!" said Pugachev. "We meet again, by the
mercy of God. Well, get on to the box-seat."

"I thank Your Highness, I thank you, oh, my Protector!"
cried Savelich, seating himself. "God send you a hundred years

of health for your goodness to an old man! I will pray for you my whole life, and I will never again mention the hareskin coat."

The hareskin coat might have enraged Pugachev in good earnest. Fortunately, however, either he did not hear what Savelich said, or ignored the inopportune hint. The horses galloped, people in the street stopped and bowed low. Pugachev nodded right and left. A minute later we were out of the village and speeding over the smooth road.

My feelings at this moment may easily be imagined. In a few hours I would be seeing her whom I had begun to regard as lost to me. I tried to picture the moment of our meeting.... I thought also of the man in whose hands my destiny lay, and who, by a series of strange coincidences, was mysteriously connected with myself. I remembered the reckless cruelty, the blood-thirsty habits of him who had offered to be the deliverer of my sweetheart. Pugachev did not know that she was the daughter of Captain Mironov. The frustrated Shvabrin might reveal all to him. Pugachev might discover the truth in some other way. Then what would become of Marya Ivanovna? A chill ran down my spine, and my hair stood on end....

Suddenly Pugachev interrupted my meditations, turning to me with the words:

"What are you thinking about, Your Honour?"

"I have plenty to think about," I told him. "I am an officer and a gentleman. Only yesterday I was fighting against you, and today I am sitting beside you in the same sleigh, and the happiness of my whole life depends on you."

"Well?" said Pugachev. "Are you afraid?"

I replied that, having once been pardoned by him, I hoped, not only for his mercy, but for his help, too.

"And you are right, by God you are!" exclaimed the Pretender. "You saw the way my lads looked at you. This very day, too, the Old One swore that you were a spy, and that you ought to be tortured and hanged. But I would not consent." He lowered his voice so that Savelich and the Tatar should not hear him. "I remembered your glass of vodka and the hareskin coat. You see I am not such a bloodthirsty monster as your fellows call me."

I remembered the taking of the Belogorsk fortress, but did not see fit to contradict him, and said no word in reply.

"What do they say of me in Orenburg?" asked Pugachev, after a short pause.

"They say that you are a hard nut to crack. You have most certainly made yourself felt."

The Pretender's face expressed satisfied vanity. "Yes," he said cheerfully. "I know how to fight. Do they know in Orenburg of the battle of Yuzeyevaya? Forty generals killed, four armies taken prisoner. What d'you think? Could the King of Prussia stand up against me?"

The presumption of the rogue amused me. "What do you think yourself?" I asked him. "Could you get the better of Friedrich?"

"Fyodor Fyodorich?* Why not? I got the better of your generals, and they beat him. Up till now my arms have been fortunate. Just you wait, wait till I get to Moscow!"

"Do you intend to march on Moscow?"

The Pretender paused for thought and went on under his breath: "God knows! I am cramped, I need more freedom. My lads are getting ideas into their heads. They are a thievish lot. I have to keep my wits about me. At the first failure they will redeem their own necks with my head."

"There you are!" I said. "Would it not be better to leave them yourself, in good time, and submit yourself to the mercy of the Empress?"

Pugachev laughed bitterly. "No," said he, "it's too late for me to repent. There will never be any mercy for me. I will go on as I have begun. Who knows? Perhaps I will be successful! After all, Grishka Otrepyev *did* rule over Moscow."

"And do you know how he ended? He was thrown out of a window, beheaded, burned, his ashes were put in the breach of a cannon, and shot into the air."

"Listen to me," said Pugachev, with a kind of wild inspiration, "I will tell you a tale told me by an old Kalmyk woman when I was a child. An eagle once asked a crow: 'Tell me, oh crow, how is it that you have lived on the earth three hundred years, and I only thirty-three years?' 'Because, Master,' the crow replied, 'you drink the blood of the living, and I live on dead flesh.'

---

* Pugachev ironically russifies the name of the Prussian king Friedrich the Second. Pugachev was a soldier in the Seven-Year War between Russia and Prussia, which ended in the defeat of Friedrich the Second, and the Russian army triumphantly entering Berlin, the capital of Prussia, in 1760.

The eagle thought to himself: 'I'll try and eat what he does.' Good. The eagle and the crow flew off together. They saw a dead horse; they flew down and perched on it. The crow began pecking and saying how good it was. The eagle pecked once, pecked twice, flapped its wings and said to the crow: 'No, brother crow, better only once drink the blood of the living, and trust in God, than live three hundred years and eat dead flesh.' How do you like the Kalmyk tale?"

"Very clever!" I said. "But to live by murder and pillage seems to me the same as pecking dead flesh."

Pugachev looked at me in astonishment and made no reply. We both fell silent, each absorbed in his thoughts. The Tatar chanted a doleful song. Savelich, dozing, swayed on the box-seat. The sleigh flew over the smooth, wintry road.... Suddenly I caught sight of the village on the steep bank of the Yaik, with its palings and belfry, and in another quarter of an hour we drove into the Belogorsk fortress.

Chapter Twelve

THE ORPHAN

> Our apple-tree
> Has no young twigs, no flowery crown
> Our little bride
> Has no father, no mother.
> No one to dress her,
> No one to bless her.
>
> *Wedding Song*

The sleigh drew up at the porch of the commandant's house. The people recognised Pugachev's sleigh bells and thronged after us. Shvabrin met the Pretender at the porch. He was in Cossack attire and had let his beard grow. The traitor helped Pugachev out of the sleigh, using the most servile expressions to show his delight and loyalty. The sight of me seemed to disconcert him but he soon recovered, holding out his hand with the words: "So you are one of us, too! High time!" I turned from him without a word.

My heart ached when I found myself in the familiar room with the late commandant's diploma still hanging on the wall, like a mournful epitaph on bygone days. Pugachev seated himself on the very sofa Ivan Kuzmich used to doze on, lulled by the nagging of his spouse. Shvabrin himself brought vodka to Pugachev, who drank a glass and told him, pointing to myself: "Wait on His Honour, too." Shvabrin approached me with his tray, but for the second time I turned away from him. He seemed to be ill at ease. With his native intuition he had guessed, of course, that Pugachev was displeased with him. Cringing before him, he glanced suspiciously at me from time to time. Pugachev enquired into the state of the fortress, the rumours about enemy troops, and so on, and then suddenly asked him: "Tell me, brother, who is this young woman you are keeping a prisoner? Show her to me."

Shvabrin turned pale as death. "She is not a prisoner, Sire," he said in faltering accents. "She is ill. She is in her chamber." "Lead me to her," said the Pretender, rising. Unable to disobey, Shvabrin led Pugachev up to the bedchamber. I followed them.

Shvabrin paused on the stairs. "You are entitled to demand of me anything you will, Sire," he said. "But do not allow a stranger to enter my wife's bedroom."

I was seized with horror. "What—you are married?" I asked him, ready to tear him to pieces.

"Hush!" interposed Pugachev. "This is my affair. And you," he continued, turning to Shvabrin, "stop trying to be clever and trumping up excuses. Whether she is your wife or not, I shall take anyone I choose to her. Follow me, Your Honour!"

At the door of the chamber Shvabrin again halted and said in a voice breaking with emotion: "I warn you, Sire, she is in high fever, and has been delirious for three days."

"Open the door," said Pugachev.

Shvabrin began feeling in his pockets, saying he had not brought the key with him. Pugachev kicked at the door. The lock gave, the door opened, and we entered.

I took one look, and my blood froze. On the floor, in a ragged peasant woman's dress, sat Marya Ivanovna, pale, thin, her hair dishevelled. Beside her stood a jug of water with a hunk of bread resting on the top of it. On seeing me she started and cried out. I was too dazed to know what became of me at that moment.

Pugachev looked at Shvabrin, saying with a bitter sneer: "A fine hospital you have here!" Then, going up to Marya Ivanovna, he said: "Tell me, my dear, what has your husband punished you for? In what way have you wronged him?"

"Husband!" she repeated. "He is no husband of mine. I will never be his wife. I have resolved to die first, and die I will, if no one delivers me."

Pugachev looked savagely at Shvabrin. "And you dared to deceive me!" he said. "Do you know, you knave, what you deserve?"

Shvabrin fell on his knees.... At that moment all my hatred and wrath were swallowed up in contempt. I looked with loathing at the gentleman sprawling at the feet of a runaway Cossack. Pugachev was softened. "I will forgive you this time," he told Shvabrin. "But know that if you offend again, this will be held against you." He then turned to Marya Ivanovna and said kindly: "Come out, my lass, I give you your liberty, I am your tsar."

Marya Ivanovna glanced swiftly at him and guessed that the murderer of her parents stood before her. Covering her face with her hands she fell back in a swoon. I rushed up to her, but at the same moment my old friend Palasha burst fearlessly into the room and began tending her mistress. Pugachev went out, and Shvabrin and I followed him down to the parlour.

"Well, Your Honour?" said Pugachev laughing. "We have delivered the fair maiden. What do you say, shall we send for the priest and make him read the marriage service over his niece? I could be the sponsor, Shvabrin the best man."

That which I had feared now occurred. Shvabrin, hearing Pugachev's proposal, was seized with a frenzy of rage. "Sire!" he cried frantically. "I am to blame—I lied to you. But Grinev deceived you, too. This girl is not the niece of the priest, she is the daughter of Ivan Mironov, who was hanged when the fortress was taken!"

Pugachev fixed his fiery gaze on me. "What's all this?" he asked me in astonished tones.

"What Shvabrin says is true," I replied firmly.

"You never told me that," remarked Pugachev, his countenance darkening.

"Judge for yourself," I said, "if I could have told you in front of your men that Mironov's daughter is alive, they would have devoured her on the spot. Nothing could have saved her!"

"That's true," said Pugachev, laughing. "My drunken sots would not have spared the poor maid. Her friend the priest's wife did well to deceive them."

"Hear me," I continued, seeing that he was favourably disposed. "I don't know what to call you, and I don't want to know.... But God knows I would gladly pay you with my life for what you have done for me. Only do not demand that which is counter to my honour and my conscience as a Christian. You are my benefactor. Finish that which you have begun— let me and the poor orphan go where God leads us. And wherever you are and whatever your fate, we will both pray for the salvation of your sinful soul every day of our lives...."

Pugachev's harsh soul seemed to be touched. "Have it your own way!" he said. "When I hang, I hang, when I pardon, I pardon. That is my way. Take away your fair maiden—take her wherever you like and may God give you love and counsel!"

At this he turned to Shvabrin and bade him provide me with a permit for all fortresses, and for the gates of all cities under his power. Shvabrin, overwhelmed, stood as if petrified. Pugachev set off to inspect the fortress. Shvabrin accompanied him. And I remained, under the pretext of preparing for my departure.

I ran back to the room. The door was locked. I knocked. "Who's there?" called out Palasha. I told them it was I. The sweet voice of Marya Ivanovna was heard through the door. "Wait a minute, Pyotr Andreich. I am changing my dress. Go to Akulina Pamfilovna. I will be there in a minute."

I obeyed, and went to the house of Father Gerasim. He and his wife came running out to meet me. Savelich had already told them of my arrival. "Greetings, Pyotr Andreich," said the priest's wife. "God has willed that we should meet again. How have you fared? We have talked about you every day. Marya Ivanovna has suffered terribly in your absence, poor thing! But tell us, good Sir, how did you manage to get on with Pugachev so well? How is it he did not have you hanged? At least we may thank the ruffian for that!" "That'll do, old woman," interrupted Father Gerasim. "You need not come out with all you know. No good ever came from a prattling tongue. Pyotr Andreich, come in, pray! It is long, long, since we have met."

The priest's wife set before me what food she had, talking incessantly. She told me how Shvabrin had forced them to give up Marya Ivanovna; how Marya Ivanovna had wept on parting with them, but had kept in touch with them through Palasha (a sharp girl, that! She had even made the sergeant dance to her tune!), how she had advised Marya Ivanovna to write me a letter, and so on. In my turn I told her my own story in brief. The priest and his wife crossed themselves on learning that Pugachev knew of the deception they had practised on him. "God have mercy on us!" said Akulina Pamfilovna. "May the Lord drive away the storm cloud. And Alexei Ivanich—a fine fellow, eh?" At that moment the door opened and Marya Ivanovna entered, a smile on her pale face. She had changed her peasant dress and was attired as before, with charming simplicity.

I seized her hand and for long could not utter a single word. The hearts of both were too full for speech. Our host and hostess, realising that we had no thoughts to spare for them, left us. We were alone. All was forgotten. We talked to our heart's content. Marya Ivanovna told me everything that had happened to her since the taking of the fortress, describing the horror of her situation, and the many ordeals to which the base Shvabrin had subjected her. We recalled the happy past, too.... We both wept.... At last I unfolded my plans. To leave her in the fortress in the power of Pugachev, and beneath the rule of Shvabrin, was out of the question. Nor could there be any thought of Orenburg, now in the throes of a siege. She had not a single relative left in the world. I proposed to her that she go to my parents in the country. At first she hesitated, for she knew and dreaded my father's animosity to her. I was able to soothe her apprehensions, assuring her that my father would regard it as a privilege and a duty to give shelter to the daughter of an honoured warrior, who had died for his country. "Dear Marya Ivanovna," I said at last, "I consider you to be my wife. Extraordinary circumstances have joined us forever. Nothing in the world can separate us." Marya Ivanovna heard me with simplicity, without the least coyness, or affected protests. She felt that her fate was joined to mine. But she repeated once more that she would only become my wife with the consent of my parents. I did not try to dissuade her. We exchanged ardent, sincere kisses—and thus we came to a decision.

In an hour's time the sergeant brought me a permit with Pugachev's scrawl affixed by way of signature, and told me the latter wished to see me. I found him ready to start on his journey. I should find it hard to explain my feelings on parting with this terrible being, this fiend, this man who was a monster of cruelty for all but myself. Why not admit the truth? At that moment I felt a strong emotion of sympathy for him. I desired ardently to tear him from the midst of the criminals he was leading, and save him from the gallows before it was too late. Shvabrin, and the people pressing round us prevented me from putting into words all that was filling my heart.

We parted friends. Pugachev, catching sight of Akulina Pamfilovna in the crowd, shook his finger at her with a meaning wink. Then he got into the sleigh, ordering the driver to make for Berda. When the horses started he thrust his head out of the

sleigh once more and shouted to me: "Farewell, Your Honour!
Perhaps we shall meet again one day!" We did, indeed, but in
what circumstances!

Pugachev was gone. I looked long at the white steppe over
which the *troika* was flying. The crowd dispersed. Shvabrin
vanished. I went back to the priest's house. All was in readiness
for our departure, and I did not wish for any further delay.
Our belongings were all stowed away on an old sleigh of the
commandant's. The driver harnessed the horses in a trice.
Marya Ivanovna went to bid farewell to the graves of her
parents, who were buried behind the church. I offered to
accompany her, but she asked me to let her go alone. A few
minutes later she came back, silently weeping. The sleigh was
in readiness. Father Gerasim and his wife came out on to their
porch. There were three of us in the sleigh—Marya Ivanovna,
Palasha and myself. Savelich clambered on to the box-seat.
"Good-bye, Marya Ivanovna, my dear one. Farewell, Pyotr
Andreich, bright falcon!" cried the priest's kindly wife. "Happy
journey and God send you both happiness!" We set off. I saw
Shvabrin standing at the window of the commandant's house.
His countenance expressed grim fury. Not wishing to triumph
over a defeated enemy, I looked away. At last we passed through
the fortress gate and left the Belogorsk fortress behind us for-
ever.

Chapter Thirteen

ARREST

> "Pray be not angry, Sir — I must not fail,
> In duty bound, to pack you off to gaol."
> "Well — I am ready. But I trust I may
> First be allowed to explain things my own way."
>
> *Knyazhnin**

I could hardly believe my good fortune in having been so unexpectedly reunited to my sweet girl, whose state only that morning had been a source of such tormenting anxiety, and I could not help wondering if all that had happened to me was not an empty dream. Marya Ivanovna gazed pensively now at my face, now at the road, as if not yet able to bring her thoughts into order. We were silent. Our hearts were too weary. Time flew by unnoticed, and two hours later we found ourselves at the nearest fortress, which was also under Pugachev's sway. Here we changed horses. By the rapidity with which fresh horses were harnessed, and the obsequiousness of the bearded Cossack promoted by Pugachev to the post of commandant, I realised that, thanks to our garrulous driver, I was taken for a court favourite.

We continued our journey. It began to get dark as we approached the small town where, according to the bearded commandant, a strong battalion marching up to join the Pretender's forces was stationed. We were stopped by sentries. To the question: "Who goes by?" the driver answered stentoriously: "A friend of the tsar and his lady!" Suddenly we were surrounded by hussars, swearing appalling oaths. "Come out,

---

* Attributed to Knyazhnin, this epigraph, too, was written by Pushkin himself.

friend of Satan!" bawled a bewhiskered sergeant-major. "You'll get it, you and your madam!"

I got out of the sleigh and demanded to be led to their chief. Seeing an officer, the soldiers ceased their swearing. The sergeant-major took me to the major. Savelich never left my side, muttering to himself: "Friend of the tsar, forsooth! Out of the frying pan into the fire! Almighty God! How will all this end?" The sleigh followed us at foot pace.

Five minutes' walking brought us to a brightly lighted hut. The sergeant-major left me under guard and went to make his report. He was back in a minute, explaining that His Honour had no time to receive me, and had ordered me to be taken to the gaol, and my wife to be taken to him.

"What's this?" I shouted in a rage. "Is he mad?"

"I do not know, Your Honour," replied the sergeant-major. "I only know His Honour has ordered Your Honour to be led to the gaol, and Her Honour to be brought to His Honour, Your Honour."

I rushed into the porch. The sentries made no attempt to restrain me and I ran straight into a room in which five or six officers of Hussars were playing faro. The major was keeping the bank. What was my astonishment to recognise in him Ivan Ivanovich Zurin, the man who had won my money in the inn at Simbirsk.

"Can it be?" I cried. "Ivan Ivanich, is it really you?"

"Why, Pyotr Andreich! What brings you here? Where have you come from? Greetings, brother! Don't you want to take a hand?"

"Thanks. It would be better if you showed me my quarters."

"Quarters? Stay with me."

"I can't. I'm not alone."

"Well, your friend can come, too."

"I'm not with a friend, I'm with—a lady."

"A lady? Where did you get hold of her? Eh, brother!" (Here Zurin whistled so expressively that everyone laughed, and I was covered with confusion.)

"Well," continued Zurin, "so be it. You shall have a room. A pity, though.... We would have made merry as we did once before. Hey, boy! Why don't you bring Pugachev's lady friend here? Or is she making trouble? Tell her not to be afraid. The gentleman's a very nice gentleman, he won't hurt her. If she's obstreperous you can just give her a good cuff."

"What's this?" I said to Zurin. "What lady friend of Pugachev? It's the daughter of the late Captain Mironov. I have taken her from captivity and now I'm accompanying her to my father's place, where I intend to leave her."

"What? So it was you they just reported about to me! Well, well! What does this mean?"

"I'll tell you all about it later. For God's sake, relieve the poor girl's fears, your hussars have terrified her to death!"

Zurin immediately gave orders. He went out himself to apologize to Marya Ivanovna for the misunderstanding, and ordered the sergeant-major to take her to the best lodgings in the town. Me he kept in his own room.

After we had supped and were alone, I related all my adventures to him. He heard me out with the utmost attention. When I had finished my narrative, he shook his head, saying: "This is all very well, brother, but there's one thing I don't like—what the devil do you want to get married for? On my honour as an officer, I'm not trying to deceive you—but believe me, marriage is all nonsense. What do you want with a wife, and a lot of babies to dandle? Forget it all! Listen to me—break it off with the captain's daughter. The road to Simbirsk has been cleared up by me, and is quite safe now. Send her off alone to your parents tomorrow, and stay here in my detachment. There's no point in returning to Orenburg. You'd only fall into the hands of the rebels again, and you will scarcely shake them off a second time. The love madness will pass, and all will be well."

While I was not entirely in agreement with him, I nevertheless felt that duty and honour demanded my presence in the troops of the Empress. I resolved to take Zurin's advice, and send Marya Ivanovna to the country, while myself remaining in his detachment.

Savelich appeared to help me to bed. I told him to be ready to take the road with Marya Ivanovna the next day. At first he opposed my wishes. "What, Sir? Am I to abandon you? Who will look after you? What will your parents say?"

Knowing the obstinacy of my tutor, I thought to win him over by affection and candour. "Arkhip Savelich, dear friend!" I said to him. "Do not refuse my request, be my benefactor!

I shall not need a servant here, and I shall have no peace if
Marya Ivanovna travels without you. Serving her, you will be
serving me, too, for I have firmly resolved that I will marry her
as soon as circumstances enable me to."

At this Savelich flung out his arms with an air of utter
astonishment. "Marry her!" he echoed. "The child is thinking
of getting married! And what will your father say? What will
your mother think?"

"They'll consent, they will certainly consent," I assured him,
"when they see what Marya Ivanovna is. I am placing my hopes
on you, too. My mother and father trust you—you will inter-
cede for us, will you not?"

The old fellow was moved. "Oh, Pyotr Andreich, Master!"
he exclaimed. "Although it is early for you to think of getting
married, Marya Ivanovna is such a good young lady that it
would be a sin to let such an opportunity slip. Be it so, then! I
will escort her, the dear angel, and humbly inform your parents
that no dowry is required with such a bride."

I thanked Savelich and went to share Zurin's bedroom for
the night. In my enthusiasm and agitation I chattered incessantly. At first Zurin lent a ready ear to my confidences, but his
words became more and more infrequent and disconnected, and
at last the only response to one of my remarks was a snore and
a whistling inhalation. I stopped talking and presently followed
his example.

I went to Marya Ivanovna the next morning to inform her of
my proposal. She admitted it to be reasonable, and agreed with
me at once. Zurin's detachment was to leave the town that same
day. There was no time for delay. I took leave of Marya Ivanovna then and there, committing her to the care of Savelich,
and giving her a letter for my parents. Marya Ivanovna wept.
"Farewell, Pyotr Andreich," she said in a low voice. "God
alone knows if you and I will ever meet again, but I shall not
forget you to the last day of my life. Your image will remain in
my heart till my dying day." I could not say a word. There were
people all round us, and I did not wish to give way to my feelings
in front of strangers. At last she went. I returned to Zurin,
melancholy and taciturn. He did his best to cheer me up and
I was myself anxious to find distraction; we spent the day in
noisy gaiety, and in the evening embarked upon the campaign.

It was the end of February. The winter, which had complicated military operations, was coming to a close, and our generals were preparing for combined, simultaneous action. Pugachev still kept Orenburg in a state of siege, but detachments were constantly joining forces, converging upon the stronghold of the brigands from every direction. At sight of our troops, disaffected villages were brought to heel, and everywhere the dastardly bands fled from us, so that everything pointed to the swift and successful issue of the struggle.

In a short time Prince Golitsin drove Pugachev from the Tatishchev fortress, scattered his followers, delivered Orenburg, and dealt what seemed like a final, decisive blow at the rebellion. At the same time Zurin was sent against a band of insurgent Bashkirs, who scattered before we got a glimpse of them. Spring confined us to a Tatar hamlet. Rivers were in spate and the roads were impassable. We consoled ourselves in our inactivity with thoughts of the rapid cessation of this tedious, trivial warfare against scoundrels and savages.

But Pugachev was not caught. He appeared at the Siberian iron works, where he rallied fresh gangs and resumed his evil activities. Once more there were rumours of his successes. We heard of the devastation of Siberian fortresses. Very soon tidings of the seizure of Kazan and the Pretender's march on Moscow came to rouse our military leaders, who were blissfully slumbering in the assurance of the despised rebels' impotence. Zurin received orders to ford the Volga.*

I will not go into the details of our campaign and the termination of the war, but will content myself with saying that the populace were reduced to the extremity of suffering. We passed through villages laid waste by the rebels, ourselves inevitably depriving the unfortunate inhabitants of the last remnants of their provisions. All attempts at administration were given up, and landowners fled to the shelter of the forests. Everywhere were gangs of ruffians, perpetrating outrages; isolated military detachments dealt out penalties and pardons arbitrarily. The condition of the whole vast region over which the conflagration raged was appalling. God defend you from the sight of a Russian rebellion in all its ruthless stupidity!

---

* Here follows the "omitted chapter", withdrawn by Pushkin, and only surviving in the first draft of the manuscript.

Pugachev fled, pursued by Ivan Ivanovich Michelson. Presently we heard of his final rout. At last Zurin received tidings of the capture of the Pretender, and simultaneously received orders to halt. The war was over. I could go home to my parents at last. The thought of embracing them and seeing Marya Ivanovna, from whom I had not received a single word all this time, sent me into ecstasies. I pranced about like a child. Zurin laughed, shrugging his shoulders and saying: "Oh, you will come to a bad end! Marry then, and be done with you!"

But my happiness was alloyed by a strange sensation. I could not shake off the thought of the miscreant, stained with the blood of so many innocent victims, and of the execution which awaited him. "Emelya! Emelya!" I sighed in vexation. "Why did you not run against a bayonet, or stop a bullet? You could have done nothing better for yourself." I could not help feeling as I did. The thought of Pugachev was inseparably associated in my mind with the mercy he had shown me in one of the most terrible moments of my life, and with the delivery of my bride from the hands of the vile Shvabrin.

Zurin gave me leave of absence. In a few days I would once more be in the midst of my family, would once more see my dear Marya Ivanovna.... And suddenly a clap of thunder broke over my head.

On the day appointed for my departure, at the very moment when I was preparing to set off on my journey, Zurin came into the hut where I was quartered, holding a sheet of paper in his hand, and looking exceedingly disturbed. I felt a pang at my heart. I feared I knew not what. He sent my orderly out of the room, and announced that he had something to tell me. "What is it?" I asked in alarm. "A slight unpleasantness," he replied, putting the paper into my hand. "Read that—I have just received it." I began reading—it was a secret order to all military authorities to arrest me wherever I happened to be, and send me forthwith under guard to Kazan, to appear before the investigatory commission formed to look into the Pugachev affair.

The paper almost slipped through my fingers. "No help for it," said Zurin. "It is my duty to carry out the order. Rumours of your friendly journeyings with Pugachev must have come to the knowledge of the government in some way or other. I trust the affair will be without ill consequences, and that you will be able to put yourself right with the commission. Do not lose heart—set out at once." My conscience was clear; I did not fear the coming trial. But the thought of postponing the sweet moment of reunion, perhaps for months to come, appalled me. The cart was ready. Zurin bade me a friendly farewell. I was seated in the cart, accompanied by two hussars with drawn sabres, and thus I drove along the highroad.

Chapter Fourteen

TRIAL

I was convinced that my only misdemeanour had been my unsanctioned absence from Orenburg. There would be no difficulty in justifying this. Far from being prohibited, skirmishing had always been strenuously encouraged. I might be accused of unnecessary zeal, but not of breach of discipline. On the other hand my friendly intercourse with Pugachev could be testified to by a host of witnesses, and was bound to appear extremely suspicious, to say the least of it. Meditating the whole way on the interrogation awaiting me, I pondered my replies, and made up my mind to lay the whole truth before the judge, relying on this as the simplest and at the same time the safest method.

I arrived at Kazan, which I found devastated and almost burnt down. The streets were lined by heaps of cinders, from which here and there protruded scorched walls without roofs or window-panes. Such were the traces left by Pugachev! I was taken to the fortress, which had survived amidst the ruins of the city. The hussars handed me over to the sentry on duty. The latter called for a smith. Fetters were placed on my ankles and tightly rivetted. I was then led to the prison and left alone in a dark, cramped cell, with bare walls and a tiny window with an iron grating.

Such a beginning boded nothing good. However, I lost neither spirits nor hope. I resorted to the consolation of all sufferers, tasting for the first time the sweetness of prayer, coming from a pure, but anguished heart, and slept peacefully, not troubling myself about what lay in store for me.

The next morning I was awakened by the jailer, who told me I was to go before the commission. Two soldiers led me across a yard to the commandant's house, where they remained in the passage, allowing me to go into the room alone.

I entered a fairly spacious hall. Two persons were seated at a table littered with papers—an elderly General, who looked cold and stern, and a young Captain of the Guards, about twenty-eight years old, pleasant-looking, agile, and easy-mannered. The secretary sat at a table of his own next the window, his quill-pen behind his ear, bending over his paper, in readiness to write down my testimony. The cross-examination began. I was asked my name and calling. The General enquired whether I was not the son of Andrei Petrovich Grinev. On my replying in the affirmative he remarked severely: "Sad that such an estimable man should have such an unworthy son!" I replied calmly that whatever the accusations against me I hoped to dispel them by a frank statement of the truth. My self-assurance seemed to displease him. "You are very sharp," he said, frowning. "But we have dealt with cleverer men than you."

The younger man then asked me in what circumstances and when I had entered the service of Pugachev, and on what commissions I had been employed by him.

I replied indignantly that, being an officer and a gentleman, I could never have entered the service of Pugachev, or accepted any commissions whatever from him.

"How was it," continued my interrogator, "that one officer and gentleman was spared by the Pretender, while all his comrades were ruthlessly slaughtered? How was it that this same officer and gentleman had feasted amicably with the rebels, received presents—a sheepskin coat, a horse, fifty kopeks—from the principal miscreant? How did this strange friendship arise, if not on the grounds of treachery, or at least of base and criminal pusillanimity?"

I was profoundly wounded by the words of the officer of the Guards, and embarked upon a heated justification of my actions. I told of my first acquaintance with Pugachev in the steppe, during the blizzard, and of how he had recognised me after the seizure of the Belogorsk fortress, and pardoned me. I said it was true I had not scrupled to accept the sheepskin and horse from

Alexander Turgenev (1784-1845). A historian, scholar and writer, who held a big government post. He accompanied the coffin with Pushkin's body from St. Petersburg to Pskov and the Svyatogorsk Monastery

Vladimir Dahl (1801-1872). A writer, scholar, linguist and physician, who attended the mortally wounded Pushkin

Pushkin's study in his house on the Moika Embankment in St. Petersburg, now the All-Union Pushkin Museum

Pushkin Memorial designed by sculptor Opekushin and built with money collected by subscription. Opened in Moscow in 1880

the Pretender, but that I had defended the Belogorsk fortress against the miscreants to the last. Finally I referred them to my General, who could testify to my zeal during the disastrous siege of Orenburg.

The man with the stern countenance picked up a letter lying on the table and began reading it aloud:

"In answer to Your Excellency's enquiry concerning Ensign Grinev, said to be involved in the present rising, and to have entered into relations with the miscreant, contrary to military regulations and the oath of allegiance, I have the honour to report to you as follows: the said Ensign Grinev served at Orenburg from the beginning of October 1773 to the 24th of February of the present year, on which date he absented himself from the town, and since when he has not been seen among the troops under my command. Deserters report that he was in the village with Pugachev, and went with him to Belogorsk fortress, where he formerly served. As regards his conduct I may...." Here he broke off, and said to me severely: "Now what have you got to say for yourself?"

I had been going to proceed as I had begun, explaining my relations with Marya Ivanovna and all the rest, with equal frankness. But suddenly I felt an insurmountable repulsion. It struck me that if I mentioned her, the commission would send for her to appear for interrogation, and the thought of her name being connected with base calumnies spread by scoundrels, and of her being brought to confront them personally—this thought was so terrible to me, that I faltered and my speech became confused.

My judges, who were beginning to listen to me with a certain indulgence, had their prejudices reawakened by the sight of my confusion. The officer of the Guards demanded that I should be confronted with the principal informer. The General called for "yesterday's miscreant" to be brought in. I turned eagerly towards the door, awaiting the appearance of my accuser. A few minutes later there was the jingling of chains, the door opened, and—Shvabrin entered. I was amazed at the change in him. He was terribly thin and pale. His hair, so recently black as pitch, had gone quite grey. His long beard was unkempt. He repeated his accusation in feeble but assured tones. According to him I had been sent to Orenburg by Pugachev as a spy; I had gone out skirmishing daily, in order to transmit written

tidings of all that went on in the town; at the last I had openly
gone over to the Pretender, driving with him from fortress to
fortress, endeavouring in every way to ruin my comrades in
treachery, so as to obtain their posts and enjoy the rewards
meted out by the Pretender. I heard him out in silence, and was
gratified by one thing—the name of Marya Ivanovna was not
uttered by the vile rascal. Perhaps his vanity suffered too much
at the thought of one who had rejected him so scornfully; perhaps some spark of that feeling which had caused me, also, to
hold my tongue, still dwelt in his heart. However this may be,
the name of the Belogorsk commandant's daughter was not
mentioned before the commission. This confirmed me still more
in my intentions, and when the judges enquired what I had to
say in refutation of Shvabrin's testimony, I replied that I
adhered to my original explanation, and had nothing to add in
my justification. The General ordered us to be taken out. We
left the room together. I looked calmly at Shvabrin, but did not
say a single word to him. He laughed spitefully, and, lifting up
his chains, preceded me from the room and hastened his footsteps. I was taken back to the prison, and not called for cross-
examination any more.

I was not an eye-witness of the events which I shall now communicate to the reader, but I heard about them so often that
they are engraved on my memory to the minutest detail, until
I feel as if I had been invisibly present during their occurrence.

Marya Ivanovna was received by my parents with the cordial
hospitality which distinguished the people of the previous century. They saw the goodness of God in the fact that they were
enabled to shelter and cherish the poor orphan. Very soon they
became sincerely attached to her, for no one could know her
without loving her. My father ceased to regard my feelings as
a mere whim, and my mother wished nothing better than the
marriage of her Petrusha with the dear daughter of the Captain.

The rumour of my arrest confounded the whole family.
Marya Ivanovna had given my parents such a simple account of
my strange acquaintance with Pugachev, that, far from perturb-
ing them, it had often moved them to hearty laughter. My
father could not bring himself to believe that I was mixed up
with the vile rebellion, the aim of which was the overthrow of
the throne and the destruction of the aristocracy. He subjected
Savelich to searching enquiries. My old tutor did not conceal

the fact that his master had been entertained by Emelka Pugachev, and that the miscreant had conferred benefits upon him,
but vowed that he had never heard of any treachery. The old
people's alarm was quieted, and they waited eagerly for favourable tidings. Marya Ivanovna, though deeply anxious, said
nothing, being blessed with modesty and discretion to a remarkable degree.

Several weeks passed.... And then my father received a
letter from our kinsman Prince B. in Petersburg. The letter
was about me. After the customary opening lines, Prince B.
wrote that the suspicions as to my participation in the plans of
the insurgents turned out, unhappily, to have been only too well-
grounded, and that I ought to receive condign punishment, but
that the Empress, in recognition of the services and declining
years of my father, had decided to pardon his infamous son, and
substitute life-long exile to a distant part of Siberia for an
inglorious death on the scaffold.

The unexpected blow almost killed my father. He quite lost
his usual firmness and poured out his grief (usually dumb) in
bitter lamentations: "What?" he repeated over and over again,
in a fury. "*My* son a party to Pugachev's schemes! Just God, to
what have I come! The Empress reprives him! As if that were
any better! It is not execution which appals me—one of my
ancestors died on the Place of Execution, in defence of what he
considered sacred; my father suffered martyrdom with Volynsky
and Kruschev.* But for a gentleman to betray his oath, to join
forces with rascals, murderers, and vagrant serfs! Shame upon
our line!" Alarmed by his despair, my mother did not dare to
weep in his presence, and endeavoured to cheer him with tales
of the falseness of rumours, the uncertainty of opinion. My
father remained inconsolable.

Marya Ivanovna suffered most of all. Convinced that I could
have justified myself with ease, she guessed at the truth, and
regarded herself as the author of my misfortunes. Concealing
her tears and sufferings from all, she sought incessantly for
some means for my deliverance.

---

* Artemy Volynsky, a Minister in the reign of Anna Ivanovna (1730-
1740), who headed the plot against Biron, the favourite of the Empress and
one of the basest foreign hirelings ever to serve at a Russian court. Andrei
Kruschev, a counsellor of the Admiralty, a participant in the plot, was
executed together with Volynsky.

One evening my father was sitting on the sofa, turning the pages of the Court Calendar. But his thoughts were far away, and the journal did not produce its customary effect on him. He was whistling an old march tune under his breath. My mother was silently knitting a woollen vest, her tears dropping on her work every now and then. Suddenly Marya Ivanovna, who was sitting beside her with her needlework, announced that circumstances made it necessary for her to go to Petersburg, and that she must ask them to let her have a conveyance. My mother was much grieved. "What have you got to go to Petersburg for?" she asked. "Surely you are not going to abandon us, too, Marya Ivanovna?" Marya Ivanovna replied that her whole future depended on this journey, that she was going to seek the protection and aid of powerful persons, as the daughter of one who had suffered for his loyalty.

My father lowered his head. Anything which recalled to him the supposed crime of his son oppressed him, and sounded like a reproach in his ears. "Go, my dear," he sighed. "We have no desire to stand in the way of your happiness. God send you a good husband, not a declared traitor." He got up and left the room.

When she found herself alone with my mother, Marya Ivanovna partially revealed her intentions to her. My mother embraced her with tears and prayed to God for the fortunate issue of her plans. Marya Ivanovna was equipped for the journey and a few days later set off accompanied by the faithful Palasha and the trusty Savelich, who, having been forcibly separated from me, consoled himself with the thought that he was at least serving my intended bride.

Marya Ivanovna arrived safely at Sofia and, learning that the court was at that time in residence at Tsarskoye Selo, determined to find a lodging there. She was given a corner behind a partition at the posting-station. The wife of the postmaster immediately got into conversation with her, declaring that she was the niece of the court stoker, and initiating Marya Ivanovna into all the secrets of court life. She told her the time the Empress usually rose, had coffee, took her walk, which courtiers would be with her then, what Her Highness had condescended to remark the day before at the dinner-table, what visitors had been received in the evening. In a word, Anna Vlasyevna's conversation was as good as a page of history, and would have been a treasure to posterity. Marya Ivanovna listened to her attentively. They went into the park. Anna Vlasyevna told her companion the history of every path and bridge, and by the time they had walked about and returned to the posting-station, they were mutually content with each other's company.

Marya Ivanovna rose early the next morning and dressed and went quietly to the park. It was a beautiful morning, the sun lighting up the tops of the lime-trees which were already turning yellow beneath the chill breath of autumn. The broad lake lay motionless and gleaming. The swans had just waked up and were solemnly gliding over the water from behind the bushes which shaded the edge of the lake. Marya Ivanovna passed a lovely meadow, in the midst of which a monument had just been erected in honour of the recent victories of Count Pyotr Alexandrovich Rumyantsev.* Suddenly a little white dog of English breed ran barking up to her. Marya Ivanovna stood still in alarm. At the same moment she heard a pleasant feminine voice say: "Don't be afraid, it doesn't bite." And Marya Ivanovna now saw a lady seated on a bench opposite the monument. Marya Ivanovna sat down at the other end of the bench. The lady gazed at her steadfastly, and Marya Ivanovna, in the course of a few sidelong glances, had surveyed her from top to toe. She wore a white morning gown, a night-cap and a quilted jacket. Marya Ivanovna guessed her to be about forty years old. Her full, highly-coloured countenance expressed dignity and calm, and there was indescribable charm in her blue eyes and slight smile. The strange lady was the first to break the silence.

"You don't live in this neighbourhood, do you?" she asked.

"No, indeed. I only arrived yesterday from the country."

"Have you come with your family?"

"No, Madam. I came all by myself."

"By yourself? You are still very young for that!"

"I have neither father nor mother."

"I presume that you have come on business of some sort."

"Yes, Madam. I have come to make a petition to the Empress."

"You are an orphan. You have probably come to complain of some injustice."

---

* An outstanding Russian general. An obelisk was erected in Tsarskoye Selo in honour of the victory gained by Rumyantsev over the Turks on July 21, 1770, on the bank of the river Kagula.

"No, Madam. I have come to ask a favour, not justice."

"May I ask who you are?"

"I am the daughter of Captain Mironov."

"Captain Mironov! The former commandant of one of the Orenburg fortresses?"

"Yes, Madam."

The lady appeared to be moved. "Forgive me," she said in a voice still more kindly, "if I interfere in your affairs. But I am attached to the Court. Explain your request to me, and I may perhaps be able to render you some assistance."

Marya Ivanovna rose and thanked her respectfully. Everything about the unknown lady won sympathy and inspired confidence. Marya Ivanovna drew a folded piece of paper from her pocket and handed it to her unknown protector, who perused it in silence.

At first she read with attention and sympathy. But soon a sudden change came over her countenance and Marya Ivanovna, following her every movement with her eyes, was alarmed by the severe expression of the face which, only a few moments before, had been so pleasant and tranquil.

"You are interceding for Grinev?" said the lady coldly. "The Empress will not be able to forgive him. It was no mere ignorance and levity which made him go over to the Pretender, his desertion was the act of an unprincipled and dangerous scoundrel."

"Oh, that is not true!" cried Marya Ivanovna.

"Not true?" echoed the lady, flushing up.

"Not true, I swear it is not true! I know all about it. I will tell you all. It was for my sake alone that he bore all that he went through. And if he did not speak up for himself at his trial, it can only have been that he did not wish to involve me." And she eagerly related the story with which the reader is acquainted.

The lady listened to her attentively. "Where are you staying?" she asked when Marya Ivanovna had finished, and hearing the name of Anna Vlasyevna, she added, smiling: "Oh, I know her! Good-bye, do not mention our meeting to anyone. I hope you will not have long to wait for a reply to your letter."

With these words she rose and entered a covered walk, while Marya Ivanovna returned to Anna Vlasyevna, filled with joyous hope.

Her hostess chided her for taking such an early walk in the autumn, which, she said, was bad for young women. She brought in the samovar and had just embarked, over a cup of tea, on one of her endless tales of the court, when a carriage from the court drew up at the porch, and a footman came into the house with the news that the Empress was graciously pleased to invite Marya Mironova to her presence.

Anna Vlasyevna was all wonder and bustle. "Gracious heavens!" she cried. "The Empress calls you to the court! How ever did she hear about you? And how can you appear before the Empress, my dear? I don't suppose you know how to behave at court.... Would it not be better for me to go with you? I could at least give you a few instructions. And how can you go in your travelling dress? Should I not send to the midwife for her yellow robe?" The court-chamberlain stated that Empress wished Marya Ivanovna to come by herself, and in the clothes she happened to be in. There was no help for it—Marya Ivanovna seated herself in the carriage and drove to the palace, pursued by the advice and good wishes of Anna Vlasyevna.

Marya Ivanovna anticipated that our fate was in the balance, and her heart beat violently, and then seemed almost to stop. A few minutes later the carriage drew up in front of the palace. Marya Ivanovna ascended the stairs in a state of trepidation. Doors opened wide before her. She traversed a long succession of splendid empty rooms, the chamberlain going before her to show her the way. At last, stopping in front of a closed door, he told her he would go in and announce her, and left her alone.

The idea of seeing the Empress face to face was so terrifying that Marya Ivanovna could hardly stand. In a few moments the door opened and she entered the Empress's boudoir.

The Empress was seated at her toilet-table. There were a few courtiers around her, who respectfully made way for Marya Ivanovna. The Empress addressed her kindly, and Marya Ivanovna recognised the lady with whom she had talked so frankly a short time before. The Empress called her to come near and said, smiling: "I am glad to be able to keep my word and fulfil your request. Your business is settled. I am convinced of the innocence of your betrothed. Here is a letter which you will be good enough to take to your future father-in-law."

Marya Ivanovna accepted the letter with a trembling hand and fell weeping at the feet of the Empress, who raised her and kissed her. The Empress then entered into conversation with her. "I know you are not rich," she said, "and consider myself indebted to the daughter of Captain Mironov. Have no anxiety for the future. I take upon myself to look after your fortune."

After treating the poor orphan with the utmost kindness, the Empress dismissed her. Marya Ivanovna went home in the same court carriage. Anna Vlasyevna, who was awaiting her return impatiently, showered her with questions, which Marya Ivanovna answered as best she could. Though vexed that she remembered so little, Anna Vlasyevna attributed it to the shyness of a provincial, and generously forgave her. Marya Ivanovna, not even stopping to have a look at Petersburg, went back to the country that same day.

The journal of Pyotr Andreyevich Grinev ends here. Family tradition has it that he was released from imprisonment at the end of 1774 by order of the Empress; that he was present at the execution of Pugachev, who recognised him in the crowd and nodded to him, bending that same head which, a minute later, dead and bloody, was held up to the sight of the people. Soon after this Pyotr Andreyevich married Marya Ivanovna. Their descendants now flourish in the Simbirsk Gubernia. Thirty *versts* from X. is a village belonging to ten proprietors. In one of the wings of a country mansion there is a framed and glazed letter in the handwriting of Catherine II. It is addressed to the father of Pyotr Andreyevich, and contains the acquittal of his son, and praises of the mind and heart of Captain Mironov's daughter. Pyotr Andreyevich Grinev's manuscript was presented to us by one of his grandchildren, who was aware of our work in connection with the period described by his grandfather. We resolved, with the permission of his relatives, to have it published separately, providing a fitting epigraph for each chapter heading, and taking the liberty of changing certain names.

October 19, 1836

THE EDITOR

OMITTED CHAPTER*

We were now approaching the banks of the Volga; our regiment entered the village of X. and we took up our quarters for the night. The village elder informed me that all the villages on the other side were in revolt, and that Pugachev's bands were prowling about everywhere. This news caused me great uneasiness. We were to cross the river on the morning of the next day.

I was a prey to impatience. My father's estate was situated about thirty *versts* from the opposite bank of the river. I asked if anyone could be found to ferry me across. All the peasants were fishermen, and there were plenty of boats. I went to Grinev and told him of my intention.

"Take care," he cautioned me. "You mustn't go alone, it would be dangerous. Wait till the morning. We'll cross with the first party and bring your parents fifty hussars as guests, in case of need."

I insisted on having my way. A boat was in readiness. I stepped into it with two boatmen. They pushed off and started plying their oars vigorously. The sky was clear and there was a bright

---

* This chapter, not included in the final version of *The Captain's Daughter*, for considerations connected with the censorship, and only preserved in manuscript form, was therefore called by Pushkin himself "Omitted Chapter". A few alterations afterwards made in the names of some of the characters have not been entered in it—notably Grinev is called *Bulanin* and Zurin, *Grinev*.

moon. It was a still evening. The Volga flowed calm and smooth. Swaying rhythmically, the boat glided over the surface of the dark water. I was plunged in a fanciful reverie.

About half an hour passed. We reached the middle of the river. Suddenly the men began whispering.

"What is it?" I asked, aroused from my dreaming.

"God knows what it is, we don't," they replied, both looking in the same direction.

My eyes followed the line of their gaze, and I discerned through the dusk, something floating downstream. A mysterious object was getting nearer and nearer to us. I ordered the men to stop rowing and wait for it to come up.

The moon hid behind a cloud. The floating phantom became still darker. Though it was quite near now, I was unable to make out what it was.

"What can it be?" said the men. "It isn't a sail and it isn't a mast...."

Suddenly the moon emerged from behind the clouds, revealing an appalling sight. Floating towards us was a raft on which was fixed a gallows, with three men hanging from its cross-beam. I was seized by morbid curiosity. I felt I must have a look at the faces of the hanged men.

On my orders the men steadied the raft with a boat-hook, and my boat jostled against the floating gallows. I jumped on to the raft and found myself between the terrible posts. The full moon shone on the mutilated visages of the unfortunates. One was an old Chuvash, another a Russian peasant, a powerful, robust lad of some twenty years. But when my eyes fell on the third, I received a violent shock, and was unable to repress a cry of horror—it was Vanya, my poor Vanya, who had joined Pugachev in a moment of folly. A fragment of blackened board was nailed over their heads, bearing in large white letters the inscription: "Thieves and rebels." The oarsmen stolidly awaited my pleasure, holding the raft in place with the boat-hook. I stepped back into the boat. The raft floated downstream. The gallows showed black in the dusk for a long time. At last it disappeared, and my boat touched the steep bank....

I rewarded the men liberally, and one of them undertook to lead me to the rebel chief of the village beside the ferry. I followed him into a hut. When the chief heard that I wanted horses, he seemed inclined to give me a rough reception, but the boatman said a few words to him in undertones, and his harsh manner immediately gave way to eager servility. A *troika* was ready in a few moments. I got into the cart and told the driver to take me to my father's village.

I was borne at a gallop along the broad highway, past sleeping villages. The only thing I feared was being held up on the road. While the nocturnal encounter on the Volga testified to the presence of the rebels, at the same time it afforded evidence of powerful resistance on the part of the authorities. In case of need I had in my pocket the permit issued to me by Pugachev, and an order from Colonel Grinev. But I did not meet anyone. And towards morning I saw the river and the fir copse beyond which our village lay. The driver whipped up his horses and in a quarter of an hour's time I was driving into X.

The manor-house stood at the other end of the village. The horses were galloping at full speed. The driver suddenly reined them in, right in the middle of the street. "Now what is it?" I asked impatiently.

"It's a picket, Sir," he replied, with difficulty checking his horses in mid-career.

And sure enough there was an improvised turnpike and a peasant on sentry duty in front of it, a club on his shoulder. He came up to me, taking off his cap, and asking for my passport.

"What's the meaning of this?" I asked. "What's the turn-pike for? Whom are you guarding?"

"Why, Sir, we have rebelled," he replied, scratching the back of his head.

"And where are your masters?" I asked, with a sinking heart.

"Our masters?" he repeated. "Our masters are in the barn."

"In the barn?"

"Well, Andryushka put shackles on them, you see, he means to take them before the tsar."

"Good heavens! Lift the bar, you fool! Don't stand there gaping!"

The sentry hesitated. I jumped out of the carriage, gave him (I regret to admit) a box on the ear and lifted the bar myself. The fellow gaped at me in bewilderment. I got back into the cart and ordered the driver to gallop on to the big house. The barn was situated in the yard. Two peasants, likewise armed with clubs, were posted at its locked door. The cart drew up right in front of them. I jumped out and made straight for them.

"Open the door!" I commanded.

There must have been something in my aspect which inspired terror. At any rate both men ran away, flinging down their clubs. I attempted to wrench the padlock off the door and then to force the door, but the door was of oak, and the huge padlock proved unyielding. Just then a tall young peasant came out of a hut and asked me insolently what I meant by creating a disturbance.

"Where is Andryushka?" I shouted. "Call him to me!"

"I am Andrei Afanasyevich, and not Andryushka," he replied defiantly, his arms akimbo. "What do you want?"

For all reply I seized him by the scruff of the neck and dragged him up to the door of the barn, commanding him to unlock it. He held out stubbornly for a moment, but on him, too, the *paternal* chastisement had its effect. He produced the key and unlocked the barn door. I rushed headlong over the threshold, and there, in a dark corner, I discerned in the dim light coming from a narrow slit in the roof, my mother and father. Their hands were bound and there were wooden shackles round their ankles. I embraced them eagerly, unable to utter a word. They gazed upon me with astonishment—three years of military life had so altered me that they were unable to recognise me. My mother gasped and burst into tears.

Suddenly I heard a dear, familiar voice behind me.

"Pyotr Andreich! Is it you?" I was dumbfounded.

Turning, I saw Marya Ivanovna in another corner, her hands and feet bound and shackled, too.

My father looked at me in silence, not daring to believe his eyes. His face was radiant with joy.

With my sword I hastily cut through the knots in the ropes binding them.

"Welcome, welcome, Petrusha," said my father, pressing me to his heart. "Thank God, we have lived to see you...."

"Petrusha, my dear one!" exclaimed my mother. "What good angel brought you here? Are you well?"

I hastened to lead them from confinement, but when I got to the door I found it again locked.

"Andryushka!" I shouted. "Open the door!"

"Not I!" he called through the door. "You can stay there yourself. We'll teach you to make trouble, and take the tsar's officials by the collar!"

I began examining the barn to look for a way of escape.

"That's no good," said my father. "There is nowhere for thieves to get in and out of my barns."

My mother, who had brightened up a little at my coming, was overcome with despair at the thought that I would share the terrible fate of the family. But I had become calmer from the moment I found myself with my parents and Marya Ivanovna. I had a sword and two pistols on me, and could have withstood a siege. Moreover I felt sure Grinev would be there before night-fall and set us free. I told my parents this and contrived to calm my mother's spirits. They now gave themselves up to the joy of reunion.

"Well, Pyotr," said my father, "you've been up to plenty of pranks, and I've been very angry with you. But we will not bring up the past. I trust you have mended your ways and sown your wild oats. I know you have served like an honourable officer. Thank you, Pyotr! You have consoled me in my old age. If I owe my deliverance to you, life will be doubly sweet to me."

I kissed his hand with tears, and looked at Marya Ivanovna, who was so overjoyed at seeing me that she seemed perfectly happy and tranquil.

About noon we heard an extraordinary noise and clamour.

"What does that mean?" said my father. "Could your colonel have arrived already?"

"Impossible," I told him. "He won't be here before nightfall."

The noise increased. The alarm was sounded. Men on horse-back could be heard galloping about the yard. Just then, the grey head of Savelich appeared at a narrow opening in the wall, and my unfortunate tutor cried in piteous tones:

"Andrei Petrovich! Avdotya Vasilyevna! Pyotr Andreich, Sir! Marya Ivanovna, Ma'am! Bad news! The scoundrels are in the village. And who do you think is leading them, Pyotr Andreich? Shvabrin, Alexei Ivanich, the devil take him!"

Hearing that hated name, Marya Ivanovna clasped her hands and stood motionless.

"Listen to me, Savelich!" I cried. "Send someone on horse-back to the ferry, to meet the hussar regiment, and tell them to let the colonel know of our danger."

"But who is there to send, Sir? All the lads have joined the rebels. And the horses have all been seized. Oh heavens! They're in the yard now, coming up to the barn."

Several voices were now heard just outside the door. Motioning to my mother and Marya Ivanovna to get into a corner, I drew my sword, and leaned against the wall next to the door. My father took the pistols, cocked them both and took up his station beside me. The lock rattled, the door opened and Andryushka's head appeared. I struck at it with my sword and he fell to the ground, blocking up the doorway. At the same moment my father fired one of the pistols through the open door. The crowd of besiegers retreated, cursing. I dragged the wounded man over the threshold and latched the door from inside.

The yard was full of armed men. In their midst I recognised Shvabrin.

"Don't be afraid," I said to the women. "There is still hope. And you, Sir, do not shoot any more. We must save the last round."

My mother was praying silently, Marya Ivanovna at her side, awaiting with saintly patience what fate had in store for us. Outside could be heard threats, oaths and curses. I stood at my post, ready to cut into pieces anyone daring to show himself. All of a sudden the noise made by the rascals died down, and Shvabrin's voice could be heard calling me by my name.

"I am here, what do you want?"

"Surrender, Bulanin, it's no good trying to resist. Have pity on your old folk. Obstinacy will not save you. I shall get at you."

"Just you try, traitor!"

"I shall neither make foolhardy attempts to get in myself, nor risk the lives of my men. I will set fire to the barn, and we'll see what you'll do then, Don Quixote of Belogorsk! It's dinnertime now. You can stay where you are for a while, and think it all over at your leisure. Farewell, Marya Ivanovna, I make no apologies to you. I don't suppose the time hangs heavy on your hands, sitting in the dark beside your knight errant!"

Shvabrin moved away, leaving sentries at the door of the barn. None of us spoke, all being absorbed in our own thoughts, which we did not dare to communicate to one another. I pictured to myself all the evil that Shvabrin, in his fury, might be able to do. I had hardly any care for my own plight. And— must I confess it?—I worried less about my parents than I did about Marya Ivanovna. I knew that my mother was adored by the peasants and the houseserfs; my father, too, for all his severity, was greatly beloved, for he was just, and knew the real needs of the people under his rule. Their rebellion was a mere delusion, a moment's intoxication, and not the expression of their wrath. And so, in the case of the old people, clemency could confidently be expected. But Marya Ivanovna? What fate did the depraved and unscrupulous man intend to mete out to her? I dared not dwell on the appalling thought, and was ready (God forgive me!) to kill her with my own hands, sooner than see her fall into the hands of this cruel enemy a second time.

Another hour passed. The sound of drunken singing came from the village. Our sentries envied the revellers, and, in their annoyance, began swearing at us, and trying to terrify us with talk of torture and death.

We waited for Shvabrin to carry out his threats. At last we became aware of a great commotion in the yard, and we once again heard Shvabrin's voice.

"Well, have you thought it over? Will you surrender yourselves into my hands of your own free will?"

There was no answer.

After a short pause, Shvabrin gave orders for straw to be brought. A few minutes later the dark barn was lit up by blazing flames, and smoke began rising from under the door. Then Marya Ivanovna came up to me, and, taking my hand, said in a low voice:

"Come, Pyotr Andreich! Why should you and your parents perish for my sake? Let me go. Shvabrin will listen to me."

"Never!" I cried hotly. "Do you know what awaits you?"

"I will not survive dishonour," she replied calmly. "But I might be able to save my deliverer and his family, so generously sheltering a poor orphan. Farewell, Andrei Petrovich! Farewell, Avdotya Vasilyevna! You have been more than benefactors to me. Give me your blessing. And farewell to you, too, Pyotr Andreich. Be assured that ... that..." here she wept, burying her face in her hands. I was nigh frantic. My mother, too, was weeping.

"No more of that, Marya Ivanovna," said my father. "As if we would let you go out to the scoundrel alone. Stay here and say not another word. If we are to die, we will all die together."

"Hark—what are they saying?"

"Are you going to surrender?" cried Shvabrin. "Look! In five minutes you will be roasted alive."

"We will never surrender, villain!" my father replied in firm accents.

His wrinkled countenance was animated by remarkable vigour, his eyes blazed from beneath the grey eyebrows. Turning to me, he said: "Now is the time."

He unlatched the door. The flames rushed in, writhing over the beams, and the dry moss stuffed into their crevices. My father fired his pistol and strode over the blazing threshold, shouting: "Follow me, all of you!" I seized the hands of my mother and Marya Ivanovna and rapidly led them out into the air. Shvabrin lay across the threshold, shot down by the unsteady hand of my father. The rascally mob, at first fleeing before our unexpected sally, took heart again, and began to surround us. It was just beginning to lay about me, when a well-aimed brick struck me full in the chest. I fell to the ground and lay unconscious for some minutes. Returning to my senses I saw Shvabrin sitting up on the blood-soaked grass, our whole family standing in front of him.

I was supported under each arm. A crowd of peasants, Cossacks and Bashkirs were closing in upon us. Shvabrin was deathly pale. With one hand he pressed his wounded side. An expression of mingled pain and rage was imprinted on his features. Slowly lifting his head, he looked at me and said in feeble, indistinct tones:

"Hang him! All of them ... except her...."

The scoundrels approached us still nearer, and dragged us to the gate with loud cries. But suddenly they let go of us and took to their heels. Grinev was riding through the gateway, followed by a whole squadron with bared swords.

The rebels dispersed in all directions; the hussars pursued them, cutting them down and taking them prisoner. Grinev jumped from the saddle, bowed to my father and mother, and pressed my hand warmly.

"I see I'm just in time," he said. "And so this is your betrothed!"

Marya Ivanovna blushed all over her face. My father, outwardly calm, though evidently deeply stirred, went up to him and thanked him. My mother embraced him, calling him our angel of deliverance.

"Welcome to our home," said my father, leading the way to the house.

As we passed Shvabrin, Grinev came to a halt.

"Who's that?" he asked, looking at the wounded man.

"That's the ringleader himself, the head of the band," replied my father with a touch of pride, betraying the old soldier. "The Lord aided my feeble hand to punish the young miscreant and avenge the blood of my son."

"It's Shvabrin," I told Grinev.

"Shvabrin! Glad to see him! Pick him up, hussars, and tell our regimental surgeon to dress his wound and look after him like the apple of his eye. Shvabrin must at all costs be brought before the secret commission at Kazan. He is one of the chief culprits, and his evidence is likely to be extremely valuable."

Shvabrin opened his eyes wearily. His features expressed nothing but physical pain. The hussars bore him away on a cloak.

We went into the house. I looked around, deeply moved, recalling the days of my childhood. Nothing had changed in the house, everything was as it had been of old. Shvabrin had not allowed it to be plundered—low as he had sunk, he evidently still felt an instinctive repugnance for base rapacity.

The servants appeared in the hall. They had taken no part in the rising and displayed heartfelt satisfaction at our deliverance. Savelich was triumphant. It may here be related that, under cover of the excitement attendant upon the attack of the rebels, he had run to the stables in which Shvabrin's horse stood, saddled it, led it noiselessly out, and, under cover of the general confusion, galloped unnoticed towards the ferry. There he had met the regiment, which had just crossed the Volga and was resting on the bank. Grinev, learning from Savelich the peril we were in, had given the order to mount, and set off at a gallop, and, thank God, they had galloped up just in time.

Grinev insisted on having the head of Andryushka exposed on a pike next to the tavern for a few hours.

The hussars returned from their pursuit, having taken a few prisoners. These were locked up in that very barn where we had withstood the memorable siege.

We all went to our own rooms. The old people needed rest. I had had no sleep the previous night, and throwing myself on my bed, I now slept soundly. Grinev went away to give his orders.

When evening came we met again in the drawing-room, around the samovar, and fell to a cheerful discussion of the danger we had so narrowly escaped. Marya Ivanovna poured out tea, I sat next to her and devoted myself entirely to her. My parents appeared to regard our mutual fondness with an indulgent eye. That evening still lives in my memory. I was happy, completely happy—and there are not too many such moments in the lives of us poor mortals.

The next day my father was informed that the peasants had assembled in front of the house to ask his pardon. He went out on the porch to talk to them. When they saw him they fell on their knees.

"Well, you fools," he said. "What put it into your heads to rebel?"

"We have erred, forgive us, Master," they replied in one voice.

"Of course you have erred. You get into mischief, and then you rue the consequences. I forgive you for the very joy that the Lord has sent my son Pyotr Andreich back to me. Well, well—"

"We have erred—forgive us!"

"Certainly you have erred. God has sent us fine weather, it's time to get in the hay, and what have you been doing for three whole days, you fools? Elder! Send everyone to mow the grass; and mind, you red-haired rascal, all the hay must be stacked by St. Ilya's day. Begone, now!"

The peasants bowed low and went to work in their master's field as if nothing at all had happened.

Shvabrin's wound was not mortal. He was sent under guard to Kazan. From my window I saw them lower him into a cart. Our eyes met, he bent his head and I moved hastily away from the window. I did not wish it to appear that I was triumphing over the misfortunes and humiliation of my enemy.

Grinev had to proceed further. I determined to go with him, despite my desire to remain a few days longer in the bosom of my family. The day before the regiment made off I went to my parents, and according to the custom at that time bowed down to the ground before them and asked for their blessing on my marriage with Marya Ivanovna. The old folks raised me with tears of joy and gave their consent. I led Marya Ivanovna, pale and trembling, up to them. They gave us their blessing.

I will not attempt to describe my feelings at that moment. Whoever has been in my position will understand me without words, and for anyone who has not been through this I have nothing but pity, and would advise such a one, before it is too late, to fall in love and receive his parents' blessing.

The regiment was ready to set out the next morning. Grinev took leave of my family. We were all sure that military operations would soon be over; I hoped, in a month's time, to be a married man. Marya Ivanovna bade me farewell, kissing me in front of everyone. I mounted my horse. Savelich followed me, once more, and the regiment departed.

I gazed as long as I could at the rural dwelling I was abandoning for the second time. I was haunted by gloomy forebodings. Something seemed to whisper to me that my misfortunes were not yet all over. In my heart I felt that there was yet another storm ahead of me.

I will not dwell in detail on our march, and the end of the Pugachev campaign. We passed through villages laid waste by Pugachev, and were compelled ourselves to take from the unfortunate inhabitants all that the insurgents had left to them.

The people did not know whom to obey. There was no semblance of government anywhere. The landowners were hiding in the forests. Bands of marauders ranged the countryside. The chiefs of the battalions sent in pursuit of Pugachev, who was by now fleeing towards Astrakhan, punished the just and the unjust alike. The condition of the territory over which the fire had raged was appalling. God defend you from the sight of Russian rebellion in all its ruthless stupidity. Those who meditate in our country impossible revolutions, are either young and do not know our people, or are hard-hearted folk, who rate the lives of others cheap, and care nothing for their own necks.

Pugachev fled, pursued by General Michelson. We soon learned of his utter defeat. Grinev received information from his general that the Pretender had been captured, together with the order to halt. At last I would be able to go home. I was in ecstasies. But strange forebodings cast a gloom over my joy.

NOTES

NOTES

Pushkin's prose marked a new stage in the work of this great poet. It began in 1827 when he sat down to write a historical novel entitled *The Blackamoor of Peter the Great*, which remained unfinished. A number of fragments and rough drafts written in the next three years and dealing with the historical events of 1812-1825 have been preserved.

In his Boldino Autumn Pushkin wrote five stories in quick succession and united them into a cycle which he called *The Tales of Ivan Belkin*. He was the first Russian writer to describe the life of different strata of Russian society with such veracity and understanding.

The position of the serf peasants troubled his mind especially. Following in Radishchev's footsteps he took up the subject in his stories *The Village of Goryukhino*, *Dubrovsky* and *The Captain's Daughter*. Thereafter, the theme was to become the leading one in progressive Russian literature.

Dubrovsky (1832) is remarkable in the first place for the embracing picture it paints of the mores and manners of the landed gentry. Belinsky wrote: "The image of the old Russian landed gentry, embodied in the person of Troyekurov, is depicted with frightening fidelity." The "pettifogging breed" of the venal officials—the hated enemies of the serfs—is described with an astute satirical pen.

In *The Captain's Daughter* (1836) Pushkin describes the peasant uprising of 1773-1775, and shows the truly popular character of Pugachev's movement aimed against serfdom. Pushkin presents Pugachev as a gifted and bold leader of the peasant revolt, an intelligent, courageous and humane person.

Commenting on this novel, Belinsky wrote: "It is something like *Evgeni Onegin* in prose. In this story the poet describes the life of Russian society in the reign of Catherine the Second. Many of the scenes in their accuracy, truthfulness and skillful exposition may well be called a miracle of perfection."

In his prose, Pushkin cultivated an extremely simple, laconic, precise and ingenuous manner of rendering. Commenting on *The Captain's Daughter* Gogol wrote: "It is positively the best Russian narrative. It is so superbly pure and ingenuous that reality itself seems artificial, as a caricature of life, in comparison."

Infinite clearness, terseness and accuracy of expression, an absence of any embellishing metaphors or epithets, and a swiftly developing plot — such are the distinctive features of Pushkin's prose. As he himself said: "Accuracy and brevity are the prime merits of prose. It calls for thoughts and more thoughts, otherwise a brilliance of expression will serve no purpose at all."

With such works as *The Queen of Spades, The Postmaster* and others, Pushkin laid the foundation for Russian realist prose.

* * *

The Tales of the Late Ivan Petrovich Belkin (p. 7)

Pushkin wrote his Tales of Ivan Belkin in the autumn of 1830 in Boldino. The manuscript of the earliest of these tales *The Undertaker* is dated September 9; next comes *The Postmaster*, September 14, *Lady Into Lassie*, September 20, *The Shot*, October 12 and 14, and *Blizzard*, October 20. Pushkin told P. A. Pletnev "very confidentially" in a letter dated December 9, that he had written five stories in prose. In April 1831, he read these stories to M. P. Pogodin in Moscow.

Pushkin decided to publish anonymously, ascribing the authorship a "late Belkin", and providing the cycle with a foreword "From the Editor". Before mailing off the stories, Pushkin changed their chronological order and shifted *The Shot* and *Blizzard* to the beginning of the collection.

The publisher was Pletnev, and he received the manuscript through Gogol. In a letter to Pletnev Pushkin wrote: "Whisper my name to Smirdin, so that he might whisper it in his turn to the buyers." The book came out in October 1831, and again with Pushkin's name on it in 1834.

Blizzard (p. 25)

The original plan, much differing from the final version of the story, has been preserved. Here it is:

A family of the landed class. An impoverished nobleman asks for the daughter's hand, is refused, and they elope. Blizzard. They stop, the girl falls ill. In despair he joins the army, and is killed. The father and mother die. The girl becomes an heiress. Many seek her hand. She is undecided. A colonel arrives. Proposal.

The Undertaker (p. 37)

The prototype was probably the coffin-maker, Adrian by name, who had his workshop opposite the Goncharovs' house in Bolshaya Nikitskaya Street in Moscow. Pushkin mentions him in a letter to his fiancée written in Boldino on November 4, 1830.

The Postmaster (p. 44)

The following plan has been preserved:

About postmasters in general—unfortunate, kindhearted people. My postmaster is a widower with a grown daughter. This post has since been closed down. I drove along this road the other day, and did not find the daughter. The daughter's story. A scribe falls in love with her. Follows her to St. Petersburg, sees her at a dance. On his return, he finds her father dead. The daughter comes home. A grave on the outskirts of the village. I drive away from this place. The scribe is dead, my driver tells me about the daughter.

The Queen of Spades (p. 75)

The story was written in Boldino in the autumn of 1833, and was published in 1834.

In 1851, P. V. Nashchokin told P. I. Bartenev that Pushkin had himself read his *Queen of Spades* to him, and told him that the main facts of the story were not fictitious. The old Countess was Natalya Petrovna Golitsyna, the mother of Moscow's Governor-General Dmitry Vladimirovich Golitsyn, and she had really lived in Paris as described by Pushkin. Her grandson had told him the following story. Once, having lost heavily at cards, he came to his grandmother for help. She did not give him the money he asked for, but instead told him of the three cards named for her in Paris by Saint Germain, and suggested that he should try it. The grandson did, and won back what he had lost. The rest of the story is pure fiction. Nashchokin remarked to Pushkin that he did not find much likeness to Golitsyna in the old Countess who had a stronger resemblance to Natalya Kirillovna Zagryazhskaya. Pushkin quite agreed, and explained that Golitsyna was easier to portray than Zagryazhskaya who was a more complex character in habits and everything else.

The story was a great success. On April 7, 1834, Pushkin wrote in his diary: "My *Queen of Spades* is very popular. Gamblers are betting on ace, three, seven."

The Captain's Daughter (p. 107)

The theme of peasant uprisings which interested Pushkin beginning from the 1830s and was only slightly touched upon in *Dubrovsky*, quite naturally turned his mind to Pugachev's uprising. For material, Pushkin travelled to Kazan, Orenburg and other places where the uprising had spread to, and worked on a *History of Pugachev*. It was in January 1833 that he decided to write a novel about the uprising and about a nobleman who was friendly with Pugachev.

It can be seen from Pushkin's draft plans how the theme of the revolt gained more and more prominence in the story, and at the same time the "romantic incident"—the love between the hero and the Captain's daughter—took shape. Changes were made in some of the names.

Work on the novel went slowly. Still, it was ready in the rough by the time Pushkin came to Boldino in the autumn of 1834. He finished it exactly two years later. When submitting it for censorship Pushkin wrote to the censor P. Korsakov in his letter dated October 25, 1836: "The name Mironova is fictitious. My novel is based on a legend I once heard about an officer who betrayed his duty and joined one of Pugachev's bands, but was later pardoned by the Empress on the request of his aged father who threw himself at her feet. The novel, as you will see, has travelled a long way from the 'truth'."

The portrait of Catherine the Second, given in *The Captain's Daughter* in conformity with the official image, was painted with the subtlest irony, that can be appreciated when we compare it with Pushkin's real opinion of the Empress given in the notes not intended for a publication that was subject to censorship.

"If reigning means knowing the weakness of the human soul and taking advantage of it, then Catherine deserves the amazement of posterity.... But in due course of time, History will appraise the influence of her reign on morals, it will expose the cruelty of her despotism covered up with meekness and tolerance, it will show the people oppressed by the vicegerents, the exchequer looted by her lovers, the serious mistakes made in political economy, the poor legislation, and the disgusting affectations in her relations with the philosophers of her age—and then the voice of the deluded Voltaire will not save her glorious memory from Russia's curse."

"May I never see a Russian revolt senseless and merciless," exclaims Grinev in *The Captain's Daughter*, but this by no means expresses the political views of Pushkin himself. To be sure, he did not support the idea of a peasant uprising, but he never thought the Pugachev movement "senseless". In his "general notes" for his *History of Pugachev* which were not intended for publication, he wrote: "All the common people were for Pugachev.... Analysing the measures undertaken by Pugachev and his accomplices, it must be admitted that the rebels had chosen the most reliable and effective means for the achievement of their aim."

Pushkin read his novel for the first time at a soiree given by P. A. Vyazemsky on November 1, 1836. *The Captain's Daughter* was first published in "Sovremennik", issue 4, 1836.

REQUEST TO READERS

Progress Publishers would be glad to have your opinion of the book, its translation and design and any suggestions you may have for future publications.
Please, send your comments to 21, Zubovsky Boulevard, Moscow, USSR.